THE WORLD'S CLASSICS
DR. WORTLE'S SCHOOL

ANTHONY TROLLOPE (1815–82), the son of a failing London barrister, was brought up an awkward and unhappy youth amidst debt and privation. His mother maintained the family by writing, but Anthony's own first novel did not appear until 1847, when he had at length established a successful Civil Service career in the Post Office, from which he retired in 1867. After a slow start, he achieved fame, with 47 novels and some 16 other books, and sales sometimes topping 100,000. He was acclaimed an unsurpassed portraitist of the lives of the professional and landed classes, especially in his perennially popular *Chronicles of Barsetshire* (1855–67), and his six brilliant Palliser novels (1864–80). His fascinating *Autobiography* (1883) recounts his successes with an enthusiasm which stems from memories of a miserable youth. Throughout the 1870s he developed new styles of fiction, but was losing critical favour by the time of his death.

JOHN HALPERIN is Centennial Professor of English at Vanderbilt University. His publications include *Trollope and Politics*, *Gissing: A Life in Books*, *C. P. Snow: An Oral Biography*, *The Life of Jane Austen*, and two books on the Victorian novel. He has edited works by Trollope, Meredith, Gissing, and Henry James, and volumes of original essays on Jane Austen, on the theory of the novel, and on Trollope. He was a Guggenheim Fellow in 1978–9.

THE WORLD'S CLASSICS

ANTHONY TROLLOPE
Dr. Wortle's School

Edited with an Introduction by
JOHN HALPERIN

Oxford   New York
OXFORD UNIVERSITY PRESS
1984

Oxford University Press, Walton Street, Oxford OX2 6DP

London New York Toronto
Delhi Bombay Calcutta Madras Karachi
Kuala Lumpur Singapore Hong Kong Tokyo
Nairobi Dar es Salaam Cape Town
Melbourne Auckland

and associated companies in
Beirut Berlin Ibadan Mexico City Nicosia

Oxford is a trade mark of Oxford University Press

Introduction, Select Bibliography, Chronology, and Notes
© John Halperin 1984

First published by Oxford University Press 1928
First issued as a World's Classics paperback, with new
editorial matter, 1984

British Library Cataloguing in Publication Data
Trollope, Anthony
Dr. Wortle's school.—(The World's classics)
I. Title   II. Halperin, John
823'.8 [F.]   PR5684.D6
ISBN 0-19-281673-X

Library of Congress Cataloging in Publication Data
Trollope, Anthony, 1815–1882.
Dr. Wortle's school.
(The World's classics)
Bibliography: p.
I. Halperin, John, 1941–   .   II. Title.
III. Title: Doctor Wortle's school.   IV. Series.
PR5684.D6 1984   823'.8   84-830
ISBN 0-19-281673-X (pbk.)

Printed in Great Britain by
Hazell Watson & Viney, Limited,
Aylesbury, Bucks

CONTENTS

ACKNOWLEDGEMENTS

I should like to thank Professors Franklin Brooks, Donald Greene, N. John Hall, and Robert Tracy, for invaluable and unstinting help during preparation of the present volume for publication.

J.H.

INTRODUCTION

As often as not one has only to take the opposite
view to the reputation created by the world in
order to judge a person accurately.

Proust

It is unlikely that Trollope was familiar with *Walden*,
but undoubtedly he would have agreed with Thoreau
that any man more right than his neighbours con-
stitutes a majority of one.

Trollope's books are full of immovably stubborn
people whose minds cannot be changed once they are
made up: readers of such novels as *He Knew He Was
Right*, *The Small House at Allington*, *Sir Harry
Hotspur of Humblethwaite*, and *John Caldigate*, to
mention just a few titles, will recognize Trollope's
fascination with various types of monomania. In
many such cases the immovable character is under a
delusion of one sort or another, often about the
nature of another person, and the failure to change
or to bend may bring with it a disaster, a disappointment, or at the very least a mistake. Frequently in
such cases the monomaniac is at odds with the vision
and values of 'Society', with the general attitudes
and conventions by which he or she is surrounded.
Indeed, it is a commonplace of Trollope criticism,
rightly or wrongly, that in his novels one goes
against the Voice of Society at one's peril, since that
collective Voice, reflected and refracted through the
narrative voice of the stories, tends to advocate what
is desirable, what is accepted—even, indeed, what
more often than not is right. Unlike such con-

temporaries as Thackeray and Wilkie Collins, Trollope is rarely 'subversive'; he usually accepts rather than questions, and contemporary codes of conduct and morality tend to be endorsed in his books.

But *Dr. Wortle's School*, a great late novel—published serially in 1880 and in two volumes in 1881, a year before the novelist's death—is a fascinating exception to these general rules in Trollope's fiction. For though, once again, the central character, having made up his mind, will not budge, he has few if any delusions about others; what is at issue is not the true nature of somebody else but rather a general principle of conduct towards others. At the centre of *Dr. Wortle's School* is what Society thinks, and whether or not it is right for an individual to go against its Voice. Here, for once, Society is portrayed by Trollope in a highly ambivalent way.

While on the one hand the novel argues that one's moral life should be a book open to one's neighbours, that the quality of life in any community is determined at least in part by the virtue or vice of those living in it, and that the well-being of all depends upon the conduct of each, *Dr. Wortle's School* is also a wide-ranging condemnation of *group* morals, of collective prejudice, and of the devastating power conventional values may have upon well-intentioned individuals who question or defy them. Like *Tess of the d'Urbervilles*, published a decade later, Trollope's little tale argues that one must take into account a person's intentions as well as his acts, and that we enforce monolithic codes of conduct at our peril—especially in unusual circumstances.

Nowhere else among Trollope's forty-seven novels

is this balance between the collective 'wisdom' of the community on the one hand, and the virtue of acting in accordance with our own personal idea of what is right on the other, so carefully struck. In some ways, *Dr. Wortle's School*, coming as it does near the end of Trollope's enormous literary output, contradicts many of the teachings of the volumes that went before it; in doing so, it stands apart from the other novels, occupying a position wholly its own. It endorses the mid-Victorian idea that the individual cannot safely live for long at variance with the conventions of the community, and at the same time anticipates the conviction held by many of the younger novelists (Hardy, Butler, and Moore, for example) that Society's values are often contemptible—hypocritical, rigid, and heartless—and that sometimes one cannot adhere to them without injury to one's moral nature. It is not unusual to find this latter point of view in the fiction of those born in the 1840s and 1850s; it is unusual to find it in a novel by a writer born in 1815. Dickens, supposedly so radical, was fond of identifying what he considered the corrupt values of his time; but in his novels, with only a few exceptions, what Society values—money, gentle breeding, a good marriage—is what his virtuous people are rewarded with and his vicious people deprived of. For all of Trollope's instinctive conservatism, his acceptance of Society's codes and its system of punishments and rewards, he managed, in *Dr. Wortle's School*, to produce a novel far more 'subversive' in this sense than anything in the Dickens canon. It is the only time he did so, and the novel is all the more fascinating for this. We might expect, in a novel by Thackeray or Collins, that

collective morality would be attacked with venom;
we might expect Dickens, Charlotte Brontë, or
Elizabeth Gaskell to show us poetic justice winning
through against difficult odds; and we might expect
this of Trollope too. He certainly obliges us in this
way again and again; most of his novels end with an
orgy of marriages, capitulations, volte-faces and
enough other manifestations of poetic justice to
resemble *A Christmas Carol*, or *Jane Eyre*, or
North and South.

Dr. Wortle's School also ends with the just rewarded and the unjust chastened. But before reaching that point we go through a story unique among
Trollope's works for the suspicious and sometimes
contemptuous treatment of convention. That the
particular convention at issue here should be, for the
time, such an apparently incontrovertible one—'A
woman should not live with a man unless she be his
wife,' as Mrs. Wortle puts it (III, ix)—is remarkable.
We could with reason and confidence anticipate a
challenge to convention from a Godwin, a Collins, a
Hardy, a Gissing, or a Samuel Butler—especially
given the complicated private circumstances of each.
Coming from Trollope, such a challenge is un-
expected and riveting. That Trollope seemed to be
treading on unusually dangerous ground in the early
chapters of *Dr. Wortle's School* surprised and
worried William Blackwood, the publisher of the
novel. He wrote to Trollope on 7 April 1880: 'I was
rather alarmed about the story when I read that
Mr. & Mrs. Peacocke were not man & wife but your
explanation of the mystery speedily dispels any
disagreeable feeling about the tone of the story that
might startle sensitive readers and I am sure that

the plot in your hands will not take any unpleasant turn.' Blackwood went on to suggest that Trollope move forward in the novel the explanation of the Peacockes' inadvertent misadventure.*

But it is no accident that Trollope chose this particular ground to mount his challenge, for the principle at issue, as Mrs. Wortle articulates it, seems indeed beyond argument—for the time and place, it must be repeated. It is precisely because Trollope wishes to show us the power and the vindictiveness of prejudice that he chooses an ostensibly uncontroversial subject in *Dr. Wortle's School*. Had he chosen instead, say, primogeniture, as the axis on which to turn his attack on convention, the issue might have been more clouded, the argument less controversial. No, he set out to put into question nothing less than the collective Wisdom of Society, and to lay before us for scrutiny nothing less than the relationship between the individual and the community. That *Dr. Wortle's School* is one of his shortest works—missing the four or five sub-plots which swell so many of his other books—testifies to the single-mindedness with which he attacked this highly complex subject. Like his early novel *The Warden* (1855), *Dr. Wortle's School* remains, in the clarity of its narrative line and its thematic focus, one of Trollope's most readable and fascinating performances.

There can be no doubt that Society, in its passive, benign state, is portrayed with some respect in *Dr. Wortle's School*; Trollope is still Trollope. It is taken for granted by everyone, even the Doctor himself, that such a man as Mr. Peacocke 'would not altogether refuse society for himself and his wife unless there were some cause for him to do so' (I, iii). For a gentleman so to cut himself and his family off from social intercourse must have seemed highly neurotic to a man living in Trollope's age. Even more so than today, people a hundred years ago believed that we cannot live completely apart from our neighbours, even should we wish to do so; the individual, by virtue of his existence in the world, is part of a community. This is a favourite theme of Trollope's contemporary, George Eliot: 'you can't isolate yourself. . . . Men's lives are as thoroughly blended with each other as the air they breathe: evil spreads as necessarily as disease' (*Adam Bede*, 1859, V, xli). So that when Dr. Wortle tells Mr. Peacocke that no man has 'a right to regard his own moral life as isolated from the lives of others around him . . . a man cannot isolate the morals, the manners, the ways of his life from the morals of others. Men, if they live together, must live together by certain laws' (III, viii–ix), we are invited—indeed, commanded—to agree. We are also reminded how dependent, for social sustenance, the individual must be on others, how subtly his moral environment can be shaped by the behaviour of those who comprise it, and how subtly, too, his own conduct can be shaped by the nature of the community he lives in. 'We are, all of us, joined together too closely to admit of isolation,' remarks Dr. Wortle, when Mr. Peacocke suggests that he 'was wrong from the first in supposing that the nature of my marriage need be of no concern to others' (III, viii). The Doctor speaks here not merely of the school or of the town, but of a general rule of existence: no man's life can be lived entirely apart from his fellows without damage to himself or to others; every man's life has some effect, for good or ill, on the life of his neighbours. It is for this reason that 'men, if they live together, must live together by certain laws'. George Eliot's novels teach a similar lesson: acts have consequences, what we do and how we live affect others, so it behoves us to act morally —for who knows what the ultimate results of our actions may turn out to be? Just as it is difficult to live a good life in a bad community, so is it difficult for a community to be a good place to live unless good lives are lived in it.

But what happens when 'the morals of others', to use Dr. Wortle's expression, are corrupted, and the standards by which Society judges its members become imperfect? Being members of a close-knit group, and unable to 'isolate' our beliefs and actions from those of others, we have an obligation, *Dr. Wortle's School* argues, not to stand passively by but rather to *change* Society's point of view—or at the very least to cling to the standards and morals which we feel to be both right and threatened. It is then that the character of the stubborn man or woman must assert itself—in the face, that is, of irrationality or injustice. As Trollope announces early in his tale (I, iii), it is 'how the Doctor bore [his ordeal that] this story is intended to tell,—and how also Mr. and Mrs. Peacocke bore it'. What is important to the novelist is not merely the story—what happens—but rather the effect of events on the characters (see first note to p. 28). Thus Trollope discloses the 'mystery' early; this book will not have the suspense of, say, *Phineas Redux*, or *Orley Farm*, or *Cousin Henry*, or *Mr. Scarborough's Family*. *Dr. Wortle's School* is a novel about character under stress; its 'suspense' is more subtle, originating as it does in the question of how some people may respond to the stimuli of unusual events and unusual questions posed—the ordinary person in extraordinary circumstances, as in a novel by Hardy.

How Dr. Wortle comports himself in the face of Society's criticism and disapproval is largely what *Dr. Wortle's School* is about. Is he a man who, in the language of the novel (III, ix), is 'prepared to face all the world, confiding in the uprightness and the humanity of his purpose' of protecting, defending, and sheltering the bigamous Peacockes? Believing them to be victims of the law rather than perpetrators of a crime, Dr. Wortle sticks to his guns, thus becoming Trollope's hero; 'There are things,' as the good Doctor says, 'which a man cannot bear and live . . . now and again a man shall make a stand in his own defence' (V, iii). He cannot bear injustice, either to those he loves and feels responsible for, or to himself for willingly taking on the responsibility and the feelings. 'It is not given to every man to be a hero,' Trollope reminds us. On the other hand, such heroism is not often called into play, if only because 'It is not often that one comes across events . . . so altogether out of the ordinary course that the common rules of life seem to be insufficient for guidance' (V, vii; again, this may remind us of Hardy, who had been publishing novels for a decade when Trollope went to work on *Dr. Wortle's School*). Faced with such a dilemma as the Doctor is, he could easily enough take refuge under the umbrella of convention; but he chooses to step away from any refuge, declaring the circumstances special and arguing that they deserve and require an unconventional response. This is the heart of Dr. Wortle's heroism: his daring to be unconventional. By placing such a man at the centre of his story, Trollope focuses our attention on what is called 'the effect and the power of character' (Conclusion, x). Should there be any doubt about Dr. Wortle's genuine heroism, should we be inclined to see him simply as cranky and contrary, it is dispelled by that moral barometer Mr. Puddicombe, who in the end tells the Doctor that he cannot help loving him 'the better for what you did' (Conclusion, xi). How does the virtuous man react to an injustice perceived by nobody else? *Dr. Wortle's School* answers this question in the person of its protagonist.

The Doctor's cause is of course helped by the corrupt perception and values of others. What Society thinks it knows here is all wrong. If, as the novel tells us (III, ix), Mr. Peacocke is a 'moral' man, then morality must be other than what the Mrs. Stantiloups of this world think it is. We are invited to see Mrs. Stantiloup as much less 'moral' than Mrs. Peacocke; for Mrs. Stantiloup is made to insist 'that nothing ought to be so dear to us as a high tone of morals' (IV, xii) and at the same time to tell lies—lies to which the blunt, unmetaphorical Trollope refers in the same chapter as 'figures of speech'. Like Dr. Wortle, the novelist is more interested in what is true than in what people think is true; and again like the Doctor, Trollope puts lying high up on his list of cardinal sins. When we read 'the Stantiloup correspondence', full of 'figures of speech', we know that its author, unlike Mrs. Peacocke, is not a lady. When we are told that Mr. Peacocke is a 'gentleman', we know that he is honest. In Trollope's mind, at least, the distinctions are clear.

Several other themes of *Dr. Wortle's School*
should be mentioned here. The idea that a man's (or a
woman's) life should be an open book, and that
secrets, like lies, are bad, and somehow infectious, is
part of the novel's leisurely attack on secretiveness
in general and its emphasis on the importance of
frankness in all our dealings with others. Trollope
had read Jane Austen carefully in the 1860s. He was
especially impressed by *Emma*, which among other
things makes a point of attacking secrecy and mystery
in interpersonal relationships and of espousing openness and candour. This theme is of course central to
Dr. Wortle's School. If the community is no better
than the lives that are lived in it, those lives had
better be lived honestly. It is significant that Dr.
Wortle 'hates' secrets: 'I haven't a secret in the
world. I know nothing of myself which you mightn't
know too' (II, iv), he tells Mr. Peacocke. In repeating
this conversation to his wife, the latter adds: 'Obscurity itself becomes mystery, and mystery of
course produces curiosity . . . A secret is always
accompanied by more or less of fear, and produces
more or less of cowardice . . . Who would not go
about, with all his affairs such as the world might
know, if it were possible?' When it is not 'possible',
the trouble starts: 'Who has a secret because he
chooses it?' Mr. Peacocke also 'hates secrets' (II, v).
Sometimes it is difficult to avoid having one, but it
is invariably a bad thing, and leads to other bad
things. The novel declares this over and over again.
Like most of the characters at the end of *Emma*, Mr.
Peacocke comes 'to hate . . . concealment' (III,
vii)—and rightly so, for it is the secret he keeps too
long that causes so much harm to Dr. Wortle, his

school, and his standing with others. The villain Robert Lefroy believes, significantly, that 'It's a good maxim to keep your own affairs quiet' (V, ix).

There are many good reasons for openness in our relations with others. The novel reminds us again and again that we must not only act morally but be *known* to do so in order to remain above the sort of suspicion that drives remorseless rumour and fuels 'figures of speech'. We must not only do what is right; we must do nothing that can lead people to suspect that we are doing what is wrong. Society is so tightly organized, so dependent for its moral verdicts upon appearances, that sometimes what we might today call 'image' can overshadow truth and determine how others perceive us. This is obviously dangerous. That Society operates in this way suggests both that its vision does not go very deep, and also that, because of this, the individual must not, by his actions, give it any cause for concern or speculation. Here Trollope gets at the heart of what has sometimes been called Victorian hypocrisy: the demand by others that we be *seen* to act properly, no matter what we are really doing. The Bishop's idea that 'It is not enough to be innocent . . . but men must know that we are so' (V, ii) expresses this most succinctly.

This ties the Church to Society as an institution equally addicted to appearances; indeed, another interesting aspect of *Dr. Wortle's School* is its highly uncharacteristic attack on the Anglican Establishment. Trollope was a worldly man, and this comes through in his books; he thought people should go out and do as well for themselves as they could. But he was also a believer, and seldom if ever is he so overtly anti-clerical as he is in this novel. This too contributes to its 'subversive' thrust.

In describing the sort of curate Dr. Wortle prefers, Trollope takes no trouble to hide his decidedly High Church (that is, anti-evangelical) bias—a bias which animates the better-known Barchester novels, and a number of others as well (see note to p. 4 (1)). But here, even those who are 'High', like the Bishop, are not easily let off (take, for example, the opening of IV, xi, a masterpiece of damnation by faint praise, in which it is made clear that the Bishop is a shallow, superficial man). That the hero of a Trollope novel should declare, 'It is often a question to me whether the religion of the world is not more odious than its want of religion' (IV, xi), is surprising enough. That a bishop should be accused of lack of breeding, 'vulgarity', 'meanness of thinking', 'meanness of intellect', and 'meanness' in general (V, iii), is astonishing. Even Bishop Proudie, who is very 'Low' indeed, gets off more easily than this in the Barchester chronicles. On the other hand, we must remember that Dr. Wortle himself, though not a devout man, is an ordained clergyman, the Rector of Bowick; in him, and in men like him, lies the Church's defence.

That much of Trollope's sympathy in *Dr. Wortle's School* is reserved for the unfortunate Mrs. Peacocke is part of the novel's attack on the old double standard—invoked, for example, by Mrs. Wortle, so often the voice of convention here. 'Anything wrong about a man', she declares, is 'of little moment' compared to 'anything wrong about a woman' (IV, xi). Mr. Peacocke knows well enough 'that a woman with a misfortune is condemned by the general voice of the world, whereas for a man to have stumbled is considered hardly more than a matter of course' (II, iv; one is reminded of the famous wedding-night scene in *Tess of the d'Urbervilles*). It is this 'general voice of the world' that Dr. Wortle seeks to combat, and rightly so; his knight-errantry is one of the most appealing aspects of his personality. That Trollope recognizes and abhors the Victorian double standard concerning the sexual conduct of men and women, at a time when Mrs. Wortle's view was the predominant one, is much to his credit. Yet again it connects him (here, at least) more closely to the younger writers then coming into prominence than to Dickens, Mrs Gaskell, or Charlotte Brontë.

The other love story is conventional enough, and not especially riveting. Trollope believed that there must be a generous dose of romance in each book for the young ladies who comprised the majority of his readers; and so we have here, in addition to the Peacockes, Mary Wortle and Lord Carstairs. But it is all very perfunctory. *Dr. Wortle's School* was written in just three weeks, 8–29 April 1879, while the novelist was staying at Lowick Rectory, Thrapston, Northamptonshire, where his friend William Lucas Collins was Rector. (Trollope enjoyed his visits to Thrapston, where he could ride with the Pytchley and Fitzwilliam hunts; he had given up riding to hounds, however, three years earlier, in 1876, when he was sixty-one.) On this occasion the Collinses were away, the Trollopes had the house to themselves, and the novelist made as always efficient use of his time. An early, discarded title was 'Bowick School'. In all likelihood the physical details of Bowick are taken from Lowick. Trollope often copied from life without much attempt at disguise (his protestations to the contrary notwithstanding); indeed, the novelist referred to *Dr. Wortle's School*, in several letters to the publisher John Blackwood written in 1879, as 'the Lowick story'. Both the rapidity and the single-mindedness with which *Dr. Wortle's School* was composed may help account for its unusual brevity among Trollope's books, and for the scant attention he pays to matters not germane to his story. This is one of the novel's strengths. In some of his other, longer tales complex, overlaid plots abound, as we have seen, and the love interests are handled with more care. We must be grateful that in *Dr. Wortle's School*, given its subject, Trollope did not work himself up to his usual sort of performance, but rather focused his creative energies on just a few ideas. The novel could go on just as well without Carstairs and Mary; its heart lies elsewhere. When Mrs. Peacocke tells Mrs. Wortle that 'It is hard to know sometimes what is right and what is wrong' (V, vii), she touches on the book's one true issue. What question could be more central—in literature or in life?

JOHN HALPERIN

NOTE ON THE TEXT

The manuscript of *Dr. Wortle's School* is in the Yale University Library; Trollope's 'Working Diary' is in the Bodleian Library, Oxford. The novel was written in three weeks in April 1879, serialized in *Blackwood's Magazine* from May to December 1880, and published in two volumes by Chapman and Hall in January 1881.

The present edition is a reproduction of the first Oxford World's Classics text of 1928 (reprinted 1944, 1951, 1960). Trollope organized the novel for serial publication into eight numbers (one number per month), each number to have three chapters. *Dr. Wortle's School* appeared in this format in *Blackwood's*. The present edition retains the 24-chapter format of the whole, and up to the end of Part IV the divisions are as they were in *Blackwood's*. The reader who wishes to follow Trollope's original organization should note that the fifth number ended with V, iii, the sixth with V, vi, and the seventh with V, ix. Thus the division of the original monthly parts may be reconstituted.

Trollope instructed *Blackwood's* to follow faithfully his original divisions for *Dr. Wortle's School*. 'In writing a story in numbers a novelist divides his points of interest, so as to make each section a whole,' he told William Blackwood on 11 February 1880. He added: 'It will often happen that his divisions should be recast to suit circumstances. But this cannot be done without a certain amount of detriment to the telling of the story.'*

SELECT BIBLIOGRAPHY

There is no collected edition of the works. A facsimile edition of thirty-six titles (62 vols.), *Selected Works of Anthony Trollope*, has been published by the Arno Press (1981; General Editor, N. John Hall). Works by Trollope are also available in the Oxford World's Classics series; in the Harting Grange Library Series (mostly the shorter works), published by the Caledonia Press; and in *Anthony Trollope: The Complete Short Stories* (forty-two stories in 5 vols.), ed. Betty Jane Slemp Breyer (1979–83). Some of Trollope's essays have been collected in *The New Zealander*, ed. N. John Hall (1972). The standard bibliography of the works is Michael Sadleir, *Trollope: A Bibliography* (1928; reprinted 1977). *The Letters of Anthony Trollope*, 2 vols., ed. N. John Hall (1983), is now the standard edition.

There is no definitive life. Among the more useful biographical volumes are Bradford A. Booth, *Anthony Trollope: Aspects of His Life and Work* (1958); James Pope Hennessy, *Anthony Trollope* (1971); Michael Sadleir, *Trollope: A Commentary* (1927); C. P. Snow, *Trollope* (1975); and L. P. and R. P. Stebbins, *The Trollopes: The Chronicle of A Writing Family* (1945). The best sources of information about Trollope's life remain T. H. S. Escott's memoir, *Anthony Trollope: His Public Services, Private Friends and Literary Originals* (1913; reprinted 1967), and the novelist's *Autobiography* (1883). Other useful tools are W. and J. Gerould, *A Guide to Trollope* (1948), and N. John Hall, *Trollope and His Illustrators* (1980).

The best bibliographies of criticism are Rafael Holling, *A Century of Trollope Criticism* (1956), and *The Reputation of Trollope: An Annotated Bibliography 1925–1975*, ed. John Charles Olmsted and Jeffrey Welch (1978). A selection of contemporary criticism may be found in *Trollope: The Critical Heritage*, ed. Donald Smalley

(1969). David Skilton, *Anthony Trollope and His Contemporaries* (1972), also discusses early critical responses. Three useful collections of essays: *The Trollope Critics*, ed. N. John Hall (1980); *Anthony Trollope*, ed. T. E. Bareham (1980); and *Trollope Centenary Essays*, ed. John Halperin (1982).

On Trollope's politics and political novels, see John Halperin, *Trollope and Politics* (1977), and Juliet McMaster, *Trollope's Palliser Novels: Theme and Pattern* (1979). Recommended critical studies: Ruth ap Roberts, *Trollope: Artist and Moralist (The Moral Trollope in US)* (1971); A. O. J. Cockshut, *Anthony Trollope: A Critical Study* (1955); James R. Kincaid, *The Novels of Anthony Trollope* (1977); Shirley R. Letwin, *The Gentleman in Trollope: Individuality and Moral Conduct* (1982); Robert M. Polhemus, *The Changing World of Anthony Trollope* (1968); Arthur Pollard, *Anthony Trollope* (1978); and Robert Tracy, *Trollope's Later Novels* (1978).

More general studies with helpful sections on Trollope: Robin Gilmour, *The Idea of the Gentleman in the Victorian Novel* (1981); J. Hillis Miller, *The Form of Victorian Fiction* (1968); Robert M. Polhemus, *Comic Faith: The Great Tradition from Austen to Joyce* (1980); and J. A. Sutherland, *Victorian Novelists and Publishers* (1976).

A CHRONOLOGY
OF ANTHONY TROLLOPE

1815   Born at 6 Keppel Street, Bloomsbury, 24 April.

1822   Sent to Harrow as a day-boy.

1825   Attends private school at Sunbury.

1827   Sent to Winchester College.

1830   Removed from Winchester and sent again to Harrow.

1834   Leaves Harrow, serves six weeks as classics teacher in a Brussels school.
Accepts junior clerkship in General Post Office; settles in London.

1841   Becomes Deputy Postal Surveyor at Banagher, in Ireland.

1844   Marries Rose Heseltine, in June. Transferred to Clonmel, in Ireland.

1845   Promoted to Surveyor in the Post Office and moves to Mallow, in Ireland.

1847   *The Macdermots of Ballycloran*, his first novel, is published (3 vols., T. C. Newby).

1848   *The Kellys and the O'Kellys; or Landlords and Tenants* (3 vols., Henry Colburn).
Rebellion in Ireland.

1850   *La Vendée: An Historical Romance* (3 vols., Henry Colburn).
Writes *The Noble Jilt* (play; published 1923).

1851   Postal duties in western England.

1853   Returns to Ireland, settles in Belfast.

1854   Leaves Belfast and settles at Donnybrook, near Dublin.

1855   *The Warden* (1 vol., Longman).

1857   *Barchester Towers* (3 vols., Longman).
        The Three Clerks (3 vols., Richard Bentley).

1858   Postal mission to Egypt; visits Palestine; postal
        mission to the West Indies; visits Malta, Gibraltar
        and Spain.
        Doctor Thorne (3 vols., Chapman & Hall).

1859   Returns to Ireland; moves to England, and settles
        at Waltham Cross, in Hertfordshire.
        The Bertrams (3 vols., Chapman & Hall).
        The West Indies and the Spanish Main (travel; 1
        vol., Chapman & Hall).

1860   Visits Florence.
        Tales of All Countries serialized in *Harper's New
        Monthly Magazine* and *Cassell's Illustrated
        Family Paper*, May–October.
        Castle Richmond (3 vols., Chapman & Hall).

1860–1 *Framley Parsonage* serialized in the *Cornhill
        Magazine*, January 1860–April 1861; its huge
        success establishes his reputation as a
        novelist.

1861   *Framley Parsonage* (3 vols., Smith, Elder).
        Tales of All Countries (1 vol., Chapman & Hall).
        Election to the Garrick Club.
        Tales of All Countries: Second Series, serialized
        in *Public Opinion*, the *London Review*, and *The
        Illustrated London News*, January–December.

1861–2 *Orley Farm* published in twenty monthly parts,
        March 1861–October 1862, by Chapman & Hall.
        Visits the United States (August 1861–May 1862).
        *The Struggles of Brown, Jones and Robinson: by
        One of the Firm*, serialized in the *Cornhill
        Magazine*, August 1861–March 1862.

1862   *Orley Farm* (2 vols., Chapman & Hall).
        North America (travel; 2 vols., Chapman & Hall).

The Struggles of Brown, Jones and Robinson (1 vol., New York: Harper; first English edition published 1870).
Rachel Ray (2 vols., Chapman & Hall).

1862–4 *The Small House at Allington*, serialized in the *Cornhill Magazine*, September 1862–April 1864.

1863 *Tales of All Countries: Second Series* (1 vol., Chapman & Hall).
Death of his mother, Frances Trollope.

1864 Election to the Athenaeum.
The Small House at Allington (2 vols., Smith, Elder).
Can You Forgive Her? (2 vols., Chapman & Hall).

1864–5 *Can You Forgive Her?* published in twenty monthly parts, January 1864–August 1865, by Chapman & Hall.

1865 *Miss Mackenzie* (2 vols., Chapman & Hall).
Hunting Sketches (1 vol., Chapman & Hall); also serialized in *Pall Mall Gazette*, February–March.
Travelling Sketches, serialized in the *Pall Mall Gazette*, August–September.

1865–6 *The Belton Estate*, serialized in the *Fortnightly Review*, May 1865–January 1866.
Clergymen of the Church of England, serialized in the *Pall Mall Gazette*, November 1865–January 1866.

1866 *The Belton Estate* (3 vols., Chapman & Hall).
Travelling Sketches (1 vol., Chapman & Hall).
Clergymen of the Church of England (1 vol., Chapman & Hall).

1866–7 *The Claverings*, serialized in the *Cornhill Magazine*, February 1866–May 1867.
Nina Balatka, serialized in *Blackwood's Magazine*, July 1866–January 1867.
The Last Chronicle of Barset, published in thirty-

two weekly parts, December 1866–July 1867, by Smith, Elder.

1867   *Nina Balatka* (2 vols., William Blackwood).
    The Last Chronicle of Barset (2 vols., Smith, Elder).
    The Claverings (2 vols., Smith, Elder).
    Lotta Schmidt: and Other Stories (contents published between 1861 and 1867; 1 vol., Alexander Strahan).
    Resigns from the Post Office and leaves the Civil Service.

1867–8   *Linda Tressel*, serialized in *Blackwood's Magazine*, October 1867–May 1868.

1867–9   *Phineas Finn: The Irish Member*, serialized in *St. Paul's Magazine*, October 1867–May 1869.

1867–70   Serves as Editor of *St. Paul's Magazine* (founded 1 October 1867).

1868   *Linda Tressel* (2 vols., William Blackwood).
    Visits United States to negotiate postal treaty.
    Stands as Liberal candidate for Beverley, in Yorkshire, in General Election; finishes at bottom of poll.

1868–9   *He Knew He Was Right*, published in thirty weekly parts, from October 1868–May 1869, by Virtue.

1869   *Phineas Finn* (2 vols., Virtue).
    He Knew He Was Right (2 vols., Alexander Strahan).
    Did He Steal It? A Comedy in Three Acts (privately printed and never performed; a dramatization of *The Last Chronicle of Barset*).

1869–70   *The Vicar of Bullhampton*, serialized in eleven monthly parts, July 1869–May 1870, by Bradbury & Evans.
    An Editor's Tales, serialized in *St. Paul's Magazine*, October 1869–May 1870.

1870   *The Vicar of Bullhampton* (1 vol., Bradbury & Evans).
           An Editor's Tales (1 vol., Alexander Strahan).
           The Commentaries of Caesar (1 vol., William Blackwood).
           Sir Harry Hotspur of Humblethwaite (1 vol., Hurst & Blackett); also serialized in *Macmillan's Magazine*, May–December.

1870–1   *Ralph the Heir*, serialized in *St. Paul's Magazine*, January 1870–July 1871.

1871   *Ralph the Heir* (3 vols., Hurst & Blackett).
           Gives up house at Waltham Cross; visits Australia.

1871–2   Travelling in Australia and New Zealand.

1871–3   *The Eustace Diamonds*, serialized in the *Fortnightly Review*, July 1871–February 1873.

1872   *The Golden Lion of Granpère* (1 vol., Tinsley); also serialized in *Good Words*, January–August.
           Returns to England and settles at 39 Montagu Square, London.

1873   *The Eustace Diamonds* (3 vols., Chapman & Hall).
           Australia and New Zealand (travel; 2 vols., Chapman & Hall).
           Phineas Redux (2 vols., Chapman & Hall).
           Harry Heathcote of Gangoil: A Tale of Australian Bush Life, published as the Christmas number of *The Graphic*.

1873–4   *Phineas Redux*, serialized in *The Graphic*, July 1873–January 1874.
           Lady Anna, serialized in the *Fortnightly Review*, April 1873–April 1874.

1874   *Lady Anna* (2 vols., Chapman & Hall).
           Harry Heathcote of Gangoil (1 vol., Sampson Low).

1874–5 *The Way We Live Now*, published in twenty monthly parts, February 1874–September 1875, by Chapman & Hall.

1875 *The Way We Live Now* (2 vols., Chapman & Hall). Travels to Ceylon and Australia, returns to England.

1875–6 *The Prime Minister*, published in eight monthly parts, November 1875–June 1876, by Chapman & Hall.

1876 *The Prime Minister* (4 vols., Chapman & Hall).

1876–7 *The American Senator*, serialized in *Temple Bar*, May 1876–July 1877.

1877 *The American Senator* (3 vols., Chapman & Hall).
Visits South Africa, returns to England.
Christmas at Thompson Hall (1 vol., New York: Harper).

1877–8 *Is He Popenjoy?: A Novel*, serialized in *All the Year Round*, October 1877–July 1878.

1878 *South Africa* (travel; 2 vols., Chapman & Hall).
Is He Popenjoy? (3 vols., Chapman & Hall).
Visits Iceland, returns to England.
How the 'Mastiffs' Went to Iceland (1 vol., Virtue).

1878–9 *An Eye for An Eye*, serialized in the *Whitehall Review*, August 1878–February 1879.
John Caldigate, serialized in *Blackwood's Magazine*, April 1878–June 1879.

1879 *An Eye for An Eye* (2 vols., Chapman & Hall).
Thackeray (1 vol., Macmillan).
John Caldigate (3 vols., Chapman & Hall).
Cousin Henry: A Novel (2 vols., Chapman & Hall); also serialized, simultaneously, in the *Manchester Weekly Times* and the *North British Weekly Mail*, May–December.

1879–80 *The Duke's Children: A Novel*, serialized in *All
the Year Round*, October 1879–July 1880.

1880 *The Duke's Children* (3 vols., Chapman & Hall).
The Life of Cicero (2 vols., Chapman & Hall).
Dr. Wortle's School: A Novel, serialized in *Black-
wood's Magazine*, May–December.
Gives up London residence and settles at Harting
Grange, near Petersfield.
London Tradesmen, serialized in the *Pall Mall
Gazette*, July–September (published 1927).

1881 *Dr. Wortle's School* (2 vols., Chapman & Hall).
Ayala's Angel (3 vols., Chapman & Hall).

1881–2 *The Fixed Period: A Novel*, serialized in *Black-
wood's Magazine*, October 1881–March 1882.
Marion Fay: A Novel, serialized in *The Graphic*,
December 1881–June 1882.

1882 Visits Ireland twice.
*Why Frau Frohmann Raised Her Prices: And
Other Stories* (stories published 1876–8; 1 vol.,
William Isbister).
Lord Palmerston (1 vol., William Isbister).
Marion Fay (3 vols., Chapman & Hall).
Kept in the Dark: A Novel (2 vols., Chatto &
Windus); also serialized in *Good Words*, May–
December.
The Fixed Period (2 vols., William Blackwood).
Death in London, 6 December.
The Two Heroines of Plumplington, Christmas
number of *Good Words* (published 1954).

1882–3 *Mr. Scarborough's Family*, written 1881, serial-
ized in *All the Year Round*, May 1882–June 1883.
The Landleaguers (unfinished), serialized in *Life*,
November 1882–October 1883.

1883 *Mr. Scarborough's Family* (3 vols., Chatto &
Windus).

The Landleaguers (3 vols., Chatto & Windus).
An Autobiography (written 1875–6; 2 vols., William Blackwood).

1884   *An Old Man's Love* (written 1882; 2 vols., William Blackwood).

CONTENTS

PART I

PART II

PART III

PART IV

PART V

CONCLUSION

DR. WORTLE'S SCHOOL

PART I

CHAPTER I

DR. WORTLE

THE Rev. Jeffrey Wortle, D.D.,* was a man much
esteemed by others,—and by himself. He combined two professions, in both of which he had been
successful,— had been, and continued to be, at the
time in which we speak of him. I will introduce
him to the reader in the present tense as Rector of
Bowick, and proprietor and head-master of the
school established in the village of that name. The
seminary at Bowick had for some time enjoyed a
reputation under him ;—not that he had ever himself used so new-fangled and unpalatable a word in
speaking of his school. Bowick School had been
established by himself as preparatory to Eton.
Dr. Wortle had been elected to an assistant-master-
ship at Eton early in life soon after he had become
a Fellow of Exeter.* There he had worked successfully for ten years, and had then retired to the
living of Bowick. On going there he had determined to occupy his leisure, and if possible to make
his fortune, by taking a few boys into his house.
By dint of charging high prices and giving good
food,—perhaps in part, also, by the quality of the
education which he imparted,—his establishment
had become popular and had outgrown the

capacity of the parsonage. He had been enabled to purchase a field or two close abutting on the glebe* gardens, and had there built convenient premises. He now limited his number to thirty boys, for each of which he charged £200 a-year. It was said of him by his friends that if he would only raise his price to £250, he might double the number, and really make a fortune. In answer to this, he told his friends that he knew his own business best;— he declared that his charge was the only sum that was compatible both with regard to himself and honesty to his customers, and asserted that the labours he endured were already quite heavy enough. In fact, he recommended all those who gave him advice to mind their own business.

It may be said of him that he knew his own so well as to justify him in repudiating counsel from others. There are very different ideas of what ' a fortune ' may be supposed to consist. It will not be necessary to give Dr. Wortle's exact idea. No doubt it changed with him, increasing as his money increased. But he was supposed to be a comfortable man. He paid ready money and high prices. He liked that people under him should thrive,—and he liked them to know that they throve by his means. He liked to be master, and always was. He was just, and liked his justice to be recognised. He was generous also, and liked that, too, to be known. He kept a carriage for his wife, who had been the daughter of a poor clergyman at Windsor, and was proud to see her as well dressed as the wife of any county squire. But he was a domineering husband. As his wife worshipped him, and regarded him as a Jupiter*on earth from whose nod

there could be and should be no appeal, but little
harm came from this. If a tyrant, he was an affectionate tyrant. His wife felt him to be so. His
servants, his parish, and his school all felt him to
be so. They obeyed him, loved him, and believed
in him.

So, upon the whole, at the time with which we
are dealing, did the diocese, the county, and that
world of parents by whom the boys were sent to
his school. But this had not come about without
some hard fighting. He was over fifty years of age,
and had been Rector of Bowick for nearly twenty.
During that time there had been a succession of
three bishops, and he had quarrelled more or less
with all of them. It might be juster to say that
they had all of them had more or less of occasion to
find fault with him. Now Dr. Wortle,—or Mr.
Wortle, as he should be called in reference to that
period,*—was a man who would bear censure from
no human being. He had left his position at Eton
because the head-master had required from him
some slight change of practice. There had been no
quarrel on that occasion, but Mr. Wortle had gone.
He at once commenced his school at Bowick, taking
half-a-dozen pupils into his own house. The bishop
of that day suggested that the cure of the souls of
the parishioners of Bowick was being subordinated
to the Latin and Greek of the sons of the nobility.
The bishop got a response which gave an additional
satisfaction to his speedy translation to a more
comfortable diocese. Between the next bishop
and Mr. Wortle there was, unfortunately, misunder-
standing, and almost feud for the entire ten years
during which his lordship reigned in the Palace of

Broughton. This Bishop of Broughton had been
one of that large batch of Low Church*prelates who
were brought forward under Lord Palmerston.
Among them there was none more low, more pious,
more sincere, or more given to interference. To
teach Mr. Wortle his duty as a parish clergyman
was evidently a necessity to such a bishop. To
repudiate any such teaching was evidently a necessity to Mr. Wortle. Consequently there were differ-
ences, in all of which Mr. Wortle carried his own.
What the good bishop suffered no one probably
knew except his wife and his domestic chaplain.
What Mr. Wortle enjoyed,—or Dr. Wortle, as he
came to be called about this time,*—was patent to
all the county and all the diocese. The sufferer
died, not, let us hope, by means of the Doctor ;
and then came the third bishop. He, too, had found
himself obliged to say a word. He was a man of
the world,—wise, prudent, not given to interference
or fault-finding, friendly by nature, one who altogether hated a quarrel, a bishop beyond all things
determined to be the friend of his clergymen ;—
and yet he thought himself obliged to say a word.
There were matters in which Dr. Wortle affected
a peculiarly anti-clerical mode of expression, if not
of feeling. He had been foolish enough to declare
openly that he was in search of a curate who should
have none of the ' grace of godliness ' about him.
He was wont to ridicule the piety of young men
who devoted themselves entirely to their religious
offices. In a letter which he wrote he spoke of one
youthful divine as ' a conceited ass who had
preached for forty minutes.' He not only disliked,
but openly ridiculed all signs of a special pietistic

bearing. It was said of him that he had been heard
to swear. There can be no doubt that he made
himself wilfully distasteful to many of his stricter
brethren. Then it came to pass that there was a
correspondence between him and the bishop as to
that outspoken desire of his for a curate without
the grace of godliness. But even here Dr. Wortle
was successful. The management of his parish was
pre-eminently good. The parish school was a
model. The farmers went to church. Dissenters*
there were none. The people of Bowick believed
thoroughly in their parson, and knew the comfort
of having an open-handed, well-to-do gentleman in
the village. This third episcopal difficulty did not
endure long. Dr. Wortle knew his man, and was
willing enough to be on good terms with his bishop
so long as he was allowed to be in all things his
own master.

There had, too, been some fighting between Dr.
Wortle and the world about his school. He was,
as I have said, a thoroughly generous man, but he
required, himself, to be treated with generosity.
Any question as to the charges made by him as
schoolmaster was unendurable. He explained to
all parents that he charged for each boy at the rate
of two hundred a-year for board, lodging, and
tuition, and that anything required for a boy's
benefit or comfort beyond that ordinarily supplied
would be charged for as an extra at such price as
Dr. Wortle himself thought to be an equivalent.
Now the popularity of his establishment no doubt
depended in a great degree on the sufficiency and
comfort of the good things of the world which he
provided. The beer was of the best ; the boys were

not made to eat fat ; their taste in the selection of
joints was consulted. The morning coffee was excellent. The cook was a great adept at cakes and
puddings. The Doctor would not himself have been
satisfied unless everything had been plentiful, and
everything of the best. He would have hated a
butcher who had attempted to seduce him with
meat beneath the usual price. But when he had
supplied that which was sufficient according to his
own liberal ideas, he did not give more without
charging for it. Among his customers there had
been a certain Honourable* Mr. Stantiloup, and,—
which had been more important,—an Honourable
Mrs. Stantiloup. Mrs. Stantiloup was a lady who
liked all the best things which the world could
supply, but hardly liked paying the best price. Dr.
Wortle's school was the best thing the world could
supply of that kind, but then the price was certainly the very best. Young Stantiloup was only
eleven, and as there were boys at Bowick as old as
seventeen,—for the school had not altogether
maintained its old character as being merely preparatory,—Mrs. Stantiloup had thought that her
boy should be admitted at a lower fee. The correspondence which had ensued had been unpleasant.
Then young Stantiloup had had the influenza, and
Mrs. Stantiloup had sent her own doctor. Champagne had been ordered, and carriage exercise.
Mr. Stantiloup had been forced by his wife to refuse
to pay sums demanded for these undoubted extras.
Ten shillings a day for a drive for a little boy
seemed to her a great deal,—seemed so to Mrs.
Stantiloup. Ought not the Doctor's wife to have
been proud to take out her little boy in her own car-

riage ? And then £2 10s. for champagne for the
little boy ! It was monstrous. Mr. Stantiloup
remonstrated. Dr. Wortle said that the little boy
had better be taken away and the bill paid at once.
The little boy was taken away and the money was
offered, short of £5. The matter was instantly put
into the hands of the Doctor's lawyer, and a suit
commenced. The Doctor, of course, got his money,
and then there followed an acrimonious correspondence in the 'Times' and other newspapers.
Mrs. Stantiloup did her best to ruin the school, and
many very eloquent passages were written not only
by her or by her own special scribe, but by others
who took the matter up, to prove that two hundred
a-year was a great deal more than ought to be paid
for the charge of a little boy during three quarters
of the year. But in the course of the next twelve
months Dr. Wortle was obliged to refuse admit-
tance to a dozen eligible pupils because he had not
room for them.

No doubt he had suffered during these contests,
—suffered, that is, in mind. There had been moments in which it seemed that the victory would be
on the other side, that the forces congregated
against him were too many for him, and that not
being able to bend he would have to be broken ;
but in every case he had fought it out, and in every
case he had conquered. He was now a prosperous
man, who had achieved his own way, and had
made all those connected with him feel that it was
better to like him and obey him, than to dislike
him and fight with him. His curates troubled him
as little as possible with the grace of godliness, and
threw off as far as they could that zeal which is so

dear to the youthful mind but which so often seems to be weak and flabby to their elders. His ushers* or assistants in the school fell in with his views implicitly, and were content to accept compensation in the shape of personal civilities. It was much better to go shares with the Doctor in a joke than to have to bear his hard words.

It is chiefly in reference to one of these ushers that our story has to be told. But before we commence it, we must say a few more words as to the Doctor and his family. Of his wife I have already spoken. She was probably as happy a woman as you shall be likely to meet on a summer's day. She had good health, easy temper, pleasant friends, abundant means, and no ambition. She went nowhere without the Doctor, and wherever he went she enjoyed her share of the respect which was always shown to him. She had little or nothing to do with the school, the Doctor having many years ago resolved that though it became him as a man to work for his bread, his wife should not be a slave. When the battles had been going on,—those between the Doctor and the bishops, and the Doctor and Mrs. Stantiloup, and the Doctor and the newspapers,—she had for a while been unhappy. It had grieved her to have it insinuated that her husband was an atheist, and asserted that her husband was a cormorant ;* but his courage had sustained her, and his continual victories had taught her to believe at last that he was indomitable.

They had one child, a daughter, Mary, of whom it was said in Bowick that she alone knew the length of the Doctor's foot.* It certainly was so that, if Mrs. Wortle wished to have anything done

which was a trifle beyond her own influence, she
employed Mary. And if the boys collectively
wanted to carry a point, they would 'collectively'
obtain Miss Wortle's aid. But all this the Doctor
probably knew very well; and though he was often
pleased to grant favours thus asked, he did so
because he liked the granting of favours when they
had been asked with a proper degree of care and
attention. She was at the present time of the age
in which fathers are apt to look upon their children
as still children, while other men regard them as
being grown-up young ladies. It was now June,
and in the approaching August she would be
eighteen. It was said of her that of the girls all
round she was the prettiest; and indeed it would
be hard to find a sweeter-favoured girl than Mary
Wortle. Her father had been all his life a man
noted for the manhood of his face. He had a broad
forehead, with bright grey eyes,—eyes that had
always a smile passing round them, though the
smile would sometimes show that touch of irony
which a smile may contain rather than the good-
humour which it is ordinarily supposed to indicate.
His nose was aquiline, not hooky like a bird's-beak,
but with that bend which seems to give to the
human face the clearest indication of individual
will. His mouth, for a man, was perhaps a little too
small, but was admirably formed, as had been the
chin with a deep dimple on it, which had now by
the slow progress of many dinners become doubled
in its folds. His hair had been chestnut, but dark
in its hue. It had now become grey, but still with
the shade of the chestnut through it here and there.
He stood five feet ten in height, with small hands

and feet. He was now perhaps somewhat stout,
but was still as upright on his horse as ever, and as
well able to ride to hounds for a few fields when by
chance the hunt came in the way of Bowick. Such
was the Doctor. Mrs. Wortle was a pretty little
woman, now over forty years of age, of whom it
was said that in her day she had been the beauty of
Windsor and those parts. Mary Wortle took mostly
after her father, being tall and comely, having
especially her father's eyes ; but still they who had
known Mrs. Wortle as a girl declared that Mary had
inherited also her mother's peculiar softness and
complexion.

For many years past none of the pupils had been
received within the parsonage,—unless when received there as guests, which was of frequent occurrence. All belonging to the school was built
outside the glebe land, as a quite separate establishment, with a door opening from the parsonage
garden to the school-yard. Of this door the rule
was that the Doctor and the gardener should have
the only two keys ; but the rule may be said to
have become quite obsolete, as the door was never
locked. Sometimes the bigger boys would come
through unasked,—perhaps in search of a game of
lawn-tennis with Miss Wortle, perhaps to ask some
favour of Mrs. Wortle, who always was delighted to
welcome them, perhaps even to seek the Doctor
himself, who never on such occasions would ask
how it came to pass that they were on that side of
the wall. Sometimes Mrs. Wortle would send her
housekeeper through for some of the little boys. It
would then be a good time for the little boys. But
this would generally be during the Doctor's absence.

Here, on the school side of the wall, there was a separate establishment of servants, and a separate kitchen. There was no sending backwards or forwards of food or of clothes,—unless it might be when some special delicacy was sent in if a boy were unwell. For these no extra charge was ever made, as had been done in the case of young Stantiloup. Then a strange doctor had come, and had ordered the wine and the carriage. There was no extra charge for the kindly glasses of wine which used to be administered in quite sufficient plenty.

Behind the school, and running down to the little river Pin, there is a spacious cricket-ground, and a court marked out for lawn-tennis. Up close to the school is a racket-court. No doubt a good deal was done to make the externals of the place alluring to those parents who love to think that their boys shall be made happy at school. Attached to the school, forming part of the building, is a pleasant, well-built residence, with six or eight rooms, intended for the senior or classical assistant-master. It had been the Doctor's scheme to find a married gentleman to occupy this house, whose wife should receive a separate salary for looking after the linen and acting as matron to the school,—doing what his wife did till he became successful,—while the husband should be in orders and take part of the church duties as a second curate. But there had been a difficulty in this.

CHAPTER II

THE NEW USHER

THE Doctor had found it difficult to carry out the scheme described in the last chapter. They indeed who know anything of such matters will be inclined to call it Utopian,*and to say that one so wise in worldly matters as our schoolmaster should not have attempted to combine so many things. He wanted a gentleman, a schoolmaster, a curate, a matron, and a lady,—we may say all in one. Curates and ushers are generally unmarried. An assistant schoolmaster is not often in orders, and sometimes is not a gentleman. A gentleman, when he is married, does not often wish to dispose of the services of his wife. A lady, when she has a husband, has generally sufficient duties of her own to employ her, without undertaking others. The scheme, if realised, would no doubt be excellent, but the difficulties were too many. The Stantiloups, who lived about twenty miles off, made fun of the Doctor and his project ; and the Bishop was said to have expressed himself as afraid that he would not be able to license as curate any one selected as usher to the school. One attempt was made after another in vain ;—but at last it was declared through the country far and wide that the Doctor had succeeded in this, as in every other enterprise that he had attempted. There had come a Rev. Mr. Peacocke and his wife. Six years since, Mr. Peacocke had been well known at Oxford as a Classic,* and had become a Fellow of Trinity.

Then he had taken orders, and had some time afterwards married, giving up his Fellowship as a matter
of course.* Mr. Peacocke, while living at Oxford,
had been well known to a large Oxford circle, but
he had suddenly disappeared from that world, and
it had reached the ears of only a few of his more
intimate friends that he had undertaken the duties
of vice-president of a classical college at Saint Louis
in the State of Missouri. Such a disruption as this
was for a time complete ; but after five years Mr.
Peacocke appeared again at Oxford, with a beautiful American wife, and the necessity of earning an
income by his erudition.

It would at first have seemed very improbable
that Dr. Wortle should have taken into his school
or into his parish a gentleman who had chosen the
United States as a field for his classical labours.
The Doctor, whose mind was by no means logical,
was a thorough-going Tory of the old school, and
therefore considered himself bound to hate the
name of a republic.* He hated rolling stones, and
Mr. Peacocke had certainly been a rolling stone.
He loved Oxford with all his heart, and some years
since had been heard to say hard things of Mr.
Peacocke, when that gentleman deserted his college
for the sake of establishing himself across the At-
lantic. But he was one who thought that there
should be a place of penitence allowed to those who
had clearly repented of their errors ; and, moreover, when he heard that Mr. Peacocke was endeavouring to establish himself in Oxford as a
' coach ' for undergraduates, and also that he was
a married man without any encumbrance in the
way of family, there seemed to him to be an

additional reason for pardoning that American escapade. Circumstances brought the two men together. There were friends at Oxford who knew how anxious the Doctor was to carry out that plan of his in reference to an usher, a curate, and a matron, and here were the very things combined. Mr. Peacocke's scholarship and power of teaching were acknowledged; he was already in orders; and it was declared that Mrs. Peacocke was undoubtedly a lady. Many inquiries were made. Many meetings took place. Many difficulties arose. But at last Mr. and Mrs. Peacocke came to Bowick, and took up their abode in the school.

All the Doctor's requirements were not at once fulfilled. Mrs. Peacocke's position was easily settled. Mrs. Peacocke, who seemed to be a woman possessed of sterling sense and great activity, undertook her duties without difficulty. But Mr. Peacocke would not at first consent to act as curate in the parish. He did, however, after a time perform a portion of the Sunday services. When he first came to Bowick he had declared that he would undertake no clerical duty. Education was his profession, and to that he meant to devote himself exclusively. Nor for the six or eight months of his sojourn did he go back from this; so that the Doctor may be said even still to have failed in carrying out his purpose. But at last the new schoolmaster appeared in the pulpit of the parish church and preached a sermon.

All that had passed in private conference between the Doctor and his assistant on the subject need not here be related. Mr. Peacocke's aversion to do more than attend regularly at the church

services as one of the parishioners had been very
strong. The Doctor's anxiety to overcome his
assistant's reasoning had also been strong. There
had no doubt been much said between them. Mr.
Peacocke had been true to his principles, whatever
those principles were, in regard to his appointment
as a curate,—but it came to pass that he for some
months preached regularly every Sunday in the
parish church, to the full satisfaction of the
parishioners. For this he had accepted no payment, much to the Doctor's dissatisfaction. Nevertheless, it was certainly the case that they who
served the Doctor gratuitously never came by the
worse of the bargain.

Mr. Peacocke was a small wiry man, anything
but robust in appearance, but still capable of great
bodily exertion. He was a great walker. Labour
in the school never seemed to fatigue him. The
addition of a sermon to preach every week seemed
to make no difference to his energies in the school.
He was a constant reader, and could pass from one
kind of mental work to another without fatigue.
The Doctor was a noted scholar, but it soon became
manifest to the Doctor himself, and to the boys,
that Mr. Peacocke was much deeper in scholarship
than the Doctor. Though he was a poor man, his
own small classical library was supposed to be a
repository of all that was known about Latin and
Greek. In fact, Mr. Peacocke grew to be a marvel;
but of all the marvels about him, the thing most
marvellous was the entire faith which the Doctor
placed in him. Certain changes even were made in
the old-established ' curriculum ' of tuition,—and
were made, as all the boys supposed, by the advice

of Mr. Peacocke. Mr. Peacocke was treated with
a personal respect which almost seemed to imply
that the two men were equal. This was supposed
by the boys to come from the fact that both the
Doctor and the assistant had been Fellows of their
colleges at Oxford; but the parsons and other
gentry around could see that there was more in it
than that. Mr. Peacocke had some power about
him which was potent over the Doctor's spirit.

Mrs. Peacocke, in her line, succeeded almost as
well. She was a woman something over thirty
years of age when she first came to Bowick, in the
very pride and bloom of woman's beauty. Her
complexion was dark and brown,—so much so,
that it was impossible to describe her colour generally by any other word. But no clearer skin was
ever given to a woman. Her eyes were brown, and
her eye-brows black, and perfectly regular. Her
hair was dark and very glossy, and always dressed
as simply as the nature of a woman's head will
allow. Her features were regular, but with a great
show of strength. She was tall for a woman, but
without any of that look of length under which
female altitude sometimes suffers. She was strong
and well made, and apparently equal to any labour
to which her position might subject her. When she
had been at Bowick about three months, a boy's
leg had been broken, and she had nursed him, not
only with assiduity, but with great capacity. The
boy was the youngest son of the Marchioness of
Altamont; and when Lady Altamont paid a
second visit to Bowick, for the sake of taking her
boy home as soon as he was fit to be moved, her
ladyship made a little mistake. With the sweetest

and most caressing smile in the world, she offered
Mrs. Peacocke a ten-pound note. 'My dear
madam,' said Mrs. Peacocke, without the slightest
reserve or difficulty, 'it is so natural that you should
do this, because you cannot of course understand
my position; but it is altogether out of the question.' The Marchioness blushed, and stammered,
and begged a hundred pardons. Being a good-
natured woman, she told the whole story to Mrs.
Wortle. 'I would just as soon have offered the
money to the Marchioness herself,' said Mrs.
Wortle, as she told it to her husband. 'I would
have done it a deal sooner,' said the Doctor. 'I am
not in the least afraid of Lady Altamont; but I
stand in awful dread of Mrs. Peacocke.' Nevertheless, Mrs. Peacocke had done her work by the little
lord's bed-side, just as though she had been a paid
nurse.

And so she felt herself to be. Nor was she in the
least ashamed of her position in that respect. If
there was aught of shame about her, as some people
said, it certainly did not come from the fact that
she was in the receipt of a salary for the performance of certain prescribed duties. Such remuneration was, she thought, as honourable as the
Doctor's income; but to her American intelligence,
the acceptance of a present of money from a Marchioness would have been a degradation.

It certainly was said of her by some persons that
there must have been something in her former life
of which she was ashamed. The Honourable Mrs.
Stantiloup, to whom all the affairs of Bowick had
been of consequence since her husband had lost his
lawsuit, and who had not only heard much, but

had inquired far and near about Mr. and Mrs.
Peacocke, declared diligently among her friends,
with many nods and winks, that there was something 'rotten in the state of Denmark '.* She did at
first somewhat imprudently endeavour to spread
a rumour abroad that the Doctor had become en-
slaved by the lady's beauty. But even those hostile
to Bowick could not accept this. The Doctor certainly was not the man to put in jeopardy the respect of the world and his own standing for the
beauty of any woman ; and, moreover, the Doctor,
as we have said before, was over fifty years of age.
But there soon came up another ground on which
calumny could found a story. It was certainly the
case that Mrs. Peacocke had never accepted any
hospitality from Mrs. Wortle or other ladies in the
neighbourhood. It reached the ears of Mrs. Stantiloup, first, that the ladies had called upon each
other, as ladies are wont to do who intend to culti-
vate a mutual personal acquaintance, and then
that Mrs. Wortle had asked Mrs. Peacocke to
dinner. But Mrs. Peacocke had refused not only
that invitation, but subsequent invitations to the
less ceremonious form of tea-drinking.

All this had been true, and it had been true also,
—though of this Mrs. Stantiloup had not heard the
particulars,—that Mrs. Peacocke had explained to
her neighbour that she did not intend to put herself
on a visiting footing with any one. ' But why not,
my dear ? ' Mrs. Wortle had said, urged to the
argument by precepts from her husband. ' Why
should you make yourself desolate here, when we
shall be so glad to have you ? ' ' It is part of my
life that it must be so,' Mrs. Peacocke had answered.

' I am quite sure that the duties I have undertaken are becoming a lady ; but I do not think that they are becoming to one who either gives or accepts entertainments.'

There had been something of the same kind between the Doctor and Mr. Peacocke. ' Why the mischief shouldn't you and your wife come and eat a bit of mutton, and drink a glass of wine, over at the Rectory, like any other decent people ? ' I never believed that accusation against the Doctor in regard to swearing; but he was no doubt addicted to expletives in conversation, and might perhaps have indulged in a strong word or two, had he not been prevented by the sanctity of his orders. ' Perhaps I ought to say,' replied Mr. Peacocke, ' because we are not like any other decent people.' Then he went on to explain his meaning. Decent people, he thought, in regard to social intercourse, are those who are able to give and take with ease among each other. He had fallen into a position in which neither he nor his wife could give anything, and from which, though some might be willing to accept him, he would be accepted only, as it were, by special favour. ' Bosh ! ' ejaculated the Doctor. Mr. Peacocke simply smiled. He said it might be bosh, but that even were he inclined to relax his own views, his wife would certainly not relax hers. So it came to pass that although the Doctor and Mr. Peacocke were really intimate, and that something of absolute friendship sprang up between the two ladies, when Mr. Peacocke had already been more than twelve months in Bowick neither had he nor Mrs. Peacocke broken bread in the Doctor's house.

And yet the friendship had become strong. An incident had happened early in the year which had served greatly to strengthen it. At the school there was a little boy, just eleven years old, the only son of a Lady De Lawle, who had in early years been a dear friend to Mrs. Wortle. Lady De Lawle was the widow of a baronet, and the little boy was the heir to a large fortune. The mother had been most loath to part with her treasure. Friends, uncles, and trustees had declared that the old prescribed form of education for British aristocrats must be followed,—a t'other school,* namely, then Eton, and then Oxford. No ; his mother might not go with him, first to one, and then to the other. Such going and living with him would deprive his education of all the real salt. Therefore Bowick was chosen as the t'other school, because Mrs. Wortle would be more like a mother to the poor desolate boy than any other lady. So it was arranged, and the ' poor desolate boy ' became the happiest of the young pickles whom it was Mrs. Wortle's special province to spoil whenever she could get hold of them.

Now it happened that on one beautiful afternoon towards the end of April, Mrs. Wortle had taken young De Lawle and another little boy with her over the foot-bridge which passed from the bottom of the parsonage garden to the glebe-meadow which ran on the other side of a little river, and with them had gone a great Newfoundland dog, who was on terms equally friendly with the inmates of the Rectory and the school. Where this bridge passed across the stream the gardens and the field were on the same level. But as the water ran down to the ground on which the school-buildings had been

erected, there arose a steep bank over a bend in the
river, or, rather, steep cliff; for, indeed, it was
almost perpendicular, the force of the current as
it turned at this spot having washed away the bank.
In this way it had come to pass that there was a
precipitous fall of about a dozen feet from the top
of the little cliff into the water, and that the water
here, as it eddied round the curve, was black and
deep, so that the bigger boys were wont to swim
in it, arrangements for bathing having been made
on the further or school side. There had sometimes been a question whether a rail should not
be placed for protection along the top of this cliff,
but nothing of the kind had yet been done. The
boys were not supposed to play in this field, which
was on the other side of the river, and could only
be reached by the bridge through the parsonage
garden.

On this day young De Lawle and his friend and
the dog rushed up the hill before Mrs. Wortle, and
there began to romp, as was their custom. Mary
Wortle, who was one of the party, followed them,
enjoining the children to keep away from the cliff.
For a while they did so, but of course returned.
Once or twice they were recalled and scolded, always asserting that the fault was altogether with
Neptune. It was Neptune that knocked them down
and always pushed them towards the river. Perhaps it was Neptune; but be that as it might,
there came a moment very terrible to them all.
The dog in one of his gyrations came violently
against the little boy, knocked him off his legs,
and pushed him over the edge. Mrs. Wortle, who
had been making her way slowly up the hill, saw

the fall, heard the splash, and fell immediately to the ground.

Other eyes had also seen the accident. The Doctor and Mr. Peacocke were at the moment walking together in the playgrounds at the school side of the brook. When the boy fell they had paused in their walk, and were standing, the Doctor with his back to the stream, and the assistant with his face turned towards the cliff. A loud exclamation broke from his lips as he saw the fall, but in a moment,— almost before the Doctor had realised the accident which had occurred,—he was in the water, and two minutes afterwards young De Lawle, drenched indeed, frightened, and out of breath, but in nowise seriously hurt, was out upon the bank; and Mr. Peacocke, drenched also, but equally safe, was standing over him, while the Doctor on his knees was satisfying himself that his little charge had received no fatal injury. It need hardly be explained that such a termination as this to such an accident had greatly increased the good feeling with which Mr. Peacocke was regarded by all the inhabitants of the school and Rectory.

CHAPTER III

THE MYSTERY

Mr. Peacocke himself said that in this matter a great deal of fuss was made about nothing. Perhaps it was so. He got a ducking, but, being a strong swimmer, probably suffered no real danger. The boy, rolling down three or four feet of bank, had then fallen down six or eight feet into deep water.

He might, no doubt, have been much hurt. He might have struck against a rock and have been killed,—in which case Mr. Peacocke's prowess would have been of no avail. But nothing of this kind happened. Little Jack De Lawle was put to bed in one of the Rectory bed-rooms, and was comforted with sherry-negus*and sweet jelly. For two days he rejoiced thoroughly in his accident, being freed from school, and subjected only to caresses. After that he rebelled, having become tired of his bed. But by that time his mother had been most unnecessarily summoned. Unless she was wanted to examine the forlorn condition of his clothes, there was nothing that she could do. But she came, and, of course, showered blessings on Mr. Peacocke's head,—while Mrs. Wortle went through to the school and showered blessings on Mrs. Peacocke. What would they have done had the Peacockes not been there ?

'You must let them have their way, whether for good or bad,' the Doctor said, when his assistant complained rather of the blessings,—pointing out at any rate their absurdity. 'One man is damned for ever, because, in the conscientious exercise of his authority, he gives a little boy a rap which happens to make a small temporary mark on his skin. Another becomes a hero because, when in the equally conscientious performance of a duty, he gives himself a ducking. I won't think you a hero ; but, of course, I consider myself very fortunate to have had beside me a man younger than myself, and quick and ready at such an emergence. Of course I feel grateful, but I shan't bother you by telling you so.'

But this was not the end of it. Lady De Lawle declared that she could not be happy unless Mr. and Mrs. Peacocke would bring Jack home for the holidays to De Lawle Park. Of course she carried her blessings up into Mrs. Peacocke's little drawing-room, and became quite convinced, as was Mrs. Wortle, that Mrs. Peacocke was in all respects a lady. She heard of Mr. Peacocke's antecedents at Oxford, and expressed her opinion that they were charming people. She could not be happy unless they would promise to come to De Lawle Park for the holidays. Then Mrs. Peacocke had to explain that in her present circumstances she did not intend to visit anywhere. She was very much flattered, and delighted to think that the dear little boy was none the worse for his accident ; but there must be an end of it. There was something in her manner, as she said this, which almost overawed Lady De Lawle. She made herself, at any rate, understood, and no further attempt was made for the next six weeks to induce her or Mr. Peacocke to enter the Rectory dining-room. But a good deal was said about Mr. Peacocke,—generally in his favour.

Generally in his favour,—because he was a fine scholar, and could swim well. His preaching per-haps did something for him, but the swimming did more. But though there was so much said of good, there was something also of evil. A man would not altogether refuse society for himself and his wife unless there were some cause for him to do so. He and she must have known themselves to be unfit to associate with such persons as they would have met at De Lawle Park. There was a mystery, and the mystery, when unravelled, would no doubt

prove to be very deleterious to the character of
the persons concerned. Mrs. Stantiloup was quite
sure that such must be the cáse. ' It might be very
well,' said Mrs. Stantiloup, ' for Dr. Wortle to
obtain the services of a well-educated usher for
his school, but it became quite another thing when
he put a man up to preach in the church, of whose
life, for five years, no one knew anything.' Somebody had told her something as to the necessity of
a bishop's authority for the appointment of a
curate ; but no one had strictly defined to her
what a curate is. She was, however, quite ready
to declare that Mr. Peacocke had no business to
preach in that pulpit, and that something very
disagreeable would come of it.

Nor was this feeling altogether confined to Mrs.
Stantiloup, though it had perhaps originated with
what she had said among her own friends. ' Don't
you think it well you should know something of
his life during these five years ? ' This had been
said to the Rector by the Bishop himself,—who
probably would have said nothing of the kind had
not these reports reached his ears. But reports,
when they reach a certain magnitude, and attain
a certain importance, require to be noticed.

So much in this world depends upon character
that attention has to be paid to bad character even
when it is not deserved. In dealing with men and
women, we have to consider what they believe, as
well as what we believe ourselves. The utility of a
sermon depends much on the idea that the audience
has of the piety of the man who preaches it. Though
the words of God should never have come with
greater power from the mouth of man, they will

come in vain if they be uttered by one who is known
as a breaker of the Commandments ;—they will
come in vain from the mouth of one who is even sus-
pected to be so. To all this, when it was said to him
by the Bishop in the kindest manner, Dr. Wortle
replied that such suspicions were monstrous, unreasonable, and uncharitable. He declared that
they originated with that abominable virago,* Mrs.
Stantiloup. 'Look round the diocese,' said the
Bishop in reply to this, ' and see if you can find a
single clergyman acting in it, of the details of whose
life for the last five years you know absolutely
nothing.' Thereupon the Doctor said that he
would make inquiry of Mr. Peacocke himself. It
might well be, he thought, that Mr. Peacocke
would not like such inquiry, but the Doctor was
quite sure that any story told to him would be true.
On returning home he found it necessary, or at any
rate expedient, to postpone his questions for a few
days. It is not easy to ask a man what he has been
doing with five years of his life, when the question
implies a belief that these five years have been
passed badly. And it was understood that the
questioning must in some sort apply to the man's
wife. The Doctor had once said to Mrs. Wortle
that he stood in awe of Mrs. Peacocke. There had
certainly come upon him an idea that she was a
lady with whom it would not be easy to meddle.
She was obedient, diligent, and minutely attentive
to any wish that was expressed to her in regard to
her duties ; but it had become manifest to the
Doctor that in all matters beyond the school she
was independent, and was by no means subject to
external influences. She was not, for instance, very

constant in her own attendance at church, and
never seemed to feel it necessary to apologise for
her absence. The Doctor, in his many and familiar
conversations with Mr. Peacocke, had not found
himself able to allude to this ; and he had observed
that the husband did not often speak of his own
wife unless it were on matters having reference to
the school. So it came to pass that he dreaded the
conversation which he proposed to himself, and
postponed it from day to day with a cowardice
which was quite unusual to him.

And now, O kind-hearted reader, I feel myself
constrained, in the telling of this little story, to
depart altogether from those principles of story-
telling to which you probably have become accustomed, and to put the horse of my romance before
the cart. There is a mystery respecting Mr. and
Mrs. Peacocke which, according to all laws recognised in such matters, ought not to be elucidated
till, let us say, the last chapter but two, so that
your interest should be maintained almost to the
end,—so near the end that there should be left only
space for those little arrangements which are necessary for the well-being, or perhaps for the evil-being,
of our personages. It is my purpose to disclose the
mystery at once, and to ask you to look for your
interest,—should you choose to go on with my
chronicle,—simply in the conduct of my persons,
during this disclosure, to others. You are to know
it all before the Doctor or the Bishop,—before Mrs.
Wortle or the Hon. Mrs. Stantiloup, or Lady De
Lawle. You are to know it all before the Peacockes
become aware that it must necessarily be disclosed
to any one. It may be that when I shall have once

told the mystery there will no longer be any room
for interest in the tale to you. That there are many
such readers of novels I know. I doubt whether
the greater number be not such. I am far from
saying that the kind of interest of which I am
speaking,—and of which I intend to deprive myself,—is not the most natural and the most efficacious. What would the ' Black Dwarf ' be if every
one knew from the beginning that he was a rich
man and a baronet ?—or ' The Pirate ', if all the
truth about Norna of the Fitful-head had been
told in the first chapter ?* Therefore, put the book
down if the revelation of some future secret be
necessary for your enjoyment. Our mystery is going to be revealed in the next paragraph,—in the
next half-dozen words. Mr. and Mrs. Peacocke
were not man and wife.

The story how it came to be so need not be very
long ;—nor will it, as I think, entail any great
degree of odious criminality either upon the man
or upon the woman. At St. Louis Mrs. Peacocke
had become acquainted with two brothers named
Lefroy, who had come up from Louisiana, and had
achieved for themselves characters which were by
no means desirable. They were sons of a planter
who had been rich in extent of acres and number
of slaves before the war of the Secession.* General
Lefroy had been in those days a great man in his
State, had held command during the war, and had
been utterly ruined. When the war was over the
two boys,—then seventeen and sixteen years of
age,—were old enough to remember and to regret
all that they had lost, to hate the idea of Abolition,*
and to feel that the world had nothing left for them

but what was to be got by opposition to the laws of the Union, which was now hateful to them. They were both handsome, and, in spite of the sufferings of their State, an attempt had been made to educate them like gentlemen. But no career of honour had been open to them, and they had fallen by degrees into dishonour, dishonesty, and brigandage.

The elder of these, when he was still little more than a stripling, had married Ella Beaufort, the daughter of another ruined planter in his State. She had been only sixteen when her father died, and not seventeen when she married Ferdinand Lefroy. It was she who afterwards came to England under the name of Mrs. Peacocke.

Mr. Peacocke was Vice-President of the College at Missouri when he first saw her, and when he first became acquainted with the two brothers, each of whom was called Colonel Lefroy. Then there arose a great scandal in the city as to the treatment which the wife received from her husband. He was about to go away South, into Mexico, with the view of pushing his fortune there with certain desperadoes, who were maintaining a perpetual war against the authorities of the United States on the borders of Texas,* and he demanded that his wife should accompany him. This she refused to do, and violence was used to force her. Then it came to pass that certain persons in St. Louis interfered on her behalf, and among these was the Reverend Mr. Peacocke, the Vice-President of the College, upon whose feelings the singular beauty and dignified demeanor of the woman, no doubt, had had much effect. The man failed to be powerful over his wife, and then the two brothers went away together. The woman was left to provide for herself, and Mr. Peacocke was generous in the aid he gave to her in doing so.

It may be understood that in this way an intimacy was created, but it must not be understood that the intimacy was of such a nature as to be injurious to the fair fame of the lady. Things went on in this way for two years, during which Mrs. Lefroy's conduct drew down upon her reproaches from no one. Then there came tidings that Colonel Lefroy had perished in making one of those raids in which the two brothers were continually concerned. But which Colonel Lefroy had perished ? If it were the younger brother, that would be nothing to Mr. Peacocke. If it were the elder, it would be everything. If Ferdinand Lefroy were dead, he would not scruple at once to ask the woman to be his wife. That which the man had done, and that which he had not done, had been of such a nature as to solve all bonds of affection. She had already allowed herself to speak of the man as one whose life was a blight upon her own ; and though there had been no word of out-spoken love from her lips to his ears, he thought that he might succeed if it could be made certain that Ferdinand Lefroy was no longer among the living.

' I shall never know,' she said in her misery. ' What I do hear I shall never believe. How can one know anything as to what happens in a country such as that ? '

Then he took up his hat and staff, and, vice-president, professor, and clergyman as he was, started off for the Mexican border. He did tell her that he was going, but barely told her. ' It's a thing that ought to be found out,' he said, ' and I want a turn of travelling. I shall be away three months.' She merely bade God bless him, but said not a word to hinder or to encourage his going.

He was gone just the three months which he had himself named, and then returned elate with his news. He had seen the younger brother, Robert Lefroy, and had learnt from him that the elder Ferdinand had certainly been killed. Robert had been most ungracious to him, having even on one occasion threatened his life ; but there had been no doubt that he, Robert, was alive, and that Ferdinand had been killed by a party of United States soldiers.

Then the clergyman had his reward, and was accepted by the widow with a full and happy heart. Not only had her release been complete, but so was her present joy ; and nothing seemed wanting to their happiness during the six first months after their union. Then one day, all of a sudden, Ferdinand Lefroy was standing within her little drawing-room at the College of St. Louis.

Dead ? Certainly he was not dead ! He did not believe that any one had said that he was dead ! She might be lying or not,—he did not care ; he, Peacocke, certainly had lied ;—so said the Colonel. He did not believe that Peacocke had ever seen his brother Robert. Robert was dead,—must have been dead, indeed, before the date given for that interview. The woman was a bigamist,—that is, if any second marriage had ever been perpetrated. Probably both had wilfully agreed to the falsehood. For himself he should resolve at once what steps he meant to take. Then he departed, it being at that moment after nine in the evening. In the morning he was gone again, and from that moment they had never either heard of him or seen him.

How was it to be with them ? They could have almost brought themselves to think it a dream, were it not that others besides themselves had seen the man, and known that Colonel Ferdinand Lefroy had been in St. Louis. Then there came to him an idea that even she might disbelieve the words which he had spoken ;—that even she might think his story to have been false. But to this she soon put an end. 'Dearest,' she said, 'I never knew a word that was true to come from his mouth, or a word that was false from yours.'

Should they part ? There is no one who reads this but will say that they should have parted. Every day passed together as man and wife must be a falsehood and a sin. There would be absolute misery for both in parting ;—but there is no law from God or man entitling a man to escape from misery at the expense of falsehood and sin. Though their hearts might have burst in the doing of it, they should have parted. Though she would have been friendless, alone, and utterly despicable in the eyes of the world, abandoning the name which she cherished, as not her own, and going back to that which she utterly abhorred, still she should have done it. And he, resolving, as no doubt he would have done under any circumstances, that he must quit the city of his adoption,—he should have left her with such material sustenance as her spirit would have enabled her to accept, should have gone his widowed way, and endured as best he might the idea that he had left the woman whom he loved behind, in the desert, all alone ! That he had not done so the reader is aware. That he had lived a life of sin,—that he and she had continued in one great falsehood,—is manifest enough. Mrs. Stantiloup, when she hears it all, will have her triumph. Lady De Lawle's soft heart will rejoice because that invitation was not accepted. The Bishop will be unutterably shocked ; but, perhaps, to the good man there will be some solace in the feeling that he had been right in his surmises. How the Doctor bore it this story is intended to tell,— and how also Mr. and Mrs. Peacocke bore it, when the sin and the falsehood were made known to all the world around them. The mystery has at any rate been told, and they who feel that on this account all hope of interest is at an end had better put down the book.

PART II

CHAPTER IV

THE DOCTOR ASKS HIS QUESTION

THE Doctor, instigated by the Bishop, had determined to ask some questions of Mr. Peacocke as to his American life. The promise had been given at the Palace, and the Doctor, as he returned home, repented himself in that he had made it. His lordship was a gossip, as bad as an old woman, as bad as Mrs. Stantiloup, and wanted to know things in which a man should feel no interest. So said the Doctor to himself. What was it to him, the Bishop, or to him, the Doctor, what Mr. Peacocke had been doing in America? The man's scholarship was patent, his morals were unexceptional, his capacity for preaching undoubted, his peculiar fitness for his place at Bowick unquestionable. Who had a right to know more? That the man had been properly educated at Oxford, and properly ordained on entering his Fellowship, was doubted by no man. Even if there had been some temporary backslidings in America,—which might be possible, for which of us have not backslided at some time of our life?—why should they be raked up? There was an uncharitableness in such a proceeding altogether opposed to the Doctor's view of life. He hated severity. It may almost be said that he hated that state of perfection which would require no pardon. He was thoroughly human, quite content with his own present position, anticipating no

millennium for the future of the world, and probably, in his heart, looking forward to heaven as
simply the better alternative when the happiness
of this world should be at an end. He himself was
in no respect a wicked man, and yet a little wickedness was not distasteful to him.

And he was angry with himself in that he had
made such a promise. It had been a rule of life
with him never to take advice. The Bishop had
his powers, within which he, as Rector of Bowick,
would certainly obey the Bishop ; but it had
been his theory to oppose his Bishop, almost more
readily than any one else, should the Bishop attempt to exceed his power. The Bishop had done
so in giving this advice, and yet he had promised.
He was angry with himself, but did not on that
account think that the promise should be evaded.
Oh no ! Having said that he would do it, he would
do it. And having said that he would do it, the
sooner that he did it the better. When three or
four days had passed by, he despised himself because he had not yet made for himself a fit occasion.
' It is such a mean, sneaking thing to do,' he said to
himself. But still it had to be done.

It was on a Saturday afternoon that he said this
to himself, as he returned back to the parsonage
garden from the cricket-ground, where he had left
Mr. Peacocke and the three other ushers playing
cricket with ten or twelve of the bigger boys of the
school. There was a French master, a German
master, a master for arithmetic and mathematics
with the adjacent sciences, besides Mr. Peacocke,
as assistant classical master. Among them Mr.
Peacocke was *facile princeps**in rank and supposed

ability ; but they were all admitted to the delights
of the playground. Mr. Peacocke, in spite of those
years of his spent in America where cricket could
not have been familiar to him, remembered well
his old pastime, and was quite an adept at the
game. It was ten thousand pities that a man
should be disturbed by unnecessary questionings
who could not only teach and preach, but play
cricket also. But nevertheless it must be done.
When, therefore, the Doctor entered his own house,
he went into his study and wrote a short note to his
assistant ;—

'MY DEAR PEACOCKE,—Could you come over
and see me in my study this evening for half an
hour ? I have a question or two which I wish to
ask you. Any hour you may name will suit me
after eight.—Yours most sincerely,
                              'JEFFREY WORTLE.'

In answer to this there came a note to say that
at half-past eight Mr. Peacocke would be with the
Doctor.

At half-past eight Mr. Peacocke came. He had
fancied, on reading the Doctor's note that some
further question would be raised as to money. The
Doctor had declared that he could no longer accept
gratuitous clerical service in the parish, and had
said that he must look out for some one else if Mr.
Peacocke could not oblige him by allowing his name
to be referred in the usual way to the Bishop. He
had now determined to say, in answer to this, that
the school gave him enough to do, and that he
would much prefer to give up the church ;—al-

though he would always be happy to take a part occasionally if he should be wanted. The Doctor had been sitting alone for the last quarter of an hour when his assistant entered the room, and had spent the time in endeavouring to arrange the conversation that should follow. He had come at last to a conclusion. He would let Mr. Peacocke know exactly what had passed between himself and the Bishop, and would then leave it to his usher either to tell his own story as to his past life, or to abstain from telling it. He had promised to ask the question, and he would ask it; but he would let the man judge for himself whether any answer ought to be given.

'The Bishop has been bothering me about you, Peacocke,' he said, standing up with his back to the fireplace, as soon as the other man had shut the door behind him. The Doctor's face was always expressive of his inward feelings, and at this moment showed very plainly that his sympathies were not with the Bishop.

'I'm sorry that his lordship should have troubled himself,' said the other, 'as I certainly do not intend to take any part in his diocese.'

'We'll sink that for the present,' said the Doctor. 'I won't let that be mixed up with what I have got to say just now. You have taken a certain part in the diocese already, very much to my satisfaction. I hope it may be continued; but I won't bother about that now. As far as I can see, you are just the man that would suit me as a colleague in the parish.' Mr. Peacocke bowed, but remained silent. 'The fact is,' continued the Doctor, 'that certain old women have got hold of the Bishop, and made him feel that he ought to answer their

objections. That Mrs. Stantiloup has a tongue as
loud as the town-crier's bell.'

'But what has Mrs. Stantiloup to say about
me?'

'Nothing, except in so far as she can hit me
through you.'

'And what does the Bishop say?'

'He thinks that I ought to know something of
your life during those five years you were in
America.'

'I think so also,' said Mr. Peacocke.

'I don't want to know anything for myself. As
far as I am concerned, I am quite satisfied. I know
where you were educated, how you were ordained,
and I can feel sure, from your present efficiency,
that you cannot have wasted your time. If you
tell me that you do not wish to say anything, I
shall be contented, and I shall tell the Bishop that,
as far as I am concerned, there must be an end
of it.'

'And what will he do?' asked Mr. Peacocke.

'Well; as far as the curacy is concerned, of
course he can refuse his licence.'

'I have not the slightest intention of applying
to his lordship for a licence.'

This the usher said with a tone of self-assertion
which grated a little on the Doctor's ear, in spite
of his good-humour towards the speaker. 'I don't
want to go into that,' he said. 'A man never can
say what his intentions may be six months hence.'

'But if I were to refuse to speak of my life in
America,' said Mr. Peacocke, 'and thus to decline
to comply with what I must confess would be no
more than a rational requirement on your part,

how then would it be with myself and my wife in regard to the school.?'

'It would make no difference whatever,' said the Doctor.

'There is a story to tell,' said Mr. Peacocke, very slowly.

'I am sure that it cannot be to your disgrace.'

'I do not say that it is,—nor do I say that it is not. There may be circumstances in which a man may hardly know whether he has done right or wrong. But this I do know,—that, had I done otherwise, I should have despised myself. I could not have done otherwise and have lived.'

'There is no man in the world,' said the Doctor, earnestly, 'less anxious to pry into the secrets of others than I am. I take things as I find them. If the cook sends me up a good dish I don't care to know how she made it. If I read a good book, I am not the less gratified because there may have been something amiss with the author.'

'You would doubt his teaching,' said Mr. Peacocke, ' who had gone astray himself.'

'Then I must doubt all human teaching, for all men have gone astray. You had better hold your tongue about the past, and let me tell those who ask unnecessary questions to mind their own business.'

'It is very odd, Doctor,' said Mr. Peacocke, 'that all this should have come from you just now.'

'Why odd just now?'

'Because I had been turning it in my mind for the last fortnight whether I ought not to ask you as a favour to listen to the story of my life. That

I must do so before I could formally accept the
curacy I had determined. But that only brought
me to the resolution of refusing the office. I think,
—I think that, irrespective of the curacy, it ought
to be told. But I have not quite made up my
mind.'

'Do not suppose that I am pressing you.'

'Oh no; nor would your pressing me influence
me. Much as I owe to your undeserved kindness
and forbearance, I am bound to say that. Nothing
can influence me in the least in such a matter but
the well-being of my wife, and my own sense of
duty. And it is a matter in which I can unfortunately take counsel from no one. She, and she
alone, besides myself, knows the circumstances,
and she is so forgetful of herself that I can hardly
ask her for an opinion.'

The Doctor by this time had no doubt become
curious. There was a something mysterious with
which he would like to become acquainted. He
was by no means a philosopher, superior to the
ordinary curiosity of mankind. But he was manly,
and even at this moment remembered his former
assurances. 'Of course,' said he, 'I cannot in the
least guess what all this is about. For myself I
hate secrets. I haven't a secret in the world. I
know nothing of myself which you mightn't know
too for all that I cared. But that is my good fortune rather than my merit. It might well have
been with me as it is with you; but, as a rule, I
think that where there is a secret it had better be
kept. No one, at any rate, should allow it to be
wormed out of him by the impertinent assiduity of
others. If there be anything affecting your wife

which you do not wish all the world on this side of the water to know, do not tell it to any one on this side of the water.'

'There is something affecting my wife that I do not wish all the world to know.'

'Then tell it to no one,' said Dr. Wortle, authoritatively.

'I will tell you what I will do,' said Mr. Peacocke; 'I will take a week to think of it, and then I will let you know whether I will tell it or whether I will not; and if I tell it I will let you know also how far I shall expect you to keep my secret, and how far to reveal it. I think the Bishop will be entitled to know nothing about me unless I ask to be recognised as one of the clergy of his diocese.'

'Certainly not; certainly not,' said the Doctor. And then the interview was at an end.

Mr. Peacocke, when he went away from the Rectory, did not at once return to his own house, but went off for a walk alone. It was now nearly mid-summer, and there was broad daylight till ten o'clock. It was after nine when he left the Doctor's, but still there was time for a walk which he knew well through the fields, which would take him round by Bowick Wood, and home by a path across the squire's park and by the church. An hour would do it, and he wanted an hour to collect his thoughts before he should see his wife, and discuss with her, as he would be bound to do, all that had passed between him and the Doctor. He had said that he could not ask her advice. In this there had been much of truth. But he knew also that he would do nothing as to which he had not received at any rate her assent. She, for his sake, would have annihilated herself, had that been possible. Again and again, since that horrible apparition had showed itself in her room at St. Louis, she had begged that she might leave him,—not on her own behalf, not from any dread of the crime that she was committing, not from shame in regard to herself should her secret be found out, but because she felt herself to be an impediment to his career in the world. As to herself, she had no pricks of conscience. She had been true to the man,—brutal, abominable as he had been to her,—until she had in truth been made to believe that he was dead ; and even when he had certainly been alive,—for she had seen him,—he had only again seen her, again to desert her. Duty to him she could owe never. There was no sting of conscience with her in that direction. But to the other man she owed, as she thought, everything that could be due from a woman to a man. He had come within her ken, and had loved her without speaking of his love. He had seen her condition, and had sympathised with her fully. He had gone out, with his life in his hand, —he, a clergyman, a quiet man of letters,—to ascertain whether she was free ; and finding her, as he believed, to be free, he had returned to take her to his heart, and to give her all that happiness which other women enjoy, but which she had hitherto only seen from a distance. Then the blow had come. It was necessary, it was natural, that she should be ruined by such a blow. Circumstances had ruined her. That fate had betaken her which so often falls upon a woman who trusts herself and her life to a man. But why should he fall also with her fall ? There was still a career before

him. He might be useful ; he might be successful ;
he might be admired. Everything might still be
open to him,—except the love of another woman.
As to that, she did not doubt his truth. Why
should he be doomed to drag her with him as a
log tied to his foot, seeing that a woman with
a misfortune is condemned by the general voice of
the world, whereas for a man to have stumbled is
considered hardly more than a matter of course ?
She would consent to take from him the means
of buying her bread ; but it would be better,—
she had said,—that she should eat it on her side of
the water, while he might earn it on the other.

We know what had come of these arguments.
He had hitherto never left her for a moment since
that man had again appeared before their eyes.
He had been strong in his resolution. If it were
a crime, then he would be a criminal. If it were a
falsehood, then would he be a liar. As to the sin,
there had no doubt been some divergence of opinion
between him and her. The teaching that he had
undergone in his youth had been that with which
we, here, are all more or less acquainted, and that
had been strengthened in him by the fact of his
having become a clergyman. She had felt herself
more at liberty to proclaim to herself a gospel of
her own for the guidance of her own soul. To herself she had never seemed to be vicious or impure,
but she understood well that he was not equally
free from the bonds which religion had imposed
upon him. For his sake,—for his sake, it would be
better that she should be away from him.

All this was known to him accurately, and all this
had to be considered by him as he walked across

the squire's park in the gloaming of the evening.
No doubt,—he now said to himself,—the Doctor
should have been made acquainted with his condition before he or she had taken their place at the
school. Reticence under such circumstances had
been a lie. Against his conscience there had been
many pricks. Living in his present condition he
certainly should not have gone up into that pulpit
to preach the Word of God. Though he had been
silent, he had known that the evil and the deceit
would work round upon him. But now what should
he do ? There was only one thing on which he
was altogether decided ;—nothing should separate
them. As he had said so often before, he said again
now,—' If there be sin, let it be sin.' But this was
clear to him,—were he to give Dr. Wortle a true
history of what had happened to him in America,
then must he certainly leave Bowick. And this
was equally certain, that before telling his tale, he
must make known his purpose to his wife.

But as he entered his own house he had determined that he would tell the Doctor everything.

CHAPTER V

' THEN WE MUST GO '

' I THOUGHT you were never going to have done
with that old Jupiter,' said Mrs. Peacocke, as she
began at that late hour of the evening to make tea
for herself and her husband.

' Why have you waited for me ? '

' Because I like company. Did you ever know
me go to tea without you when there was a chance

of your coming ? What has Jupiter been talking about all this time ? '

' Jupiter has not been talking all this time. Jupiter talked only for half an hour. Jupiter is a very good fellow.'

' I always thought so. Otherwise I should never have consented to have been one of his satellites, or have been contented to see you doing chief moon. But you have been with him an hour and a half.'

' Since I left him I have walked all round by Bowick Lodge. I had something to think of before I could talk to you,—something to decide upon, indeed, before I could return to the house.'

' What have you decided ? ' she asked. Her voice was altogether changed. Though she was seated in her chair and had hardly moved, her appearance and her carriage of herself were changed. She still held the cup in her hand which she had been about to fill, but her face was turned towards his, and her large brown speaking eyes were fixed upon him.

' Let me have my tea,' he said, ' and then I will tell you.' While he drank his tea she remained quite quiet, not touching her own, but waiting patiently till it should suit him to speak. ' Ella,' he said, ' I must tell it all to Dr. Wortle.'

' Why, dearest ? ' As he did not answer at once, she went on with her question. ' Why now more than before ? '

' Nay, it is not now more than before. As we have let the before go by, we can only do it now.'

' But why at all, dear ? Has the argument, which was strong when we came, lost any of its force ? '

'It should have had no force. We should not have taken the man's good things, and have subjected him to the injury which may come to him by our bad name.'

'Have we not given him good things in return?'

'Not the good things which he had a right to expect,—not that respectability which is all the world to such an establishment as this.'

'Let me go,' she said, rising from her chair and almost shrieking.

'Nay, Ella, nay; if you and I cannot talk as though we were one flesh, almost with one soul between us, as though that which is done by one is done by both, whether for weal or woe,—if you and I cannot feel ourselves to be in a boat together either for swimming or for sinking, then I think that no two persons on this earth ever can be bound together after that fashion. "Whither thou goest, I will go; and where thou lodgest, I will lodge. The Lord do so to me, and more also, if aught but death part thee and me." '* Then she rose from her chair, and flinging herself on her knees at his feet, buried her face in his lap. 'Ella,' he said, 'the only injury you can do me is to speak of leaving me. And it is an injury which is surely unnecessary because you cannot carry it beyond words. Now, if you will sit up and listen to me, I will tell you what passed between me and the Doctor.' Then she raised herself from the ground and took her seat at the tea-table, and listened patiently as he began his tale. 'They have been talking about us here in the county.'

'Who has found it necessary to talk about one so obscure as I?'

' What does it matter who they might be ? The Doctor in his kindly wrath,—for he is very wroth, —mentions this name and the other. What does it matter ? Obscurity itself becomes mystery, and mystery of course produces curiosity. It was bound to be so. It is not they who are in fault, but we. If you are different from others, of course you will be inquired into.'

' Am I so different ? '

' Yes ;—different in not eating the Doctor's dinners when they are offered to you ; different in not accepting Lady De Lawle's hospitality ; different in contenting yourself simply with your duties and your husband. Of course we are different. How could we not be different ? And as we are different, so of course there will be questions and wonderings, and that sifting and searching which always at last finds out the facts. The Bishop says that he knows nothing of my American life.'

' Why should he want to know anything ? '

' Because I have been preaching in one of his churches. It is natural ;—natural that the mothers of the boys should want to know something. The Doctor says that he hates secrets. So do I.'

' Oh, my dearest ! '

' A secret is always accompanied by more or less of fear, and produces more or less of cowardice. But it can no more be avoided than a sore on the flesh or a broken bone. Who would not go about, with all his affairs such as the world might know, if it were possible ? But there come gangrenes in the heart, or perhaps in the pocket. Wounds come, undeserved wounds, as those did to you, my darling ; but wounds which may not be laid bare to all eyes. Who has a secret because he chooses it?'

'But the Bishop?'

'Well,—yes, the Bishop. The Bishop has told the Doctor to examine me, and the Doctor has done it. I give him the credit of saying that the task has been most distasteful to him. I do him the justice of acknowledging that he has backed out of the work he had undertaken. He has asked the question, but has said in the same breath that I need not answer it unless I like.'

'And you? You have not answered it yet?'

'No; I have answered nothing as yet. But I have, I think, made up my mind that the question must be answered.'

'That everything should be told?'

'Everything,—to him. My idea is to tell everything to him, and to leave it to him to decide what should be done. Should he refuse to repeat the story any further, and then bid us go away from Bowick, I should think that his conduct had been altogether straightforward and not uncharitable.'

'And you,—what would you do then?'

'I should go. What else?'

'But whither?'

'Ah! on that we must decide. He would be friendly with me. Though he might think it necessary that I should leave Bowick, he would not turn against me violently.'

'He could do nothing.'

'I think he would assist me rather. He would help me, perhaps, to find some place where I might still earn my bread by such skill as I possess;—where I could do so without dragging in aught of

my domestic life, as I have been forced to do
here.'

'I have been a curse to you,' exclaimed the
unhappy wife.

'My dearest blessing,' he said. 'That which you
call a curse has come from circumstances which are
common to both of us. There need be no more
said about it. That man has been a source of
terrible trouble to us. The trouble must be discussed from time to time, but the necessity of
enduring it may be taken for granted.'

'I cannot be a philosopher such as you are,' she
said.

'There is no escape from it. The philosophy is
forced upon us. When an evil thing is necessary,
there remains only the consideration how it may be
best borne.'

'You must tell him, then ? '

'I think so. I have a week to consider of it ;
but I think so. Though he is very kind at this
moment in giving me the option, and means what
he says in declaring that I shall remain even though
I tell him nothing, yet his mind would become
uneasy, and he would gradually become discon-
tented. Think how great is his stake in the school !
How would he feel towards me, were its success to
be gradually diminished because he kept a master
here of whom people believed some unknown evil ?'

'There has been no sign of any such falling off ?'

'There has been no time for it. It is only now
that people are beginning to talk. Had nothing of
the kind been said, had this Bishop asked no questions, had we been regarded as people simply obscure, to whom no mystery attached itself, the

thing might have gone on ; but as it is, I am bound
to tell him the truth.'

' Then we must go ? '

' Probably.'

' At once ? '

' When it has been so decided, the sooner the
better. How could we endure to remain here when
our going shall be desired ? '

' Oh no ! '

' We must flit, and again seek some other home.
Though he should keep our secret,—and I believe
he will if he be asked,—it will be known that there
is a secret, and a secret of such a nature that its
circumstances have driven us hence. If I could get
literary work in London, perhaps we might live
there.'

' But how,—how would you set about it ? The
truth is, dearest, that for work such as yours you
should either have no wife at all, or else a wife of
whom you need not be ashamed to speak the whole
truth before the world.'

' What is the use of it ? ' he said, rising from his
chair as in anger. ' Why go back to all that which
should be settled between us, as fixed by fate ? Each
of us has given to the other all that each has to
give, and the partnership is complete. As far as
that is concerned, I at any rate am contented.'

' Ah, my darling ! ' she exclaimed, throwing her
arms round his neck.

' Let there be an end to distinctions and differ-
ences, which, between you and me, can have no
effect but to increase our troubles. You are a
woman, and I am a man ; and therefore, no doubt,
your name, when brought in question, is more sub-

ject to remark than mine,—as is my name, being
that of a clergyman, more subject to remark than
that of one not belonging to a sacred profession.
But not on that account do I wish to unfrock myself ; nor certainly on that account do I wish to be
deprived of my wife. For good or bad, it has to be
endured together ; and expressions of regret as to
that which is unavoidable, only aggravate our
trouble.' After that, he seated himself, and took
up a book as though he were able at once to carry
off his mind to other matters. She probably knew
that he could not do so, but she sat silent by him
for a while, till he bade her take herself to bed,
promising that he would follow without delay.

For three days nothing further was said between
them on the subject, nor was any allusion made to
it between the Doctor and his assistant. The school
went on the same as ever, and the intercourse between the two men was unaltered as to its general
mutual courtesy. But there did undoubtedly grow
in the Doctor's mind a certain feverish feeling of
insecurity. At any rate, he knew this, that there
was a mystery, that there was something about the
Peacockes,—something referring especially to Mrs.
Peacocke,—which, if generally known, would be
held to be deleterious to their character. So much
he could not help deducing from what the man had
already told him. No doubt he had undertaken, in
his generosity, that although the man should decline to tell his secret, no alteration should be made
as to the school arrangements ; but he became conscious that in so promising he had in some degree
jeopardised the well-being of the school. He began
to whisper to himself that persons in such a position

as that filled by this Mr. Peacocke and his wife
should not be subject to peculiar remarks from ill-
natured tongues. A weapon was afforded by such
a mystery to the Stantiloups of the world, which
the Stantiloups would be sure to use with all their
virulence. To such an establishment as his school,
respectability was everything. Credit, he said to
himself, is a matter so subtle in its essence, that,
as it may be obtained almost without reason, so,
without reason, may it be made to melt away.
Much as he liked Mr. Peacocke, much as he ap-
proved of him, much as there was in the man of
manliness and worth which was absolutely dear to
him,—still he was not willing to put the character
of his school in peril for the sake of Mr. Peacocke.
Were he to do so, he would be neglecting a duty
much more sacred than any he could owe to Mr.
Peacocke. It was thus that, during these three days,
he conversed with himself on the subject, although
he was able to maintain outwardly the same manner
and the same countenance as though all things were
going well between them. When they parted after
the interview in the study, the Doctor, no doubt, had
so expressed himself as rather to dissuade his usher
from telling his secret than to encourage him to do
so. He had been free in declaring that the telling
of the secret should make no difference in his assistant's position at Bowick. But in all that, he had
acted from his habitual impulse. He had since told
himself that the mystery ought to be disclosed. It
was not right that his boys should be left to the
charge of one who, however competent, dared not
speak of his own antecedents. It was thus he
thought of the matter, after consideration. He

must wait, of course, till the week should be over before he made up his mind to anything further.

'So Peacocke isn't going to take the curacy?'

This was said to the Doctor by Mr. Pearson, the squire, in the course of those two or three days of which we are speaking. Mr. Pearson was an old gentleman, who did not live often at Bowick, being compelled, as he always said, by his health, to spend the winter and spring of every year in Italy, and the summer months by his family in London. In truth, he did not much care for Bowick, but had always been on good terms with the Doctor, and had never opposed the school. Mr. Pearson had been good also as to Church matters,—as far as goodness can be shown by generosity,—and had interested himself about the curates. So it had come to pass that the Doctor did not wish to snub his neighbour when the question was asked. 'I rather think not,' said the Doctor. 'I fear I shall have to look out for some one else.' He did not prolong the conversation; for, though he wished to be civil, he did not wish to be communicative. Mr. Pearson had shown his parochial solicitude, and did not trouble himself with further questions.

'So Mr. Peacocke isn't going to take the curacy?' This, the very same question in the very same words, was put to the Doctor on the next morning by the vicar of the next parish. The Rev. Mr. Puddicombe, a clergyman without a flaw who did his duty excellently in every station of life, was one who would preach a sermon or take a whole service for a brother parson in distress, and never think of reckoning up that return sermons or return services were due to him,—one who gave dinners, too, and had pretty daughters;—but still our Doctor did not quite like him. He was a little too pious, and perhaps given to ask questions. 'So Mr. Peacocke isn't going to take the curacy?'

There was a certain animation about the asking of this question by Mr. Puddicombe very different from Mr. Pearson's listless manner. It was clear to the Doctor that Mr. Puddicombe wanted to know. It seemed to the Doctor that something of condemnation was implied in the tone of the question, not only against Mr. Peacocke, but against himself also, for having employed Mr. Peacocke. 'Upon my word I can't tell you,' he said, rather crossly.

'I thought that it had been all settled. I heard that it was decided.'

'Then you have heard more than I have.'

'It was the Bishop told me.'

Now it certainly was the case that in that fatal conversation which had induced the Doctor to interrogate Mr. Peacocke about his past life, the Doctor himself had said that he intended to look out for another curate. He probably did not remember that at the moment. 'I wish the Bishop would confine himself to asserting things that he knows,' said the Doctor, angrily.

'I am sure the Bishop intends to do so,' said Mr. Puddicombe, very gravely. 'But I apologise. I had not intended to touch a subject on which there may perhaps be some reserve. I was only going to tell you of an excellent young man of whom I have heard. But, good morning.' Then Mr. Puddicombe withdrew.

CHAPTER VI

LORD CARSTAIRS

DURING the last six months Mr. Peacocke's most intimate friend at Bowick, excepting of course his wife, had been one of the pupils at the school. The lad was one of the pupils, but could not be said to be one of the boys. He was the young Lord Carstairs, eldest son of Earl Bracy. He had been sent to Bowick now six years ago, with the usual purpose of progressing from Bowick to Eton. And from Bowick to Eton he had gone in due course. But there, things had not gone well with the young lord. Some school disturbance had taken place when he had been there about a year and a half, in which he was, or was supposed to have been, a ringleader. It was thought necessary, for the preservation of the discipline of the school, that a victim should be made ;—and it was perhaps thought well, in order that the impartiality of the school might be made manifest, that the victim should be a lord. Earl Bracy was therefore asked to withdraw his son ; and young Lord Carstairs, at the age of seventeen, was left to seek his education where he could. It had been, and still was, the Earl's purpose to send his son to Oxford, but there was now an interval of two years before that could be accomplished. During one year he was sent abroad to travel with a tutor, and was then reported to have been all that a well-conducted lad ought to be. He was declared to be quite worthy of all that Oxford would do for him. It was even suggested that Eton had done badly for herself in throwing off from her such a young nobleman. But though Lord Carstairs had done well with his French and German on the Continent, it would certainly be necessary that he should rub up his Greek and Latin before he went to Christ Church. Then a request was made to the Doctor to take him in at Bowick in some sort as a private pupil. After some demurring the Doctor consented. It was not his wont to run counter to earls who treated him with respect and deference. Earl Bracy had in a special manner been his friend, and Lord Carstairs himself had been a great favourite at Bowick. When that expulsion from Eton had come about, the Doctor had interested himself, and had declared that a very scant measure of justice had been shown to the young lord. He was thus in a measure compelled to accede to the request made to him, and Lord Carstairs was received back at Bowick, not without hesitation, but with a full measure of affectionate welcome. His bed-room was in the parsonage-house, and his dinner he took with the Doctor's family. In other respects he lived among the boys.

'Will it not be bad for Mary?' Mrs. Wortle had said anxiously to her husband when the matter was first discussed.

'Why should it be bad for Mary?'

'Oh, I don't know;—but young people together, you know? Mightn't it be dangerous?'

'He is a boy, and she is a mere child. They are both children. It will be a trouble, but I do not think it will be at all dangerous in that way.' And so it was decided. Mrs. Wortle did not at all agree

as to their both being children. She thought that
her girl was far from being a child. But she had
argued the matter quite as much as she ever argued
anything with the Doctor. So the matter was
arranged, and young Lord Carstairs came back to
Bowick.

As far as the Doctor could see, nothing could be
nicer than his young pupil's manners. He was not
at all above playing with the other boys. He took
very kindly to his old studies and his old haunts,
and of an evening, after dinner, went away from
the drawing-room to the study in pursuit of his
Latin and his Greek, without any precocious attempt at making conversation with Miss Wortle.
No doubt there was a good deal of lawn-tennis of
an afternoon, and the lawn-tennis was generally
played in the rectory garden. But then this had
ever been the case, and the lawn-tennis was always
played with two on a side ; there were no *tête-à-
tête* games between his lordship and Mary, and
whenever the game was going on, Mrs. Wortle was
always there to see fair-play. Among other amuse-
ments the young lord took to walking far afield
with Mr. Peacocke. And then, no doubt, many
things were said about that life in America. When
a man has been much abroad, and has passed his
time there under unusual circumstances, his doings
will necessarily become subjects of conversation to
his companions. To have travelled in France, Ger-
many, or in Italy, is not uncommon ; nor is it
uncommon to have lived a year or years in Florence
or in Rome. It is not uncommon now to have
travelled all through the United States. The Rocky
Mountains or Peru are hardly uncommon, so much

has the taste for travelling increased. But for an
Oxford Fellow of a college, and a clergyman of the
Church of England, to have established himself as
a professor in Missouri, is uncommon, and it could
hardly be but that Lord Carstairs should ask questions respecting that far-away life.

Mr. Peacocke had no objection to such questions.
He told his young friend much about the manners
of the people of St. Louis,—told him how far the
people had progressed in classical literature, in
what they fell behind, and in what they excelled
youths of their own age in England, and how far
the college was a success. Then he described his
own life,—both before and after his marriage. He
had liked the people of St. Louis well enough,—but
not quite well enough to wish to live among them.
No doubt their habits were very different from
those of Englishmen. He could, however, have
been happy enough there,—only that circumstances arose.

'Did Mrs. Peacocke like the place?' the young
lord asked one day.

'She is an American, you know.'

'Oh yes; I have heard. But did she come from
St. Louis?'

'No; her father was a planter in Louisiana, not
far from New Orleans, before the abolition of
slavery.'

'Did she like St. Louis?'

'Well enough, I think, when we were first
married. She had been married before, you know.
She was a widow.'

'Did she like coming to England among
strangers?'

'She was glad to leave St. Louis. Things happened there which made her life unhappy. It was on that account I came here, and gave up a position higher and more lucrative than I shall ever now get in England.'

'I should have thought you might have had a school of your own,' said the lad. 'You know so much, and get on so well with boys. I should have thought you might have been tutor at a college.'

'To have a school of my own would take money,' said he, 'which I have not got. To be tutor at a college would take—— But never mind. I am very well where I am, and have nothing to complain of.' He had been going to say that to be tutor of a college he would want high standing. And then he would have been forced to explain that he had lost at his own college that standing which he had once possessed.

'Yes,' he said on another occasion, 'she is unhappy; but do not ask her any questions about it.'

'Who,—I ? Oh dear, no ! I should not think of taking such a liberty.'

'It would be as a kindness, not as a liberty. But still, do not speak to her about it. There are sorrows which must be hidden, which it is better to endeavour to bury by never speaking of them, by not thinking of them, if that were possible.'

'Is it as bad as that ? ' the lad asked.

'It is bad enough sometimes. But never mind. You remember that Roman wisdom,—" Dabit Deus his quoque finem."* And I think that all things are bearable if a man will only make up his mind to bear them. Do not tell any one that I have complained.'

'Who,—I? Oh, never!'

'Not that I have said anything which all the
world might not know; but that it is unmanly to
complain. Indeed I do not complain, only I wish
that things were lighter to her.' Then he went off
to other matters; but his heart was yearning to
tell everything to this young lad.

Before the end of the week had arrived, there
came a letter to him which he had not at all expected, and a letter also to the Doctor,—both from
Lord Bracy. The letter to Mr. Peacocke was as
follows :—

'MY DEAR SIR,—I have been much gratified by
what I have heard both from Dr. Wortle and my
son as to his progress. He will have to come home
in July, when the Doctor's school is broken up, and,
as you are probably aware, will go up to Oxford in
October. I think it would be very expedient that
he should not altogether lose the holidays, and I am
aware how much more he would do with adequate
assistance than without it. The meaning of all
this is, that I and Lady Bracy will feel very much
obliged if you and Mrs. Peacocke will come and
spend your holidays with us at Carstairs. I have
written to Dr. Wortle on the subject, partly to tell
him of my proposal, because he has been so kind
to my son, and partly to ask him to fix the amount
of remuneration, should you be so kind as to accede
to my request.

'His mother has heard on more than one occasion from her son how very good-natured you have
been to him.—Yours faithfully,

                                        'BRACY.'

It was, of course, quite out of the question. Mr.
Peacocke, as soon as he had read the letter, felt
that it was so. Had things been smooth and easy
with him, nothing would have delighted him more.
His liking for the lad was most sincere, and it would
have been a real pleasure to him to have worked
with him during the holidays. But it was quite out
of the question. He must tell Lord Carstairs that
it was so, and must at the moment give such explanation as might occur to him. He almost felt that
in giving that explanation he would be tempted to
tell his whole story.

But the Doctor met him before he had an opportunity of speaking to Lord Carstairs. The Doctor
met him, and at once produced the Earl's letter.
' I have heard from Lord Bracy, and you, I suppose, have had a letter too,' said the Doctor. His
manner was easy and kind, as though no disagreeable communication was due to be made on the
following day.

' Yes,' said Mr. Peacocke. ' I have had a letter.'
' Well ? '
' His lordship has asked me to go to Carstairs for
the holidays ; but it is out of the question.'
' It would do Carstairs all the good in the world,'
said the Doctor ; ' and I do not see why you should
not have a pleasant visit and earn twenty-five
pounds at the same time.'
' It is quite out of the question.'
' I suppose you would not like to leave Mrs.
Peacocke,' said the Doctor.
' Either to leave her or to take her ! To go my-
self under any circumstances would be altogether
out of the question. I shall come to you to-morrow,

Doctor, as I said I would last Saturday. What hour
will suit you ? ' Then the Doctor named an hour in
the afternoon, and knew that the revelation was to
be made to him. He felt, too, that that revelation
would lead to the final departure of Mr. and Mrs.
Peacocke from Bowick, and he was unhappy in his
heart. Though he was anxious for his school, he
was anxious also for his friend. There was a gratifi-
cation in the feeling that Lord Bracy thought so
much of his assistant,—or would have been but for
this wretched mystery !

' No,' said Mr. Peacocke to the lad. ' I regret to
say that I cannot go. I will tell you why, perhaps,
another time, but not now. I have written to your
father by this post, because it is right that he should
be told at once. I have been obliged to say that it
is impossible.'

' I am so sorry ! I should so much have liked it.
My father would have done everything to make you
comfortable, and so would mamma.' In answer to
all this Mr. Peacocke could only say that it was
impossible. This happened on Friday afternoon,
Friday being a day on which the school was always
very busy. There was no time for the doing of anything special, as there would be on the following
day, which was a half-holiday. At night, when the
work was altogether over, he showed the letter to
his wife, and told her what he had decided.

' Couldn't you have gone without me ? ' she
asked.

' How can I do that,' he said, ' when before this
time to-morrow I shall have told everything to Dr.
Wortle ? After that, he would not let me go. He
would do no more than his duty in telling me that

if I proposed to go he must make it all known to
Lord Bracy. But this is a trifle. I am at the present moment altogether in the dark as to what I
shall do with myself when to-morrow evening
comes. I cannot guess, because it is so hard to
know what are the feelings in the breast of another
man. It may so well be that he should refuse me
permission to go to my desk in the school again.'

' Will he be hard like that ? '

' I can hardly tell myself whether it would be
hard. I hardly know what I should feel it my
duty to do in such a position myself. I have
deceived him.'

' No ! ' she exclaimed.

' Yes ; I have deceived him. Coming to him as
I did, I gave him to understand that there was
nothing wrong ;—nothing to which special objection could be made in my position.'

' Then we are deceiving all the world in calling
ourselves man and wife.'

' Certainly we are ; but to that we had made up
our mind ! We are not injuring all the world. No
doubt it is a lie,—but there are circumstances in
which a lie can hardly be a sin. I would have been
the last to say so before all this had come upon me,
but I feel it to be so now. It is a lie to say that you
are my wife.'

' Is it ? Is it ? '

' Is it not ? And yet I would rather cut my
tongue out than say otherwise. To give you my
name is a lie,—but what should I think of myself
were I to allow you to use any other ? What would
you have thought if I had asked you to go away and
leave me when that bad hour came upon us ? '

'I would have borne it.'

'I could not have borne it. There are worse
things than a lie. I have found, since this came
upon us, that it may be well to choose one sin in
order that another may be shunned. To cherish
you, to comfort you, to make the storm less sharp
to you,—that has already been my duty as well as
my pleasure. To do the same to me is your duty.'

'And my pleasure; and my pleasure,—my only
pleasure.'

'We must cling to each other, let the world call
us what names it may. But there may come a
time in which one is called on to do a special act
of justice to others. It has come now to me.
From the world at large I am prepared, if possible,
to keep my secret, even though I do it by lying;
—but to this one man I am driven to tell it, because
I may not return his friendship by doing him an
evil.'

Morning school at this time of the year at Bowick
began at half-past seven. There was an hour of
school before breakfast, at which the Doctor did
not himself put in an appearance. He was wont to
tell the boys that he had done all that when he was
young, and that now in his old age it suited him
best to have his breakfast before he began the work
of the day. Mr. Peacocke, of course, attended the
morning school. Indeed, as the matutinal performances were altogether classical, it was impossible
that much should be done without him. On this
Saturday morning, however, he was not present;
and a few minutes after the proper time, the mathe-
matical master took his place. 'I saw him coming
across out of his own door,' little Jack Talbot said

to the younger of the two Clifford boys, ' and there was a man coming up from the gate who met him.'

' What sort of a man ? ' asked Clifford.

' He was a rummy-looking fellow, with a great beard, and a queer kind of coat. I never saw any one like him before.'

' And where did they go ? '

' They stood talking for a minute or two just before the front door, and then Mr. Peacocke took him into the house. I heard him tell Carstairs to go through and send word up to the Doctor that he wouldn't be in school this morning.'

It had all happened just as young Talbot had said. A very ' rummy-looking fellow ' had at that early hour been driven over from Broughton to Bowick, and had caught Mr. Peacocke just as he was going into the school. He was a man with a beard, loose, flowing on both sides, as though he were winged like a bird,—a beard that had been black, but was now streaked through and through with grey hairs. The man had a coat with frogged buttons*that must have been intended to have a military air when it was new, but which was now much the worse for wear. The coat was so odd as to have caught young Talbot's attention at once. And the man's hat was old and seedy. But there was a look about him as though he were by no means ashamed either of himself or of his present purpose. ' He came in a gig,' said Talbot to his friend ; ' for I saw the horse standing at the gate, and the man sitting in the gig.'

' You remember me, no doubt,' the stranger said, when he encountered Mr. Peacocke.

' I do not remember you in the least,' the school-master answered.

' Come, come ; that won't do. You know me well enough. I'm Robert Lefroy.'

Then Mr. Peacocke, looking at him again, knew that the man was the brother of his wife's husband. He had not seen him often, but he recognised him as Robert Lefroy, and having recognised him he took him into the house.

PART III

CHAPTER VII

ROBERT LEFROY

FERDINAND LEFROY, the man who had in truth
been the woman's husband, had, during that one
interview which had taken place between him and
the man who had married his wife, on his return to
St. Louis, declared that his brother Robert was
dead. But so had Robert, when Peacocke encountered him down at Texas, declared that Ferdinand was dead. Peacocke knew that no word
of truth could be expected from the mouths of
either of them. But seeing is believing. He had
seen Ferdinand alive at St. Louis after his marriage,
and by seeing him, had been driven away from his
home back to his old country. Now he also saw
this other man, and was aware that his secret was
no longer in his own keeping.

' Yes, I know you now. Why, when I saw you
last, did you tell me that your brother was dead ?
Why did you bring so great an injury on your
sister-in-law ? '

' I never told you anything of the kind.'

' As God is above us you told me so.'

' I don't know anything about that, my friend.
Maybe I was cut.* I used to be drinking a good
deal them days. Maybe I didn't say anything of
the kind,—only it suited you to go back and tell
her so. Anyways I disremember it altogether.
Anyways he wasn't dead. And I ain't dead now.'

D. W. S.—6

'I can see that.'

'And I ain't drunk now. But I am not quite so well off as a fellow would wish to be. Can you get me breakfast?'

'Yes, I can get you breakfast,' he said, after pausing for a while. Then he rang the bell and told the girl to bring some breakfast for the gentleman as soon as possible into the room in which they were sitting. This was in a little library in which he was in the habit of studying and going through lessons with the boys. He had brought the man here so that his wife might not come across him. As soon as the order was given, he ran upstairs to her room, to save her from coming down.

'A man;—what man?' she asked.

'Robert Lefroy. I must go to him at once. Bear yourself well and boldly, my darling. It is he, certainly. I know nothing yet of what he may have to say, but it will be well that you should avoid him if possible. When I have heard anything I will tell you all.' Then he hurried down and found the man examining the book-shelves.

'You have got yourself up pretty tidy again, Peacocke,' said Lefroy.

'Pretty well.'

'The old game, I suppose. Teaching the young idea. Is this what you call a college, now, in your country?'

'It is a school.'

'And you're one of the masters.'

'I am the second master.'

'It ain't as good, I reckon, as the Missouri College.'

'It's not so large, certainly.'

' What's the screw ? ' he said.

' The payment, you mean. It can hardly serve us now to go into matters such as that. What is it that has brought you here, Lefroy ? '

' Well, a big ship, an uncommonly bad sort of railway car, and the ricketiest little buggy that ever a man trusted his life to. Them's what's brought me here.'

' I suppose you have something to say, or you would not have come,' said Peacocke.

' Yes, I've a good deal to say of one kind or another. But here's the breakfast, and I'm well-nigh starved. What, cold meat ! I'm darned if I can eat cold meat. Haven't you got anything hot, my dear ? ' Then it was explained to him that hot meat was not to be had, unless he would choose to wait, to have some lengthened cooking accomplished. To this, however, he objected, and then the girl left the room.

' I've a good many things to say of one kind or another,' he continued. ' It's difficult to say, Peacocke, how you and I stand with each other.'

' I do not know that we stand with each other at all, as you call it.'

' I mean as to relationship. Are you my brother-in-law, or are you not ? ' This was a question which in very truth the schoolmaster found it hard to answer. He did not answer it at all, but remained silent. ' Are you my brother-in-law, or are you not ? You call her Mrs. Peacocke, eh ? '

' Yes, I call her Mrs. Peacocke.'

' And she is here living with you ? '

' Yes, she is here.'

'Had she not better come down and see me? She is my sister-in-law, anyway.'

'No,' said Mr. Peacocke; 'I think, on the whole, that she had better not come down and see you.'

'You don't mean to say she isn't my sister-in-law? She's that, whatever else she is. She's that, whatever name she goes by. If Ferdinand had been ever so much dead, and that marriage at St. Louis had been ever so good, still she'd been my sister-in-law.'

'Not a doubt about it,' said Mr. Peacocke. 'But still, under all the circumstances, she had better not see you.'

'Well, that's a queer beginning, anyway. But perhaps you'll come round by-and-by. She goes by Mrs. Peacocke?'

'She is regarded as my wife,' said the husband, feeling himself to become more and more indignant at every word, but knowing at the same time how necessary it was that he should keep his indignation hidden.

'Whether true or false?' asked the brother-in-law.

'I will answer no such question as that.'

'You ain't very well disposed to answer any question, as far as I can see. But I shall have to make you answer one or two before I've done with you. There's a Doctor here, isn't there, as this school belongs to?'

'Yes, there is. It belongs to Dr. Wortle.'

'It's him these boys are sent to?'

'Yes, he is the master; I am only his assistant.'

'It's him they comes to for education, and morals, and religion?'

' Quite so.'

' And he knows, no doubt, all about you and my
sister-in-law;—how you came and married her
when she was another man's wife, and took her
away when you knew as that other man was alive
and kicking ? ' Mr. Peacocke, when these questions
were put to him, remained silent, because literally
he did not know how to answer them. He was
quite prepared to take his position as he found it.
He had told himself before this dreadful man had
appeared, that the truth must be made known at
Bowick, and that he and his wife must pack up and
flit. It was not that the man could bring upon him
any greater evil than he had anticipated. But the
questions which were asked him were in themselves
so bitter ! The man, no doubt, was his wife's
brother-in-law. He could not turn him out of the
house as he would a stranger, had a stranger come
there asking such questions without any claim of
family. Abominable as the man was to him, still
he was there with a certain amount of right upon
his side.

' I think,' said he, ' that questions such as those
you've asked can be of no service to you. To me
they are intended only to be injurious.'

' They're as a preface to what is to come,' said
Robert Lefroy, with an impudent leer upon his
face. ' The questions, no doubt, are disagreeable
enough. She ain't your wife no more than she's
mine. You've no business with her ; and that you
knew when you took her away from St. Louis. You
may, or you mayn't, have been fooled by some one
down in Texas when you went back and married
her in all that hurry. But you knew what you

were doing well enough when you took her away. You won't dare to tell me that you hadn't seen Ferdinand when you two mizzled off from the College?' Then he paused, waiting again for a reply.

'As I told you before,' he said, 'no further conversation on the subject can be of avail. It does not suit me to be cross-examined as to what I knew or what I did not know. If you have anything for me to hear, you can say it. If you have anything to tell to others, go and tell it to them.'

'That's just it,' said Lefroy.

'Then go and tell it.'

'You're in a terrible hurry, Mister Peacocke. I don't want to drop in and spoil your little game. You're making money of your little game. I can help you as to carrying on your little game, better than you do at present. I don't want to blow upon you. But as you're making money out of it, I'd like to make a little too. I am precious hard up, —I am.'

'You will make no money of me,' said the other.

'A little will go a long way with me; and remember, I have got tidings now which are worth paying for.'

'What tidings?'

'If they're worth paying for, it's not likely that you are going to get them for nothing.'

'Look here, Colonel Lefroy; whatever you may have to say about me will certainly not be prevented by my paying you money. Though you might be able to ruin me to-morrow I would not give you a dollar to save myself.'

'But her,' said Lefroy, pointing as it were upstairs, with his thumb over his shoulder.

' Nor her,' said Peacocke.

' You don't care very much about her, then ? '

' How much I may care I shall not trouble myself to explain to you. I certainly shall not endeavour to serve her after that fashion. I begin to understand why you have come, and can only beg you to believe that you have come in vain.'

Lefroy turned to his food, which he had not yet finished, while his companion sat silent at the window, trying to arrange in his mind the circumstances of the moment as best he might. He declared to himself that had the man come but one day later, his coming would have been matter of no moment. The story, the entire story, would then have been told to the Doctor, and the brother-in-law, with all his malice, could have added nothing to the truth. But now it seemed as though there would be a race which should tell the story first. Now the Doctor would, no doubt, be led to feel that the narration was made because it could no longer be kept back. Should this man be with the Doctor first, and should the story be told as he would tell it, then it would be impossible for Mr. Peacocke, in acknowledging the truth of it all, to bring his friend's mind back to the condition in which it would have been had this intruder not been in the way. And yet he could not make a race of it with the man. He could not rush across, and, all but out of breath with his energy, begin his narration while Lefroy was there knocking at the door. There would be an absence of dignity in such a mode of proceeding which alone was sufficient to deter him. He had fixed an hour already with the Doctor. He had said that he would be there in the house at a certain time. Let the man do what he would he would keep exactly to his purpose, unless the Doctor should seek an earlier interview. He would, in no tittle, be turned from his purpose by the unfortunate coming of this wretched man. ' Well ! ' said Lefroy, as soon as he had eaten his last mouthful.

' I have nothing to say to you,' said Peacocke.

' Nothing to say ? '

' Not a word.'

' Well, that's queer. I should have thought there'd have been a many words. I've got a lot to say to somebody, and mean to say it ;—precious soon too. Is there any hotel here, where I can put this horse up ? I suppose you haven't got stables of your own ? I wonder if the Doctor would give me accommodation ? '

' I haven't got a stable, and the Doctor certainly will not give you accommodation. There is a public-house less than a quarter of a mile further on, which no doubt your driver knows very well. You had better go there yourself, because after what has taken place, I am bound to tell you that you will not be admitted here.'

' Not admitted ? '

' No. You must leave this house, and will not be admitted into it again as long as I live in it.'

' The Doctor will admit me.'

' Very likely. I, at any rate, shall do nothing to dissuade him. If you go down to the road you'll see the gate leading up to his house. I think you'll find that he is down-stairs by this time.'

' You take it very cool, Peacocke.'

' I only tell you the truth. With you I will have

nothing more to do. You have a story which you wish to tell to Dr. Wortle. Go and tell it to him.'

' I can tell it to all the world,' said Lefroy.

' Go and tell it to all the world.'

' And I ain't to see my sister ? '

' No ; you will not see your sister-in-law here. Why should she wish to see one who has only injured her ? '

' I ain't injured her ;—at any rate not as yet. I ain't done nothing ;—not as yet. I've been as dark as the grave ;—as yet. Let her come down, and you go away for a moment, and let us see if we can't settle it.'

' There is nothing for you to settle. Nothing that you can do, nothing that you can say, will influence either her or me. If you have anything to tell, go and tell it.'

' Why should you smash up everything in that way, Peacocke ? You're comfortable here ; why not remain so ? I don't want to hurt you. I want to help you ;—and I can. Three hundred dollars wouldn't be much to you. You were always a fellow as had a little money by you.'

' If this box were full of gold,' said the school-master, laying his hand upon a black desk which stood on the table, ' I would not give you one cent to induce you to hold your tongue for ever. I would not condescend even to ask it of you as a favour. You think that you can disturb our happiness by telling what you know of us to Dr. Wortle. Go and try.'

Mr. Peacocke's manner was so firm that the other man began to doubt whether in truth he had a secret to tell. Could it be possible that Dr. Wortle knew it all, and that the neighbours knew it all, and that, in spite of what had happened, the position of the man and of the woman was accepted among them? They certainly were not man and wife, and yet they were living together as such. Could such a one as this Dr. Wortle know that it was so? He, when he had spoken of the purposes for which the boys were sent there, asking whether they were not sent for education, for morals and religion, had understood much of the Doctor's position. He had known the peculiar value of his secret. He had been aware that a schoolmaster with a wife to whom he was not in truth married must be out of place in an English seminary such as this. But yet he now began to doubt. 'I am to be turned out, then?' he asked.

'Yes, indeed, Colonel Lefroy. The sooner you go the better.'

'That's a pretty sort of welcome to your wife's brother-in-law, who has just come over all the way from Mexico to see her.'

'To get what he can out of her by his unwelcome presence,' said Peacocke. 'Here you can get nothing. Go and do your worst. If you remain much longer I shall send for the policeman to remove you.'

'You will?'

'Yes, I shall. My time is not my own, and I cannot go over to my work leaving you in my house. You have nothing to get by my friendship. Go and see what you can do as my enemy.'

'I will,' said the Colonel, getting up from his chair; 'I will. If I'm to be treated in this way it shall not be for nothing. I have offered you the right hand of an affectionate brother-in-law.'

' Bosh,' said Mr. Peacocke.

' And you tell me that I am an enemy. Very well; I will be an enemy. I could have put you altogether on your legs, but I'll leave you without an inch of ground to stand upon. You see if I don't.' Then he put his hat on his head, and stalked out of the house, down the road towards the gate.

Mr. Peacocke, when he was left alone, remained in the room collecting his thoughts, and then went up-stairs to his wife.

' Has he gone ? ' she asked.

' Yes, he has gone.'

' And what has he said ? '

' He has asked for money,—to hold his tongue.'

' Have you given him any ? '

' Not a cent. I have given him nothing but hard words. I have bade him go and do his worst. To be at the mercy of such a man as that would be worse for you and for me than anything that fortune has sent us even yet.'

' Did he want to see me ? '

' Yes ; but I refused. Was it not better ? '

' Yes ; certainly, if you think so. What could I have said to him ? Certainly it was better. His presence would have half killed me. But what will he do, Henry ? '

' He will tell it all to everybody that he sees.'

' Oh, my darling ! '

' What matter though he tells it at the town-cross ? It would have been told to-day by myself.'

' But only to one.'

' It would have been the same. For any purpose

of concealment it would have been the same. I
have got to hate the concealment. What have we
done but clung together as a man and woman
should who have loved each other, and have had a
right to love ? What have we done of which we
should be ashamed ? Let it be told. Let it all be
known. Have you not been good and pure ? Have
not I been true to you ? Bear up your courage, and
let the man do his worst. Not to save even you
would I cringe before such a man as that. And
were I to do so, I should save you from nothing.'

CHAPTER VIII

THE STORY IS TOLD

DURING the whole of that morning the Doctor
did not come into the school. The school hours
lasted from half-past nine to twelve, during a portion of which time it was his practice to be there.
But sometimes, on a Saturday, he would be absent,
when it was understood generally that he was preparing his sermon for the Sunday. Such, no doubt,
might be the case now ; but there was a feeling
among the boys that he was kept away by some
other reason. It was known that during the hour
of morning school Mr. Peacocke had been occupied
with that uncouth stranger, and some of the boys
might have observed that the uncouth stranger
had not taken himself altogether away from the
premises. There was at any rate a general feeling
that the uncouth stranger had something to do with
the Doctor's absence.

Mr. Peacocke did his best to go on with the work

as though nothing had occurred to disturb the
usual tenor of his way, and as far as the boys were
aware he succeeded. He was just as clear about
his Greek verbs, just as incisive about that passage
of Cæsar, as he would have been had Colonel
Lefroy remained on the other side of the water.
But during the whole time he was exercising his
mind in that painful process of thinking of two
things at once. He was determined that Cæsar
should be uppermost; but it may be doubted
whether he succeeded. At that very moment
Colonel Lefroy might be telling the Doctor that his
Ella was in truth the wife of another man. At that
moment the Doctor might be deciding in his anger
that the sinful and deceitful man should no longer
be ' officer of his.' The hour was too important to
him to leave his mind at his own disposal. Nevertheless he did his best. ' Clifford, junior,' he said,
' I shall never make you understand what Cæsar
says here or elsewhere if you do not give your
entire mind to Cæsar.'

' I do give my entire mind to Cæsar,' said Clifford, junior.

' Very well; now go on and try again. But
remember that Cæsar wants all your mind.' As he
said this he was revolving in his own mind how he
would face the Doctor when the Doctor should look
at him in his wrath. If the Doctor were in any
degree harsh with him, he would hold his own
against the Doctor as far as the personal contest
might go. At twelve the boys went out for an hour
before their dinner, and Lord Carstairs asked him
to play a game of rackets.

' Not to-day, my Lord,' he said.

'Is anything wrong with you?'

'Yes, something is very wrong.' They had strolled out of the building, and were walking up and down the gravel terrace in front when this was said.

'I knew something was wrong, because you called me my Lord.'

'Yes, something is so wrong as to alter for me all the ordinary ways of my life. But I wasn't thinking of it. It came by accident,—just because I am so troubled.'

'What is it?'

'There has been a man here,—a man whom I knew in America.'

'An enemy?'

'Yes,—an enemy. One who is anxious to do me all the injury he can.'

'Are you in his power, Mr. Peacocke?'

'No, thank God; not that. I am in no man's power. He cannot do me any material harm. Anything which may happen would have happened whether he had come or not. But I am unhappy.'

'I wish I knew.'

'So do I,—with all my heart. I wish you knew; I wish you knew. I would that all the world knew. But we shall live through it, no doubt. And if we do not, what matter. "Nil conscire sibi,—nulla pallescere culpa."* That is all that is necessary to a man. I have done nothing of which I repent;—nothing that I would not do again; nothing of which I am ashamed to speak as far as the judgment of other men is concerned. Go, now. They are making up sides for cricket. Perhaps I can tell you more before the evening is over.'

Both Mr. and Mrs. Peacocke were accustomed to dine with the boys at one, when Carstairs, being a private pupil, only had his lunch. But on this occasion she did not come into the dining-room. 'I don't think I can to-day,' she said, when he bade her to take courage, and not be altered more than she could help, in her outward carriage, by the misery of her present circumstances. 'I could not eat if I were there, and then they would look at me.'

'If it be so, do not attempt it. There is no necessity. What I mean is, that the less one shrinks the less will be the suffering. It is the man who shivers on the brink that is cold, and not he who plunges into the water. If it were over,—if the first brunt of it were over, I could find means to comfort you.'

He went through the dinner, as he had done the Cæsar, eating the roast mutton and the baked potatoes, and the great plateful of currant-pie that was brought to him. He was fed and nourished, no doubt, but it may be doubtful whether he knew much of the flavour of what he ate. But before the dinner was quite ended, before he had said the grace which it was always his duty to pronounce, there came a message to him from the rectory. 'The Doctor would be glad to see him as soon as dinner was done.' He waited very calmly till the proper moment should come for the grace, and then, very calmly, he took his way over to the house. He was certain now that Lefroy had been with the Doctor, because he was sent for considerably before the time fixed for the interview.

It was his chief resolve to hold his own before the Doctor. The Doctor, who could read a character well, had so read that of Mr. Peacocke as to have been aware from the first that no censure, no fault-finding, would be possible if the connection were to be maintained. Other ushers, other curates, he had occasionally scolded. He had been very careful never even to seem to scold Mr. Peacocke. Mr. Peacocke had been aware of it too,—aware that he could not endure it, and aware also that the Doctor avoided any attempt at it. He had known that, as a consequence of this, he was bound to be more than ordinarily prompt in the performance of all his duties. The man who will not endure censure has to take care that he does not deserve it. Such had been this man's struggle, and it had been altogether successful. Each of the two understood the other, and each respected the other. Now their position must be changed. It was hardly possible, Mr. Peacocke thought, as he entered the house, that he should not be rebuked with grave severity, and quite out of the question that he should bear any rebuke at all.

The library at the rectory was a spacious and handsome room, in the centre of which stood a large writing-table, at which the Doctor was accustomed to sit when he was at work,—facing the door, with a bow-window at his right hand. But he rarely remained there when any one was summoned into the room, unless some one were summoned with whom he meant to deal in a spirit of severity. Mr. Peacocke would be there perhaps three or four times a-week, and the Doctor would always get up from his chair and stand, or seat himself elsewhere in the room, and would probably move about with vivacity, being a fidgety man of quick motions, who sometimes seemed as though he could not hold his own body still for a moment. But now when Mr. Peacocke entered the room he did not leave his place at the table. ' Would you take a chair ? ' he said; 'there is something that we must talk about.'

' Colonel Lefroy has been with you, I take it.'

' A man calling himself by that name has been here. Will you not take a chair ? '

' I do not know that it will be necessary. What he has told you,—what I suppose he has told you, —is true.'

' You had better at any rate take a chair. I do not believe that what he has told me is true.'

' But it is.'

' I do not believe that what he has told me is true. Some of it cannot, I think, be true. Much of it is not so,—unless I am more deceived in you than I ever was in any man. At any rate sit down.' Then the schoolmaster did sit down. ' He has made you out to be a perjured, wilful, cruel bigamist.'

' I have not been such,' said Peacocke, rising from his chair.

' One who has been willing to sacrifice a woman to his passion.'

' No ; no.'

' Who deceived her by false witnesses.'

' Never.'

' And who has now refused to allow her to see her own husband's brother, lest she should learn the truth.'

' She is there,—at any rate for you to see.'

' Therefore the man is a liar. A long story has to be told, as to which at present I can only guess what may be the nature. I presume the story will be the same as that you would have told had the man never come here.'

'Exactly the same, Dr. Wortle.'

'Therefore you will own that I am right in asking you to sit down. The story may be very long,—that is, if you mean to tell it.'

'I do,—and did. I was wrong from the first in supposing that the nature of my marriage need be of no concern to others, but to herself and to me.'

'Yes,—Mr. Peacocke; yes. We are, all of us, joined together too closely to admit of isolation such as that.' There was something in this which grated against the schoolmaster's pride, though nothing had been said as to which he did not know that much harder things must meet his ears before the matter could be brought to an end between him and the Doctor. The 'Mister' had been pre-fixed to his name, which had been omitted for the last three or four months in the friendly intercourse which had taken place between them; and then, though it had been done in the form of agreeing with what he himself had said, the Doctor had made his first complaint by declaring that no man had a right to regard his own moral life as isolated from the lives of others around him. It was as much as to declare at once that he had been wrong in bringing this woman to Bowick, and calling her Mrs. Peacocke. He had said as much himself, but that did not make the censure lighter when it came to him from the mouth of the Doctor. 'But come,' said the Doctor, getting up from his seat at the table, and throwing himself into an easy-chair, so as to mitigate the austerity of the position; 'let us hear the true story. So big a liar as that American

gentleman probably never put his foot in this room
before.'

Then Mr. Peacocke told the story, beginning
with all those incidents of the woman's life which
had seemed to be so cruel both to him and to others
at St. Louis before he had been in any degree
intimate with her. Then came the departure of
the two men, and the necessity for pecuniary assistance, which Mr. Peacocke now passed over lightly,
saying nothing specially of the assistance which he
himself had rendered. 'And she was left quite
alone ? ' asked the Doctor.

' Quite alone.'

' And for how long ? '

' Eighteen months had passed before we heard
any tidings. Then there came news that Colonel
Lefroy was dead.'

' The husband ? '

' We did not know which. They were both
Colonels.'

' And then ? '

'Did he tell you that I went down into Mexico ? '

' Never mind what he told me. All that he told
me were lies. What you tell me I shall believe.
But tell me everything.'

There was a tone of complete authority in the
Doctor's voice, but mixed with this there was a
kindliness which made the schoolmaster determined that he would tell everything as far as he
knew how. ' When I heard that one of them was
dead, I went away down to the borders of Texas,
in order that I might learn the truth.'

' Did she know that you were going ? '

' Yes ;—I told her the day I started.'

'And you told her why ?'

'That I might find out whether her husband were still alive.'

'But——' The Doctor hesitated as he asked the next question. He knew, however, that it had to be asked, and went on with it. 'Did she know that you loved her ?' To this the other made no immediate answer. The Doctor was a man who, in such a matter, was intelligent enough, and he therefore put his question in another shape. 'Had you told her that you loved her ?'

'Never,—while I thought that other man was living.'

'She must have guessed it,' said the Doctor.

'She might guess what she pleased. I told her that I was going, and I went.'

'And how was it, then ?'

'I went, and after a time I came across the very man who is here now, this Robert Lefroy. I met him and questioned him, and he told me that his brother had been killed while fighting. It was a lie.'

'Altogether a lie ?' asked the Doctor.

'How altogether ?'

'He might have been wounded and given over for dead. The brother might have thought him to be dead.'

'I do not think so. I believe it to have been a plot in order that the man might get rid of his wife. But I believed it. Then I went back to St. Louis,—and we were married.'

'You thought there was no obstacle but what you might become man and wife legally ?'

'I thought she was a widow.'

'There was no further delay ?'

' Very little. Why should there have been delay ? '

' I only ask.'

' She had suffered enough, and I had waited long enough.'

' She owed you a great deal,' said the Doctor.

' It was not a case of owing,' said Mr. Peacocke. ' At least I think not. I think she had learnt to love me as I had learnt to love her.'

' And how did it go with you then ? '

' Very well,—for some months. There was nothing to mar our happiness,—till one day he came and made his way into our presence.'

' The husband ? '

' Yes ; the husband, Ferdinand Lefroy, the elder brother ;—he of whom I had been told that he was dead ; he was there standing before us, talking to us,—half drunk, but still well knowing what he was doing.'

' Why had he come ? '

' In want of money, I suppose,—as this other one has come here.'

' Did he ask for money ? '

' I do not think he did then, though he spoke of his poor condition. But on the next day he went away. We heard that he had taken the steamer down the river for New Orleans. We have never heard more of him from that day to this.'

' Can you imagine what caused conduct such as that ? '

' I think money was given to him that night to go ; but if so, I do not know by whom. I gave him none. During the next day or two I found that many in St. Louis knew that he had been there.'

'They knew then that you——'

'They knew that my wife was not my wife. That is what you mean to ask?' The Doctor nodded his head. 'Yes, they knew that.'

'And what then?'

'Word was brought to me that she and I must part if I chose to keep my place at the College.'

'That you must disown her?'

'The President told me that it would be better that she should go elsewhere. How could I send her from me?'

'No, indeed;—but as to the facts?'

'You know them all pretty well now. I could not send her from me. Nor could I go and leave her. Had we been separated then, because of the law or because of religion, the burden, the misery, the desolation, would all have been upon her.'

'I would have clung to her, let the law say what it might,' said the Doctor, rising from his chair.

'You would?'

'I would;—and I think that I could have reconciled it to my God. But I might have been wrong,' he added; 'I might have been wrong. I only say what I should have done.'

'It was what I did.'

'Exactly; exactly. We are both sinners. Both might have been wrong. Then you brought her over here, and I suppose I know the rest?'

'You know everything now,' said Mr. Peacocke.

'And believe every word I have heard. Let me say that, if that may be any consolation to you. Of my friendship you may remain assured. Whether you can remain here is another question.'

'We are prepared to go.'

'You cannot expect that I should have thought it all out during the hearing of the story. There is much to be considered ;—very much. I can only say this, as between man and man, that no man ever sympathized with another more warmly than I do with you. You had better let me have till Monday to think about it.'

CHAPTER IX

MRS. WORTLE AND MR. PUDDICOMBE

In this way nothing was said at the first telling of the story to decide the fate of the schoolmaster and of the lady whom we shall still call his wife. There certainly had been no horror displayed by the Doctor. 'Whether you can remain here is another question.' The Doctor, during the whole interview, had said nothing harder than that. Mr. Peacocke, as he left the rectory, did feel that the Doctor had been very good to him. There had not only been no horror, but an expression of the kindest sympathy. And as to the going, that was left in doubt. He himself felt that he ought to go ;—but it would have been so very sad to have to go without a friend left with whom he could consult as to his future condition !

'He has been very kind, then ? ' said Mrs. Peacocke to her husband when he related to her the particulars of the interview.

'Very kind.'

'And he did not reproach you.'

'Not a word.'

'Nor me ? '

'He declared that had it been he who was in question he would have clung to you for ever and ever.'

'Did he ? Then will he leave us here ? '

'That does not follow. I should think not. He will know that others must know it. Your brother-in-law will not tell him only. Lefroy, when he finds that he can get no money here, from sheer revenge will tell the story everywhere. When he left the rectory, he was probably as angry with the Doctor as he is with me. He will do all the harm that he can to all of us.'

'We must go, then ? '

'I should think so. Your position here would be insupportable even if it could be permitted. You may be sure of this ;—everybody will know it.'

'What do I care for everybody ? ' she said. ' It is not that I am ashamed of myself.'

'No, dearest ; nor am I,—ashamed of myself or of you. But there will be bitter words, and bitter words will produce bitter looks and scant respect. How would it be with you if the boys looked at you as though they thought ill of you ? '

'They would not ;—oh, they would not ! '

'Or the servants,—if they reviled you ? '

'Could it come to that ? '

'It must not come to that. But it is as the Doctor said himself just now ;—a man cannot isolate the morals, the manners, the ways of his life from the morals of others. Men, if they live together, must live together by certain laws.'

'Then there can be no hope for us.'

'None that I can see, as far as Bowick is concerned. We are too closely joined in our work with other people. There is not a boy here with whose father and mother and sisters we are not more or less connected. When I was preaching in the church, there was not one in the parish with whom I was not connected. Would it do, do you think, for a priest to preach against drunkenness, whilst he himself was a noted drunkard ? '

' Are we like that ? '

' It is not what the drunken priest might think of himself, but what others might think of him. It would not be with us the position which we know that we hold together, but that which others would think it to be. If I were in Dr. Wortle's case, and another were to me as I am to him, I should bid him go.'

' You would turn him away from you ; him and his—wife ? '

' I should. My first duty would be to my parish and to my school. If I could befriend him otherwise I would do so ;—and that is what I expect from Dr. Wortle. We shall have to go, and I shall be forced to approve of our dismissal.'

In this way Mr. Peacocke came definitely and clearly to a conclusion in his own mind. But it was very different with Dr. Wortle. The story so disturbed him, that during the whole of that afternoon he did not attempt to turn his mind to any other subject. He even went so far as to send over to Mr. Puddicombe and asked for some assistance for the afternoon service on the following day. He was too unwell, he said, to preach himself, and the one curate would have the two entire services unless Mr. Puddicombe could help him. Could Mr. Puddicombe come himself and see him on the Sunday afternoon? This note he sent away by a messenger, who came back with a reply, saying that Mr. Puddicombe would himself preach in the afternoon, and would afterwards call in at the rectory.

For an hour or two before his dinner, the Doctor went out on horseback, and roamed about among the lanes, endeavouring to make up his mind. He was hitherto altogether at a loss as to what he should do in this present uncomfortable emergency. He could not bring his conscience and his inclination to come square together. And even when he counselled himself to yield to his conscience, his very conscience,—a second conscience, as it were,—revolted against the first. His first conscience told him that he owed a primary duty to his parish, a second duty to his school, and a third to his wife and daughter. In the performance of all these duties he would be bound to rid himself of Mr. Peacocke. But then there came that other conscience, telling him that the man had been more ' sinned against than sinning,'*—that common humanity required him to stand by a man who had suffered so much, and had suffered so unworthily. Then this second conscience went on to remind him that the man was pre-eminently fit for the duties which he had undertaken,—that the man was a God-fearing, moral, and especially intellectual assistant in his school,—that were he to lose him he could not hope to find any one that would be his equal, or at all approaching to him in capacity. This second conscience went further, and assured him that the man's excellence as a schoolmaster was even increased by the peculiarity of his position. Do we

not all know that if a man be under a cloud the
very cloud will make him more attentive to his
duties than another ? If a man, for the wages
which he receives, can give to his employer high
character as well as work, he will think that he may
lighten his work because of his character. And as
to this man, who was the very phœnix of school
assistants, there would really be nothing amiss with
his character if only this piteous incident as to his
wife were unknown. In this way his second conscience almost got the better of the first.

But then it would be known. It would be impossible that it should not be known. He had already
made up his mind to tell Mr. Puddicombe, absolutely not daring to decide in such an emergency
without consulting some friend. Mr. Puddicombe
would hold his peace if he were to promise to do so.
Certainly he might be trusted to do that. But
others would know it ; the Bishop would know it ;
Mrs. Stantiloup would know it. That man, of
course, would take care that all Broughton, with
its close full of cathedral clergymen, would know
it. When Mrs. Stantiloup should know it there
would not be a boy's parent through all the school
who would not know it. If he kept the man he
must keep him resolving that all the world should
know that he kept him, that all the world should
know of what nature was the married life of the
assistant in whom he trusted. And he must be
prepared to face all the world, confiding in the
uprightness and the humanity of his purpose.

In such case he must say something of this kind
to all the world ; ' I know that they are not
married. I know that their condition of life is

opposed to the law of God and man. I know that she bears a name that is not, in truth, her own ; but I think that the circumstances in this case are so strange, so peculiar, that they excuse a disregard even of the law of God and man.' Had he courage enough for this ? And if the courage were there, was he high enough and powerful enough to carry out such a purpose ? Could he beat down the Mrs. Stantiloups ? And, indeed, could he beat down the Bishop and the Bishop's phalanx ;—for he knew that the Bishop and the Bishop's phalanx would be against him ? They could not touch him in his living, because Mr. Peacocke would not be concerned in the services of the church ; but would not his school melt away to nothing in his hands, if he were to attempt to carry it on after this fashion ? And then would he not have destroyed himself without advantage to the man whom he was anxious to assist ?

To only one point did he make up his mind certainly during that ride. Before he slept that night he would tell the whole story to his wife. He had at first thought that he would conceal it from her. It was his rule of life to act so entirely on his own will, that he rarely consulted her on matters of any importance. As it was, he could not endure the responsibility of acting by himself. People would say of him that he had subjected his wife to contamination, and had done so without giving her any choice in the matter. So he resolved that he would tell his wife.

' Not married,' said Mrs. Wortle, when she heard the story.

' Married ; yes. They were married. It was not

their fault that the marriage was nothing. What was he to do when he heard that they had been deceived in this way ? '

' Not married properly ! Poor woman ! '

' Yes, indeed. What should I have done if such had happened to me when we had been six months married ? '

' It couldn't have been.'

' Why not to you as well as to another ? '

' I was only a young girl.'

' But if you had been a widow ? '

' Don't, my dear ; don't ! It wouldn't have been possible.'

' But you pity her ? '

' Oh yes.'

' And you see that a great misfortune has fallen upon her, which she could not help ? '

' Not till she knew it,' said the wife who had been married quite properly.

' And what then ? What should she have done then ? '

' Gone,' said the wife, who had no doubt as to the comfort, the beauty, the perfect security of her own position.

' Gone ? '

' Gone away at once.'

' Whither should she go ? Who would have taken her by the hand ? Who would have supported her ? Would you have had her lay herself down in the first gutter and die ? '

' Better that than what she did do,' said Mrs. Wortle.

' Then, by all the faith I have in Christ, I think you are hard upon her. Do you think what it is to

have to go out and live alone ;—to have to look for
your bread in desolation ? '

' I have never been tried, my dear,' said she,
clinging close to him. ' I have never had anything
but what was good.'

' Ought we not to be kind to one to whom Fortune has been so unkind ? '

' If we can do so without sin.'

' Sin ! I despise the fear of sin which makes us
think that its contact will soil us. Her sin, if it be
sin, is so near akin to virtue, that I doubt whether
we should not learn of her rather than avoid
her.'

' A woman should not live with a man unless she
be his wife.' Mrs. Wortle said this with more of
obstinacy than he had expected.

' She was his wife, as far as she knew.'

' But when she knew that it was not so any
longer,—then she should have left him.'

' And have starved ? '

' I suppose she might have taken bread from
him.'

' You think, then, that she should go away from
here ? '

' Do not you think so ?   What will Mrs. Stantiloup say ? '

' And I am to turn them out into the cold because
of a virago such as she is ? You would have no
more charity than that ? '

' Oh, Jeffrey ! what would the Bishop say ? '

' Cannot you get beyond Mrs. Stantiloup and
beyond the Bishop, and think what Justice de-
mands ? '

' The boys would all be taken away. If you had

a son, would you send him where there was a school-master living,—living——. Oh, you wouldn't.'

It is very clear to the Doctor that his wife's mind was made up on the subject ; and yet there was no softer-hearted woman than Mrs. Wortle anywhere in the diocese, or one less likely to be severe upon a neighbour. Not only was she a kindly, gentle woman, but she was one who always had been willing to take her husband's opinion on all questions of right and wrong. She, however, was decided that they must go.

On the next morning, after service, which the schoolmaster did not attend, the Doctor saw Mr. Peacocke, and declared his intention of telling the story to Mr. Puddicombe. ' If you bid me hold my tongue,' he said, ' I will do so. But it will be better that I should consult another clergyman. He is a man who can keep a secret.' Then Mr. Peacocke gave him full authority to tell everything to Mr. Puddicombe. He declared that the Doctor might tell the story to whom he would. Everybody might know it now. He had, he said, quite made up his mind about that. What was the good of affecting secrecy when this man Lefroy was in the country ?

In the afternoon, after service, Mr. Puddicombe came up to the house, and heard it all. He was a dry, thin, apparently unsympathetic man, but just withal, and by no means given to harshness. He could pardon whenever he could bring himself to believe that pardon would have good results ; but he would not be driven by impulses and softness of heart to save the faulty one from the effect of his fault, merely because that effect would be painful.

He was a man of no great mental calibre,—not sharp, and quick, and capable of repartee as was the Doctor, but rational in all things, and always guided by his conscience. 'He has behaved very badly to you,' he said, when he heard the story.

'I do not think so ; I have no such feeling myself.'

'He behaved very badly in bringing her here without telling you all the facts. Considering the position that she was to occupy, he must have known that he was deceiving you.'

'I can forgive all that,' said the Doctor vehemently. 'As far as I myself am concerned, I forgive everything.'

'You are not entitled to do so.'

'How—not entitled ? '

'You must pardon me if I seem to take a liberty in expressing myself too boldly in this matter. Of course I should not do so unless you asked me.'

'I want you to speak freely,—all that you think.'

'In considering his conduct, we have to consider it all. First of all there came a great and terrible misfortune which cannot but excite our pity. According to his own story, he seems, up to that time, to have been affectionate and generous.'

'I believe every word of it,' said the Doctor.

'Allowing for a man's natural bias on his own side, so do I. He had allowed himself to become attached to another man's wife ; but we need not, perhaps, insist upon that.' The Doctor moved himself uneasily in his chair, but said nothing. 'We will grant that he put himself right by his marriage, though in that, no doubt, there should have been more of caution. Then came his great misfortune. He knew that his marriage had been no marriage. He saw the man and had no doubt.'

' Quite so; quite so,' said the Doctor, impatiently.

' He should, of course, have separated himself from her. There can be no doubt about it. There is no room for any quibble.'

' Quibble ! ' said the Doctor.

' I mean that no reference in our own minds to the pity of the thing, to the softness of the moment, —should make us doubt about it. Feelings such as these should induce us to pardon sinners, even to receive them back into our friendship and respect,—when they have seen the error of their ways and have repented.'

' You are very hard.'

' I hope not. At any rate I can only say as I think. But, in truth, in the present emergency you have nothing to do with all that. If he asked you for counsel you might give it to him, but that is not his present position. He has told you his story, not in a spirit of repentance, but because such telling had become necessary.'

' He would have told it all the same though this man had never come.'

' Let us grant that it is so, there still remains his relation to you. He came here under false pretences, and has done you a serious injury.'

' I think not,' said the Doctor.

' Would you have taken him into your establishment had you known it all before ? Certainly not. Therefore I say that he has deceived you. I do not advise you to speak to him with severity ; but he should, I think, be made to know that you appreciate what he has done.'

' And you would turn him off ;—send him away at once, out about his business ? '

' Certainly I would send him away.'

' You think him such a reprobate that he should not be allowed to earn his bread anywhere ? '

' I have not said so. I know nothing of his means of earning his bread. Men living in sin earn their bread constantly. But he certainly should not be allowed to earn his here.'

' Not though that man who was her husband should now be dead, and he should again marry, —legally marry,—this woman to whom he has been so true and loyal ? '

' As regards you and your school,' said Mr. Puddicombe, ' I do not think it would alter his position.'

With this the conference ended, and Mr. Puddicombe took his leave. As he left the house the Doctor declared to himself that the man was a strait-laced, fanatical, hard-hearted bigot. But though he said so to himself, he hardly thought so ; and was aware that the man's words had had effect upon him.

PART IV

CHAPTER X

MR. PEACOCKE GOES

THE Doctor had been all but savage with his wife, and, for the moment, had hated Mr. Puddicombe, but still what they said had affected him. They were both of them quite clear that Mr. Peacocke should be made to go at once. And he, though he hated Mr. Puddicombe for his cold logic, could not but acknowledge that all the man had said was true. According to the strict law of right and wrong the two unfortunates should have parted when they found that they were not in truth married. And, again, according to the strict law of right and wrong, Mr. Peacocke should not have brought the woman there, into his school, as his wife. There had been deceit. But then would not he, Dr. Wortle himself, have been guilty of similar deceit had it fallen upon him to have to defend a woman who had been true and affectionate to him ? Mr. Puddicombe would have left the woman to break her heart and have gone away and done his duty like a Christian, feeling no tugging at his heart-strings. It was so that our Doctor spoke to himself of his counsellor, sitting there alone in his library.

During his conference with Lefroy something had been said which had impressed him suddenly with an idea. A word had fallen from the Colonel, an unintended word, by which the Doctor was made to believe that the other Colonel was dead, at any rate now. He had cunningly tried to lead up to the subject, but Robert Lefroy had been on his guard as soon as he had perceived the Doctor's object, and had drawn back, denying the truth of the word he had before spoken. The Doctor at last asked him the question direct. Lefroy then declared that his brother had been alive and well when he left Texas, but he did this in such a manner as to strengthen in the Doctor's mind the impression that he was dead. If it were so, then might not all these crooked things be made straight ?

He had thought it better to raise no false hopes. He had said nothing of this to Peacocke on discussing the story. He had not even hinted it to his wife, from whom it might probably make its way to Mrs. Peacocke. He had suggested it to Mr. Puddicombe,—asking whether there might not be a way out of all their difficulties. Mr. Puddicombe had declared that there could be no such way as far as the school was concerned. Let them marry, and repent their sins, and go away from the spot they had contaminated, and earn their bread in some place in which there need be no longer additional sin in concealing the story of their past life. That seemed to have been Mr. Puddicombe's final judgment. But it was altogether opposed to Dr. Wortle's feelings.

When Mr. Puddicombe came down from the church to the rectory, Lord Carstairs was walking home after the afternoon service with Miss Wortle. It was his custom to go to church with the family, whereas the school went there under the charge of one of the ushers and sat apart in a portion of the church appropriated to themselves. Mrs. Wortle, when she found that the Doctor was not going to the afternoon service, declined to go herself. She was thoroughly disturbed by all these bad tidings, and was, indeed, very little able to say her prayers in a fit state of mind. She could hardly keep herself still for a moment, and was as one who thinks that the crack of doom is coming ;—so terrible to her was her vicinity and connection with this man, and with the woman who was not his wife. Then, again, she became flurried when she found that Lord Carstairs and Mary would have to walk alone together ; and she made little abortive attempts to keep first the one and then the other from going to church. Mary probably saw no reason for staying away, while Lord Carstairs possibly found an additional reason for going. Poor Mrs. Wortle had for some weeks past wished that the charming young nobleman had been at home with his father and mother, or anywhere but in her house. It had been arranged, however, that he should go in July and not return after the summer holidays. Under these circumstances, having full confidence in her girl, she had refrained from again expressing her fears to the Doctor. But there were fears. It was evident to her, though the Doctor seemed to see nothing of it, that the young lord was falling in love. It might be that his youth and natural bash-fulness would come to her aid, and that nothing should be said before that day in July which would separate them. But when it suddenly occurred to her that they two would walk to and fro from church together, there was cause for additional uneasiness.

If she had heard their conversation as they came back she would have been in no way disturbed by its tone on the score of the young man's tenderness towards her daughter, but she might perhaps have been surprised by his vehemence in another respect. She would have been surprised also at finding how much had been said during the last twenty-four hours by others besides herself and her husband about the affairs of Mr. and Mrs. Peacocke.

'Do you know what he came about?' asked Mary. The 'he' had of course been Robert Lefroy.

'Not in the least; but he came up there looking so queer, as though he certainly had come about something unpleasant.'

'And then he was with papa afterwards,' said Mary. 'I am sure papa and mamma not coming to church has something to do with it. And Mr. Peacocke hasn't been to church all day.'

'Something has happened to make him very unhappy,' said the boy. 'He told me so even before this man came here. I don't know any one whom I like so much as Mr. Peacocke.'

'I think it is about his wife,' said Mary.

'How about his wife?'

'I don't know, but I think it is. She is so very quiet.'

'How quiet, Miss Wortle?' he asked.

'She never will come in to see us. Mamma has asked her to dinner and to drink tea ever so often, but she never comes. She calls perhaps once in two or three months in a formal way, and that is all we see of her.'

'Do you like her?' he asked.

'How can I say, when I so seldom see her.'

'I do. I like her very much. I go and see her often ; and I'm sure of this ;—she is quite a lady. Mamma asked her to go to Carstairs for the holidays because of what I said.'

'She is not going ? '

'No ; neither of them will come. I wish they would ; and oh, Miss Wortle, I do so wish you were going to be there too.' This is all that was said of peculiar tenderness between them on that walk home.

Late in the evening,—so late that the boys had already gone to bed,—the Doctor sent again for Mr. Peacocke. 'I should not have troubled you to-night,' he said, ' only that I have heard something from Pritchett.' Pritchett was the rectory gardener who had charge also of the school buildings, and was a person of great authority in the establishment. He, as well the Doctor, held Mr. Peacocke in great respect, and would have been almost as unwilling as the Doctor himself to tell stories to the schoolmaster's discredit. ' They are saying down at the Lamb '—the Lamb was the Bowick public-house—' that Lefroy told them all yesterday——' the Doctor hesitated before he could tell it.

' That my wife is not my wife ? '

' Just so.'

' Of course I am prepared for it. I knew that it would be so ; did not you ? '

' I expected it.'

' I was sure of it. It may be taken for granted at once that there is no longer a secret to keep. I would wish you to act just as though all the facts were known to the entire diocese.' After this there

was a pause, during which neither of them spoke
for a few moments. The Doctor had not intended
to declare any purpose of his own on that occasion,
but it seemed to him now as though he were almost
driven to do so. Then Mr. Peacocke seeing the
difficulty at once relieved him from it. ' I am quite
prepared to leave Bowick,' he said, ' at once. I
know that it must be so. I have thought about it,
and have perceived that there is no possible alternative. I should like to consult with you as to
whither I had better go. Where shall I first take
her ? '

' Leave her here,' said the Doctor.

' Here ! Where ? '

' Where she is in the school-house. No one will
come to fill your place for a while.'

' I should have thought,' said Mr. Peacocke very
slowly, ' that her presence—would have been worse
almost,—than my own.'

' To me,'—said the Doctor,—' to me she is as
pure as the most unsullied matron in the country.'
Upon this Mr. Peacocke, jumping from his chair,
seized the Doctor's hand, but could not speak for
his tears ; then he seated himself again, turning
his face away towards the wall. ' To no one could
the presence of either of you be an evil. The evil
is, if I may say so, that the two of you should be
here together. You should be apart,—till some
better day has come upon you.'

' What better day can ever come ? ' said the poor
man through his tears.

Then the Doctor declared his scheme. He told
what he thought as to Ferdinand Lefroy, and his
reason for believing that the man was dead. ' I

felt sure from his manner that his brother is now dead in truth. Go to him and ask him boldly,' he said.

'But his word would not suffice for another marriage ceremony.'

To this the Doctor agreed. It was not his intention, he said, that they should proceed on evidence as slight as that. No ; a step must be taken much more serious in its importance, and occupying a considerable time. He, Peacocke, must go again to Missouri and find out all the truth. The Doctor was of opinion that if this were resolved upon, and that if the whole truth were at once proclaimed, then Mr. Peacocke need not hesitate to pay Robert Lefroy for any information which might assist him in his search. ' While you are gone,' continued the Doctor almost wildly, ' let bishops and Stantiloups and Puddicombes say what they may, she shall remain here. To say that she will be happy is of course vain. There can be no happiness for her till this has been put right. But she will be safe ; and here, at my hand, she will, I think, be free from insult. What better is there to be done ? '

' There can be nothing better,' said Peacocke drawing his breath,—as though a gleam of light had shone in upon him.

' I had not meant to have spoken to you of this till to-morrow. I should not have done so, but that Pritchett had been with me. But the more I thought of it, the more sure I became that you could not both remain,—till something had been done ; till something had been done.'

' I was sure of it, Dr. Wortle.'

' Mr. Puddicombe saw that it was so. Mr. Puddi-

combe is not all the world to me by any means, but
he is a man of common sense. I will be frank with
you. My wife said that it could not be so.'

'She shall not stay. Mrs. Wortle shall not be
annoyed.'

'You don't see it yet,' said the Doctor. 'But
you do. I know you do. And she shall stay. The
house shall be hers, as her residence, for the next
six months. As for money——'

'I have got what will do for that, I think.'

'If she wants money she shall have what she
wants. There is nothing I will not do for you in
your trouble,—except that you may not both be
here together till I shall have shaken hands with
her as Mrs. Peacocke in very truth.'

It was settled that Mr. Peacocke should not go
again into the school, or Mrs. Peacocke among the
boys, till he should have gone to America and have
come back. It was explained in the school by the
Doctor early,—for the Doctor must now take the
morning school himself,—that circumstances of
very grave import made it necessary that Mr.
Peacocke should start at once for America. That
the tidings which had been published at the Lamb
would reach the boys, was more than probable.
Nay; was it not certain? It would of course
reach all the boys' parents. There was no use, no
service, in any secrecy. But in speaking to the
school not a word was said of Mrs. Peacocke. The
Doctor explained that he himself would take the
morning school, and that Mr. Rose, the mathe-
matical master, would take charge of the school
meals. Mrs. Cane, the housekeeper, would look to
the linen and the bed-rooms. It was made plain

that Mrs. Peacocke's services were not to be required ; but her name was not mentioned,—except that the Doctor, in order to let it be understood that she was not to be banished from the house, begged the boys as a favour that they would not interrupt Mrs. Peacocke's tranquillity during Mr. Peacocke's absence.

On the Tuesday morning Mr. Peacocke started, remaining, however, a couple of days at Broughton, during which the Doctor saw him. Lefroy declared that he knew nothing about his brother,—whether he were alive or dead. He might be dead, because he was always in trouble, and generally drunk. Robert, on the whole, thought it probable that he was dead, but could not be got to say so. For a thousand dollars he would go over to Missouri, and, if necessary, to Texas, so as to find the truth. He would then come back and give undeniable evidence. While making this benevolent offer, he declared, with tears in his eyes, that he had come over intending to be a true brother to his sister-in-law, and had simply been deterred from prosecuting his good intentions by Peacocke's austerity. Then he swore a most solemn oath that if he knew anything about his brother Ferdinand he would reveal it. The Doctor and Peacocke agreed together that the man's word was worth nothing ; but that the man's services might be useful in enabling them to track out the truth. They were both convinced, by words which fell from him, that Ferdinand Lefroy was dead ; but this would be of no avail unless they could obtain absolute evidence.

During these two days there were various conversations at Broughton between the Doctor, Mr. Peacocke, and Lefroy, in which a plan of action was at length arranged. Lefroy and the schoolmaster were to proceed to America together, and there obtain what evidence they could as to the life or death of the elder brother. When absolute evidence had been obtained of either, a thousand dollars was to be handed to Robert Lefroy. But when this agreement was made the man was given to understand that his own uncorroborated word would go for nothing.

'Who is to say what is evidence, and what not?' asked the man, not unnaturally.

'Mr. Peacocke must be the judge,' said the Doctor.

'I ain't going to agree to that,' said the other. 'Though he were to see him dead, he might swear he hadn't, and not give me a red cent. Why ain't I to be judge as well as he?'

'Because you can trust him, and he cannot in the least trust you,' said the Doctor. 'You know well enough that if he were to see your brother alive, or to see him dead, you would get the money. At any rate, you have no other way of getting it but what we propose.' To all this Robert Lefroy at last assented.

The prospect before Mr. Peacocke for the next three months was certainly very sad. He was to travel from Broughton to St. Louis, and possibly from thence down into the wilds of Texas, in company with this man, whom he thoroughly despised. Nothing could be more abominable to him than such an association; but there was no other way in which the proposed plan could be carried out.

He was to pay Lefroy's expenses back to his own country, and could only hope to keep the man true to his purpose by doing so from day to day. Were he to give the man money, the man would at once disappear. Here in England, and in their passage across the ocean, the man might, in some degree, be amenable and obedient. But there was no knowing to what he might have recourse when he should find himself nearer to his country, and should feel that his companion was distant from his own.

'You'll have to keep a close watch upon him,' whispered the Doctor to his friend. 'I should not advise all this if I did not think you were a man of strong nerve.'

'I am not afraid,' said the other ; 'but I doubt whether he may not be too many for me. At any rate, I will try it. You will hear from me as I go on.'

And so they parted as dear friends part. The Doctor had, in truth, taken the man altogether to his heart since all the circumstances of the story had come home to him. And it need hardly be said that the other was aware how deep a debt of gratitude he owed to the protector of his wife. Indeed the very money that was to be paid to Robert Lefroy, if he earned it, was advanced out of the Doctor's pocket. Mr. Peacocke's means were sufficient for the expenses of the journey, but fell short when these thousand dollars had to be provided.

CHAPTER XI

THE BISHOP

MR. PEACOCKE had been quite right in saying that the secret would at once be known through the whole diocese. It certainly was so before he had been gone a week, and it certainly was the case also that the diocese generally did not approve of the Doctor's conduct. The woman ought not to have been left there. So said the diocese. It was of course the case, that though the diocese knew much, it did not know all. It is impossible to keep such a story concealed, but it is quite as impossible to make known all its details. In the eyes of the diocese the woman was of course the chief sinner, and the chief sinner was allowed to remain at the school ! When this assertion was made to him the Doctor became very angry, saying that Mrs. Peacocke did not remain at the school ; that, according to the arrangement as at present made, Mrs. Peacocke had nothing to do with the school ; that the house was his own, and that he might lend it to whom he pleased. Was he to turn the woman out houseless, when her husband had gone, on such an errand, on his advice ? Of course the house was his own, but as clergyman of the parish he had not a right to do what he liked with it. He had no right to encourage evil. And the man was not the woman's husband. That was just the point made by the diocese. And she was at the school,—living under the same roof with the boys ! The diocese was clearly of opinion that all the boys would be taken away.

The diocese spoke by the voice of its bishop, as a diocese should do. Shortly after Mr. Peacocke's departure, the Doctor had an interview with his lordship, and told the whole story. The doing this went much against the grain with him, but he hardly dared not to do it. He felt that he was bound to do it on the part of Mrs. Peacocke if not on his own. And then the man, who had now gone, though he had never been absolutely a curate, had preached frequently in the diocese. He felt that it would not be wise to abstain from telling the bishop.

The bishop was a goodly man, comely in his person, and possessed of manners which had made him popular in the world. He was one of those who had done the best he could with his talent, not wrapping it up in a napkin, but getting from it the best interest which the world's market could afford. But not on that account was he other than a good man. To do the best he could for himself and his family,—and also to do his duty,—was the line of conduct which he pursued. There are some who reverse this order, but he was not one of them. He had become a scholar in his youth, not from love of scholarship, but as a means to success. The Church had become his profession, and he had worked hard at his calling. He had taught himself to be courteous and urbane, because he had been clever enough to see that courtesy and urbanity are agreeable to men in high places. As a bishop he never spared himself the work which a bishop ought to do. He answered letters, he studied the characters of the clergymen under him, he was just with his patronage, he endeavoured to be efficacious with his charges, he confirmed children in cold weather as well as in warm, he occasionally preached sermons, and he was beautiful and decorous in his gait of manner, as it behoves a clergyman of the Church of England to be. He liked to be master; but even to be master he would not encounter the abominable nuisance of a quarrel. When first coming to the diocese he had had some little difficulty with our Doctor, but the Bishop had abstained from violent assertion, and they had, on the whole, been friends. There was, however, on the Bishop's part, something of a feeling that the Doctor was the bigger man; and it was probable that, without active malignity, he would take advantage of any chance which might lower the Doctor a little, and bring him more within episcopal power. In some degree he begrudged the Doctor his manliness.

He listened with many smiles and with perfect courtesy to the story as it was told to him, and was much less severe on the unfortunates than Mr. Puddicombe had been. It was not the wickedness of the two people in living together, or their wickedness in keeping their secret, which offended him so much, as the evil which they were likely to do,—and to have done. 'No doubt,' he said, 'an ill-living man may preach a good sermon, perhaps a better one than a pious God-fearing clergyman, whose intellect may be inferior though his morals are much better;—but coming from tainted lips, the better sermon will not carry a blessing with it.' At this the Doctor shook his head. 'Bringing a blessing' was a phrase which the Doctor hated. He shook his head not too civilly, saying that he had not intended to trouble his lordship on so difficult a point in ecclesiastical morals. 'But we cannot but remember,' said the Bishop, 'that he has been preaching in your parish church, and the people will know that he has acted among them as a clergyman.'

'I hope the people, my lord, may never have the Gospel preached to them by a worse man.'

'I will not judge him; but I do think that it has been a misfortune. You, of course, were in ignorance.'

'Had I known all about it, I should have been very much inclined to do the same.'

This was, in fact, not true, and was said simply in a spirit of contradiction. The Bishop shook his head and smiled. 'My school is a matter of more importance,' said the Doctor.

'Hardly, hardly, Dr. Wortle.'

'Of more importance in this way, that my school may probably be injured, whereas neither the morals nor the faith of the parishioners will have been hurt.'

'But he has gone.'

'He has gone;—but she remains.'

'What!' exclaimed the Bishop.

'He has gone, but she remains.' He repeated the words very distinctly, with a frown on his brow, as though to show that on that branch of the subject he intended to put up with no opposition,—hardly even with an adverse opinion.

'She had a certain charge, as I understand,—as to the school.'

'She had, my lord; and very well she did her work. I shall have a great loss in her,—for the present.'

' But you said she remained.'

' I have lent her the use of the house till her husband shall come back.'

' Mr. Peacocke, you mean,' said the Bishop, who was unable not to put in a contradiction against the untruth of the word which had been used.

' I shall always regard them as married.'

' But they are not.'

' I have lent her the house, at any rate, during his absence. I could not turn her into the street.'

' Would not a lodging here in the city have suited her better ? '

' I thought not. People here would have refused to take her,—because of her story. The wife of some religious grocer, who sands his sugar regularly, would have thought her house contaminated by such an inmate.'

' So it would have been, Doctor, to some extent.' At hearing this the Doctor made very evident signs of discontent. ' You cannot alter the ways of the world suddenly, though by example and precept you may help to improve them slowly. In our present imperfect condition of moral culture, it is perhaps well that the company of the guilty should be shunned.'

' Guilty ! '

' I am afraid that I must say so. The knowledge that such a feeling exists no doubt deters others from guilt. The fact that wrong-doing in women is scorned helps to maintain the innocence of women. Is it not so ? '

' I must hesitate before I trouble your lordship by arguing such difficult questions. I thought it right to tell you the facts after what had occurred.

He has gone, she is there,—and there she will remain for the present. I could not turn her out. Thinking her, as I do, worthy of my friendship, I could not do other than befriend her.'

' Of course you must be the judge yourself.'

' I had to be the judge, my lord.'

' I am afraid that the parents of the boys will not understand it.'

' I also am afraid. It will be very hard to make them understand it. There will be some who will work hard to make them misunderstand it.'

' I hope not that.'

' There will. I must stand the brunt of it. I have had battles before this, and had hoped that now, when I am getting old, they might have been at an end. But there is something left of me, and I can fight still. At any rate, I have made up my mind about this. There she shall remain till he comes back to fetch her.' And so the interview was over, the Bishop feeling that he had in some slight degree had the best of it,—and the Doctor feeling that he, in some slight degree, had had the worst. If possible, he would not talk to the Bishop on the subject again.

He told Mr. Puddicombe also. ' With your generosity and kindness of heart I quite sympathise,' said Mr. Puddicombe, endeavouring to be pleasant in his manner.

' But not with my prudence.'

' Not with your prudence,' said Mr. Puddicombe, endeavouring to be true at the same time.

But the Doctor's greatest difficulty was with his wife, whose conduct it was necessary that he should guide, and whose feelings and conscience he was

most anxious to influence. When she first heard
his decision she almost wrung her hands in despair.
If the woman could have gone to America, and the
man have remained, she would have been satisfied.
Anything wrong about a man was but of little
moment,—comparatively so, even though he were
a clergyman ; but anything wrong about a woman,
—and she so near to herself ! O dear ! And the
poor dear boys,—under the same roof with her !
And the boys' mammas ! How would she be able
to endure the sight of that horrid Mrs. Stantiloup ;
—or Mrs. Stantiloup's words, which would certainly be conveyed to her ? But there was something much worse for her even than all this. The
Doctor insisted that she should go and call upon
the woman ! 'And take Mary ? ' asked Mrs.
Wortle.

'What would be the good of taking Mary ? Who
is talking of a child like that ? It is for the sake of
charity,—for the dear love of Christ, that I ask you
to do it. Do you ever think of Mary Magdalene ? '

'Oh yes.'

'This is no Magdalene. This is a woman led into
no faults by vicious propensities. Here is one who
has been altogether unfortunate,—who has been
treated more cruelly than any of whom you have
ever read.'

'Why did she not leave him ? '

'Because she was a woman, with a heart in her
bosom.'

'I am to go to her ? '

'I do not order it. I only ask it.' Such asking
from her husband was, she knew, very near alike
to ordering.

'What shall I say to her?'

'Bid her keep up her courage till he shall return. If you were all alone, as she is, would not you wish that some other woman should come to comfort you? Think of her desolation.'

Mrs. Wortle did think of it, and after a day or two made up her mind to obey her husband's— request. She made her call, but very little came of it, except that she promised to come again. 'Mrs. Wortle,' said the poor woman, 'pray do not let me be a trouble to you. If you stay away I shall quite understand that there is sufficient reason. I know how good your husband has been to us.' Mrs. Wortle said, however, as she took her leave, that she would come again in a day or two.

But there were other troubles in store for Mrs. Wortle. Before she had repeated her visit to Mrs. Peacocke, a lady, who lived about ten miles off, the wife of the Rector of Buttercup, called upon her. This was the Lady Margaret Momson, a daughter of the Earl of Brigstock, who had, thirty years ago, married a young clergyman. Nevertheless, up to the present day, she was quite as much the Earl's daughter as the parson's wife. She was first cousin to that Mrs. Stantiloup between whom and the Doctor internecine war was always being waged ; and she was also aunt to a boy at the school, who, however, was in no way related to Mrs. Stantiloup, young Momson being the son of the parson's eldest brother. Lady Margaret had never absolutely and openly taken the part of Mrs. Stantiloup. Had she done so, a visit even of ceremony would have been impossible. But she was supposed to have Stantiloup proclivities, and was not, therefore, much liked at Bowick. There had been a question indeed whether young Momson should be received at the school,—because of the *quasi**connection with the arch-enemy ; but Squire Momson of Buttercup, the boy's father, had set that at rest by bursting out, in the Doctor's hearing, into violent abuse against ' the close-fisted, vulgar old faggot.'* The son of a man imbued with such proper feelings was, of course, accepted.

But Lady Margaret was proud,—especially at the present time. ' What a romance this is, Mrs. Wortle,' she said, ' that has gone all through the diocese ! ' The reader will remember that Lady Margaret was also the wife of a clergyman.

' You mean—the Peacockes ? '

' Of course I do.'

' He has gone away.'

' We all know that, of course ;—to look for his wife's husband. Good gracious me ! What a story ! '

' They think that he is—dead now.'

' I suppose they thought so before,' said Lady Margaret.

' Of course they did.'

' Though it does seem that no inquiry was made at all. Perhaps they don't care about those things over there as we do here. He couldn't have cared very much,—nor she.'

' The Doctor thinks that they are very much to be pitied.'

' The Doctor always was a little Quixotic*—eh ? '

' I don't think that at all, Lady Margaret.'

' I mean in the way of being so very good-natured and kind. Her brother came ;—didn't he ? '

'Her first husband's brother,' said Mrs. Wortle, blushing.

'Her first husband!'

'Well;—you know what I mean, Lady Margaret.'

'Yes; I know what you mean. It is so very shocking; isn't it? And so the two men have gone off together to look for the third. Goodness me;—what a party they will be if they meet! Do you think they'll quarrel?'

'I don't know, Lady Margaret.'

'And that he should be a clergyman of the Church of England! Isn't it dreadful? What does the Bishop say? Has he heard all about it?'

'The Bishop has nothing to do with it. Mr. Peacocke never held a curacy in the diocese.'

'But he has preached here very often,—and has taken her to church with him! I suppose the Bishop has been told?'

'You may be sure that he knows it as well as you.'

'We are so anxious, you know, about dear little Gus.' Dear little Gus was Augustus Momson, the lady's nephew, who was supposed to be the worst-behaved, and certainly the stupidest boy in the school.

'Augustus will not be hurt, I should say.'

'Perhaps not directly. But my sister has, I know, very strong opinions on such subjects. Now, I want to ask you one thing. Is it true that—she—remains here?'

'She is still living in the school-house.'

'Is that prudent, Mrs. Wortle?'

'If you want to have an opinion on that subject, Lady Margaret, I would recommend you to ask the

Doctor.' By which she meant to assert that Lady
Margaret would not, for the life of her, dare to ask
the Doctor such a question. ' He has done what he
has thought best.'

' Most good-natured, you mean, Mrs. Wortle.'

' I mean what I say, Lady Margaret. He has
done what he has thought best, looking at all the circumstances. He thinks that they are very worthy
people, and that they have been most cruelly ill-
used. He has taken that into consideration. You
call it good-nature. Others perhaps may call it—
charity.' The wife, though she at her heart de-
plored her husband's action in the matter, was not
going to own to another lady that he had been
imprudent.

' I am sure I hope they will,' said Lady Margaret.
Then as she was taking her leave, she made a
suggestion. ' Some of the boys will be taken away,
I suppose. The Doctor probably expects that.'

' I don't know what he expects,' said Mrs. Wortle.
' Some are always going, and when they go, others
come in their places. As for me, I wish he would
give the school up altogether.'

' Perhaps he means it,' said Lady Margaret;
' otherwise, perhaps he wouldn't have been so good-
natured.' Then she took her departure.

When her visitor was gone Mrs. Wortle was very
unhappy. She had been betrayed by her wrath
into expressing that wish as to the giving up of the
school. She knew well that the Doctor had no such
intention. She herself had more than once suggested it in her timid way, but the Doctor had
treated her suggestions as being worth nothing. He
had his ideas about Mary, who was undoubtedly

a very pretty girl. Mary might marry well, and £20,000 would probably assist her in doing so.

When he was told of Lady Margaret's hints, he said in his wrath that he would send young Momson away instantly if a word was said to him by the boy's mamma. ' Of course,' said he, ' if the lad turns out a scapegrace, as is like enough, it will be because Mrs. Peacocke had two husbands. It is often a question to me whether the religion of the world is not more odious than its want of religion.' To this terrible suggestion poor Mrs. Wortle did not dare to make any answer whatever.

CHAPTER XII

THE STANTILOUP CORRESPONDENCE

WE will now pass for a moment out of Bowick parish, and go over to Buttercup. There, at Buttercup Hall, the squire's house, in the drawing-room, were assembled Mrs. Momson, the squire's wife; Lady Margaret Momson, the Rector's wife ; Mrs. Rolland, the wife of the Bishop ; and the Hon. Mrs. Stantiloup. A party was staying in the house, collected for the purpose of entertaining the Bishop ; and it would perhaps not have been possible to have got together in the diocese, four ladies more likely to be hard upon our Doctor. For though Squire Momson was not very fond of Mrs. Stantiloup, and had used strong language respecting her when he was anxious to send his boy to the Doctor's school, Mrs. Momson had always been of the other party, and had in fact adhered to Mrs. Stantiloup from the beginning of the quarrel. ' I do trust,' said

Mrs. Stantiloup, ' that there will be an end to all this kind of thing now.'

' Do you mean an end to the school ? ' asked Lady Margaret.

' I do indeed. I always thought it matter of great regret that Augustus should have been sent there, after the scandalous treatment that Bob received.' Bob was the little boy who had drank the champagne and required the carriage exercise.

' But I always heard that the school was quite popular,' said Mrs. Rolland.

' I think you'll find,' continued Mrs. Stantiloup, ' that there won't be much left of its popularity now. Keeping that abominable woman under the same roof with the boys ! No master of a school that wasn't absolutely blown up with pride, would have taken such people as those Peacockes without making proper inquiry. And then to let him preach in the church ! I suppose Mr. Momson will allow you to send for Augustus at once ? ' This she said turning to Mrs. Momson.

' Mr. Momson thinks so much of the Doctor's scholarship,' said the mother, apologetically. 'And we are so anxious that Gus should do well when he goes to Eton.'

' What is Latin and Greek as compared to his soul ? ' asked Lady Margaret.

' No, indeed,' said Mrs. Rolland. She had found herself compelled, as wife of the Bishop, to assent to the self-evident proposition which had been made. She was a quiet, silent little woman, whom the Bishop had married in the days of his earliest preferment, and who, though she was delighted to find herself promoted to the society of the big

people in the diocese, had never quite lifted herself
up into their sphere.   Though she had her ideas as
to what it was to be a Bishop's wife, she had never
yet been quite able to act up to them.

' I know that young Talbot is to leave,' said Mrs.
Stantiloup.   ' I wrote to Mrs. Talbot immediately
when all this occurred, and I've heard from her
cousin Lady Grogram that the boy is not to go back
after the holidays.'   This happened to be altogether
untrue.   What she probably meant was, that the
boy should not go back if she could prevent his
doing so.

' I feel quite sure,' said Lady Margaret, ' that
Lady Anne will not allow her boys to remain when
she finds out what sort of inmates the Doctor
chooses to entertain.'   The Lady Anne spoken of
was Lady Anne Clifford, the widowed mother of
two boys who were intrusted to the Doctor's care.

' I do hope you'll be firm about Gus,' said Mrs.
Stantiloup to Mrs. Momson.   ' If we're not to put
down this kind of thing, what is the good of having
any morals in the country at all ?   We might
just as well live like pagans, and do without any
marriage services, as they do in so many parts of
the United States.'

' I wonder what the Bishop does think about it ?'
asked Mrs. Momson of the Bishop's wife.

' It makes him very unhappy ; I know that,'
said Mrs. Rolland.   ' Of course he cannot interfere
about the school.   As for licensing the gentleman
as a curate, that was of course quite out of the
question.'

At this moment Mr. Momson, the clergyman, and
the Bishop came into the room, and were offered,

as is usual on such occasions, cold tea and the remains of the buttered toast. The squire was not there. Had he been with the other gentlemen, Mrs. Stantiloup, violent as she was, would probably have held her tongue ; but as he was absent, the opportunity was not bad for attacking the Bishop on the subject under discussion. ' We were talking, my lord, about the Bowick school.'

Now the Bishop was a man who could be very confidential with one lady, but was apt to be guarded when men are concerned. To any one of those present he might have said what he thought, had no one else been there to hear. That would have been the expression of a private opinion ; but to speak before the four would have been tanta- mount to a public declaration.

' About the Bowick school ? ' said he ; ' I hope there is nothing going wrong with the Bowick school.'

' You must have heard about Mr. Peacocke,' said Lady Margaret.

' Yes ; I have certainly heard of Mr. Peacocke. He, I believe, has left Dr. Wortle's seminary.'

' But she remains ! ' said Mrs. Stantiloup, with tragic energy.

' So I understand ;—in the house ; but not as part of the establishment.'

' Does that make so much difference ? ' asked Lady Margaret.

' It does make a very great difference,' said Lady Margaret's husband, the parson, wishing to help the Bishop in his difficulty.

' I don't see it at all,' said Mrs. Stantiloup. ' The main spirit in the matter is just as manifest whether the lady is or is not allowed to look after the boys' linen. In fact, I despise him for making the pretence. Her doing menial work about the house would injure no one. It is her presence there,—the presence of a woman who has falsely pretended to be married, when she knew very well that she had no husband.'

' When she knew that she had two,' said Lady Margaret.

' And fancy, Lady Margaret,—Lady Bracy absolutely asked her to go to Carstairs ! That woman was always infatuated about Dr. Wortle. What would she have done if they had gone, and this other man had followed his sister-in-law there. But Lord and Lady Bracy would ask any one to Carstairs,—just any one that they could get hold of ! '

Mr. Momson was one whose obstinacy was wont to give way when sufficiently attacked. Even he, after having been for two days subjected to the eloquence of Mrs. Stantiloup, acknowledged that the Doctor took a great deal too much upon himself. ' He does it,' said Mrs. Stantiloup, ' just to show that there is nothing that he can't bring parents to assent to. Fancy,—a woman living there as house-keeper with a man as usher, pretending to be husband and wife, when they knew all along that they were not married ! '

Mr. Momson, who didn't care a straw about the morals of the man whose duty it was to teach his little boy his Latin grammar, or the morals of the woman who looked after his little boy's waistcoats and trousers, gave a half-assenting grunt. ' And you are to pay,' continued Mrs. Stantiloup, with considerable emphasis,—' you are to pay two hundred and fifty pounds a-year for such conduct as that ! '

' Two hundred,' suggested the squire, who cared as little for the money as he did for the morals.

' Two hundred and fifty,—every shilling of it, when you consider the extras.'

' There are no extras, as far as I can see. But then my boy is strong and healthy, thank God,' said the squire, taking his opportunity of having one fling at the lady. But while all this was going on, he did give a half-assent that Gus should be taken away at midsummer, being partly moved thereto by a letter from the Doctor, in which he was told that his boy was not doing any good at the school.

It was a week after that that Mrs. Stantiloup wrote the following letter to her friend Lady Grogram, after she had returned home from Buttercup Hall. Lady Grogram was a great friend of hers, and was first cousin to that Mrs. Talbot who had a son at the school. Lady Grogram was an old woman of strong mind but small means, who was supposed to be potential over those connected with her. Mrs. Stantiloup feared that she could not be efficacious herself, either with Mr. or Mrs. Talbot ; but she hoped that she might carry her purpose through Lady Grogram. It may be remembered that she had declared at Buttercup Hall that young Talbot was not to go back to Bowick. But this had been a figure of speech, as has been already explained :—

' MY DEAR LADY GROGRAM,—Since I got your last letter I have been staying with the Momsons at Buttercup. It was awfully dull. He and she are,

I think, the stupidest people that ever I met. None of those Momsons have an idea among them. They are just as heavy and inharmonious as their name. Lady Margaret was one of the party. She would have been better, only that our excellent Bishop was there too, and Lady Margaret thought it well to show off all her graces before the Bishop and the Bishop's wife. I never saw such a dowdy in all my life as Mrs. Rolland. He is all very well, and looks at any rate like a gentleman. It was, I take it, that which got him his diocese. They say the Queen saw him once, and was taken by his manners.

'But I did one good thing at Buttercup. I got Mr. Momson to promise that that boy of his should not go back to Bowick. Dr. Wortle has become quite intolerable. I think he is determined to show that whatever he does, people shall put up with it. It is not only the most expensive establishment of the kind in all England, but also the worst conducted. You know, of course, how all this matter about that woman stands now. She is remaining there at Bowick, absolutely living in the house, calling herself Mrs. Peacocke, while the man she was living with has gone off with her brother-in-law to look for her husband! Did you ever hear of such a mess as that?

'And the Doctor expects that fathers and mothers will still send their boys to such a place as that? I am very much mistaken if he will not find it altogether deserted before Christmas. Lord Carstairs is already gone.' [This was at any rate disingenuous, as she had been very severe when at Buttercup on all the Carstairs family because of their declared and perverse friendship for the

Doctor.] 'Mr. Momson, though he is quite incapable
of seeing the meaning of anything, has determined
to take his boy away. She may thank me at any
rate for that. I have heard that Lady Anne Clifford's two boys will both leave.' [In one sense she
had heard it, because the suggestion had been made
by herself at Buttercup.] 'I do hope that Mr.
Talbot's dear little boy will not be allowed to return
to such contamination as that ! Fancy,—the man
and the woman living there in that way together ;
and the Doctor keeping the woman on after he
knew it all ! It is really so horrible that one doesn't
know how to talk about it. When the Bishop was
at Buttercup I really felt almost obliged to be
silent.

'I know very well that Mrs. Talbot is always
ready to take your advice. As for him, men very
often do not think so much about these things as
they ought. But he will not like his boy to be
nearly the only one left at the school. I have not
heard of one who is to remain for certain. How
can it be possible that any boy who has a mother
should be allowed to remain there ?

'Do think of this, and do your best. I need not
tell you that nothing ought to be so dear to us as
a high tone of morals.—Most sincerely yours,

'JULIANA STANTILOUP.'

We need not pursue this letter further than to
say that when it reached Mr. Talbot's hands, which
it did through his wife, he spoke of Mrs. Stantiloup
in language which shocked his wife considerably,
though she was not altogether unaccustomed to
strong language on his part. Mr. Talbot and the

Doctor had been at school together, and at Oxford, and were friends.

I will give now a letter that was written by the Doctor to Mr. Momson in answer to one in which that gentleman signified his intention of taking little Gus away from the school.

'MY DEAR MR. MOMSON,—After what you have said, of course I shall not expect your boy back after the holidays. Tell his mamma, with my compliments, that he shall take all his things home with him. As a rule I do charge for a quarter in advance when a boy is taken away suddenly, without notice, and apparently without cause. But I shall not do so at the present moment either to you or to any parent who may withdraw his son. A circumstance has happened which, though it cannot impair the utility of my school, and ought not to injure its character, may still be held as giving offence to certain persons. I will not be driven to alter my conduct by what I believe to be foolish misconception on their part. But they have a right to their own opinions, and I will not mulct them because of their conscientious convictions.— Yours faithfully,

'JEFFREY WORTLE.'

'If you come across any friend who has a boy here, you are perfectly at liberty to show him or her this letter.'

The defection of the Momsons wounded the Doctor, no doubt. He was aware that Mrs. Stantiloup had been at Buttercup, and that the Bishop also had been there—and he could put two and two together ; but it hurt him to think that one so 'staunch' though so 'stupid' as Mrs. Momson, should be turned from her purpose by such a woman as Mrs. Stantiloup. And he got other letters on the subject. Here is one from Lady Anne Clifford.

'DEAR DOCTOR,—You know how safe I think my dear boys are with you, and how much obliged I am both to you and your wife for all your kindness. But people are saying things to me about one of the masters at your school and his wife. Is there any reason why I should be afraid ? You will see how thoroughly I trust you when I ask you the question.—Yours very sincerely,

'ANNE CLIFFORD.'

Now Lady Anne Clifford was a sweet, confiding, affectionate, but not very wise woman. In a letter, written not many days before to Mary Wortle, who had on one occasion been staying with her, she said that she was at that time in the same house with the Bishop and Mrs. Rolland. Of course the Doctor knew again how to put two and two together.

Then there came a letter from Mr. Talbot—

'DEAR WORTLE,—So you are boiling for yourself another pot of hot water. I never saw such a fellow as you are for troubles ! Old Mother Shipton*has been writing such a letter to our old woman, and explaining that no boy's soul would any longer be worth looking after if he be left in your hands. Don't you go and get me into a scrape more than you can help ; but you may be quite sure of this that if I had as many sons as Priam*I should send them all to you ;—only I think that the cheques would be very long in coming.—Yours always,

'JOHN TALBOT.'

The Doctor answered this at greater length than he had done in writing to Mr. Momson, who was not specially his friend.

'MY DEAR TALBOT,—You may be quite sure that I shall not repeat to any one what you have told me of Mother Shipton. I knew, however, pretty well what she was doing and what I had to expect from her. It is astonishing to me that such a woman should still have the power of persuading any one,—astonishing also that any human being should continue to hate as she hates me. She has often tried to do me an injury, but she has never succeeded yet. At any rate she will not bend me. Though my school should be broken up to-morrow, which I do not think probable, I should still have enough to live upon,—which is more, by all accounts, than her unfortunate husband can say for himself.

'The facts are these. More than twelve months ago I got an assistant named Peacocke, a clergyman, an Oxford man, and formerly a Fellow of Trinity ;—a man quite superior to anything I have a right to expect in my school. He had gone as a Classical Professor to a college in the United States ;—a rash thing to do, no doubt ;—and had there married a widow, which was rasher still. The lady came here with him and undertook the charge of the school-house,—with a separate salary; and an admirable person in the place she was. Then it turned out, as no doubt you have heard, that her former husband was alive when they were married. They ought probably to have separated, but they didn't. They came here instead, and here they were followed by the brother of the husband,— who I take it is now dead, though of that we know nothing certain.

'That he should have told me his position is more than any man has a right to expect from another. Fortune had been most unkind to him, and for her sake he was bound to do the best that he could with himself. I cannot bring myself to be angry with him, though I cannot defend him by strict laws of right and wrong. I have advised him to go back to America and find out if the man be in truth dead. If so, let him come back and marry the woman again before all the world. I shall be ready to marry them and to ask him and her to my house afterwards.

'In the mean time what was to become of her? "Let her go into lodgings," said the Bishop. Go to lodgings at Broughton! You know what sort of lodgings she would get there among psalm-singing greengrocers who would tell her of her misfortune every day of her life! I would not subject her to the misery of going and seeking for a home. I told him, when I persuaded him to go, that she should have the rooms they were then occupying while he was away. In settling this, of course I had to make arrangements for doing in our own establishment the work which had lately fallen to her share. I mention this for the sake of explaining that she has got nothing to do with the school. No doubt the boys are under the same roof with her. Will your boy's morals be the worse? It seems that Gustavus Momson's will. You know the father; do you not? I wonder whether anything will ever affect his morals?

'Now, I have told you everything. Not that I have doubted you; but, as you have been told so much, I have thought it well that you should have the whole story from myself. What effect it may have upon the school I do not know. The only boy of whose secession I have yet heard is young Momson. But probably there will be others. Four new boys were to have come, but I have already heard from the father of one that he has changed his mind. I think I can trace an acquaintance between him and Mother Shipton. If the body of the school should leave me I will let you know at once as you might not like to leave your boy under such circumstances.

'You may be sure of this, that here the lady remains until her husband returns. I am not going to be turned from my purpose at this time of day by anything that Mother Shipton may say or do.— Yours always,

'JEFFREY WORTLE.'

PART V

CHAPTER I

MR. PUDDICOMBE'S BOOT

It was not to be expected that the matter should be kept out of the county newspaper, or even from those in the metropolis. There was too much of romance in the story, too good a tale to be told, for any such hope. The man's former life and the woman's, the disappearance of her husband and his reappearance after his reported death, the departure of the couple from St. Louis and the coming of Lefroy to Bowick, formed together a most attractive subject. But it could not be told without reference to Dr. Wortle's school, to Dr. Wortle's position as clergyman of the parish,—and also to the fact which was considered by his enemies to be of all the facts the most damning, that Mr. Peacocke had for a time been allowed to preach in the parish church. The 'Broughton Gazette,' a newspaper which was supposed to be altogether devoted to the interest of the diocese, was very eloquent on this subject. 'We do not desire,' said the 'Broughton Gazette,' 'to make any remarks as to the management of Dr. Wortle's school. We leave all that between him and the parents of the boys who are educated there. We are perfectly aware that Dr. Wortle himself is a scholar, and that his school has been deservedly successful. It is advisable, no doubt, that in such an establishment none

should be employed whose lives are openly immoral ;—but as we have said before, it is not our
purpose to insist upon this. Parents, if they feel
themselves to be aggrieved, can remedy the evil by
withdrawing their sons. But when we consider the
great power which is placed in the hands of an
incumbent of a parish, that he is endowed as it
were with the freehold of his pulpit, that he may
put up whom he will to preach the Gospel to his
parishioners, even in a certain degree in opposition
to his bishop, we think that we do no more than
our duty in calling attention to such a case as this.'
Then the whole story was told at great length, so
as to give the ' we ' of the ' Broughton Gazette ' a
happy opportunity of making its leading article not
only much longer, but much more amusing, than
usual. ' We must say,' continued the writer, as he
concluded his narrative, ' that this man should not
have been allowed to preach in the Bowick pulpit.
He is no doubt a clergyman of the Church of England, and Dr. Wortle was within his rights in asking
for his assistance ; but the incumbent of a parish is
responsible for those he employs, and that responsibility now rests on Dr. Wortle.'

There was a great deal in this that made the
Doctor very angry,—so angry that he did not know
how to restrain himself. The matter had been
argued as though he had employed the clergyman
in his church after he had known the history. ' For
aught I know,' he said to Mrs. Wortle, ' any curate
coming to me might have three wives, all alive.'

' That would be most improbable,' said Mrs.
Wortle.

' So was all this improbable,—just as improbable.

Nothing could be more improbable. Do we not all
feel overcome with pity for the poor woman because
she encountered trouble that was so improbable ?
How much more improbable was it that I should
come across a clergyman who had encountered such
improbabilities.' In answer to this Mrs. Wortle
could only shake her head, not at all understanding
the purport of her husband's argument.

But what was said about his school hurt him
more than what was said about his church. In
regard to his church he was impregnable. Not
even the Bishop could touch him,—or even annoy
him much. But this ' penny-a-liner,'*as the Doctor
indignantly called him, had attacked him in his
tenderest point. After declaring that he did not
intend to meddle with the school, he had gone on
to point out that an immoral person had been
employed there, and had then invited all parents
to take away their sons. ' He doesn't know what
moral and immoral means,' said the Doctor, again
pleading his own case to his own wife. ' As far as
I know, it would be hard to find a man of a higher
moral feeling than Mr. Peacocke, or a woman than
his wife.'

' I suppose they ought to have separated when it
was found out,' said Mrs. Wortle.

' No, no,' he shouted ; ' I hold that they were
right. He was right to cling to her, and she was
bound to obey him. Such a fellow as that,'—and
he crushed the paper up in his hand in his wrath,
as though he were crushing the editor himself,—
' such a fellow as that knows nothing of morality,
nothing of honour, nothing of tenderness. What
he did I would have done, and I'll stick to him

through it all in spite of the Bishop, in spite of the newspapers, and in spite of all the rancour of all my enemies.' Then he got up and walked about the room in such a fury that his wife did not dare to speak to him. Should he or should he not answer the newspaper? That was a question which for the first two days after he had read the article greatly perplexed him. He would have been very ready to advise any other man what to do in such a case. ' Never notice what may be written about you in a newspaper,' he would have said. Such is the advice which a man always gives to his friend. But when the case comes to himself he finds it sometimes almost impossible to follow it. 'What's the use? Who cares what the "Broughton Gazette" says? let it pass, and it will be forgotten in three days. If you stir the mud yourself, it will hang about you for months. It is just what they want you to do. They cannot go on by themselves, and so the subject dies away from them; but if you write rejoinders they have a contributor working for them for nothing, and one whose writing will be much more acceptable to their readers than any that comes from their own anonymous scribes. It is very disagreeable to be worried like a rat by a dog; but why should you go into the kennel and unnecessarily put yourself in the way of it?' The Doctor had said this more than once to clerical friends who were burning with indignation at some-thing that had been written about them. But now he was burning himself, and could hardly keep his fingers from pen and ink.

In this emergency he went to Mr. Puddicombe, not, as he said to himself, for advice, but in order that he might hear what Mr. Puddicombe would have to say about it. He did not like Mr. Puddicombe, but he believed in him,—which was more than he quite did with the Bishop. Mr. Puddicombe would tell him his true thoughts. Mr. Puddicombe would be unpleasant very likely; but he would be sincere and friendly. So he went to Mr. Puddicombe. 'It seems to me,' he said, 'almost necessary that I should answer such allegations as these for the sake of truth.'

'You are not responsible for the truth of the "Broughton Gazette,"' said Mr. Puddicombe.

'But I am responsible to a certain degree that false reports shall not be spread abroad as to what is done in my church.'

'You can contradict nothing that the newspaper has said.'

'It is implied,' said the Doctor, 'that I allowed Mr. Peacocke to preach in my church after I knew his marriage was informal.'

'There is no such statement in the paragraph,' said Mr. Puddicombe, after attentive reperusal of the article. 'The writer has written in a hurry, as such writers generally do, but has made no statement such as you presume. Were you to answer him, you could only do so by an elaborate statement of the exact facts of the case. It can hardly be worth your while, in defending yourself against the "Broughton Gazette," to tell the whole story in public of Mr. Peacocke's life and fortunes.'

'You would pass it over altogether?'

'Certainly I would.'

'And so acknowledge the truth of all that the newspaper says.'

'I do not know that the paper says anything untrue,' said Mr. Puddicombe, not looking the Doctor in the face, with his eyes turned to the ground, but evidently with the determination to say what he thought, however unpleasant it might be. 'The fact is that you have fallen into a— misfortune.'

'I don't acknowledge it at all,' said the Doctor.

'All your friends at any rate will think so, let the story be told as it may. It was a misfortune that this lady whom you had taken into your establishment should have proved not to be the gentleman's wife. When I am taking a walk through the fields and get one of my feet deeper than usual into the mud, I always endeavour to bear it as well as I may before the eyes of those who meet me rather than make futile efforts to get rid of the dirt and look as though nothing had happened. The dirt, when it is rubbed and smudged and scraped, is more palpably dirt than the honest mud.'

'I will not admit that I am dirty at all,' said the Doctor.

'Nor do I, in the case which I describe. I admit nothing; but I let those who see me form their own opinion. If any one asks me about my boot I tell him that it is a matter of no consequence. I advise you to do the same. You will only make the smudges more palpable if you write to the "Broughton Gazette."'

'Would you say nothing to the boys' parents?' asked the Doctor.

'There, perhaps, I am not a judge, as I never

kept a school;—but I think not. If any father writes to you, then tell him the truth.'

If the matter had gone no farther than this, the Doctor might probably have left Mr. Puddicombe's house with a sense of thankfulness for the kindness rendered to him; but he did go farther, and endeavoured to extract from his friend some sense of the injustice shown by the Bishop, the Stantiloups, the newspaper, and his enemies in general through the diocese. But here he failed signally. ' I really think, Dr. Wortle, that you could not have expected it otherwise.'

' Expect that people should lie ? '

' I don't know about lies. If people have told lies I have not seen them or heard them. I don't think the Bishop has lied.'

' I don't mean the Bishop; though I do think that he has shown a great want of what I may call liberality towards a clergyman in his diocese.'

' No doubt he thinks you have been wrong. By liberality you mean sympathy. Why should you expect him to sympathise with your wrong-doing ? '

'What have I done wrong ? '

' You have countenanced immorality and deceit in a brother clergyman.'

'I deny it,' said the Doctor, rising up impetuously from his chair.

' Then I do not understand the position, Dr. Wortle. That is all I can say.'

' To my thinking, Mr. Puddicombe, I never came across a better man than Mr. Peacocke in my life.'

' I cannot make comparisons. As to the best man I ever met in my life I might have to acknowledge that even he had done wrong in certain cir-

cumstances. As the matter is forced upon me, I
have to express my opinion that a great sin was
committed both by the man and by the woman.
You not only condone the sin, but declare both by
your words and deeds that you sympathise with
the sin as well as with the sinners. You have no
right to expect that the Bishop will sympathise
with you in that ;—nor can it be but that in such
a country as this the voices of many will be loud
against you.'

'And yours as loud as any,' said the Doctor,
angrily.

'That is unkind and unjust,' said Mr. Puddicombe. 'What I have said, I have said to yourself, and not to others ; and what I have said, I
have said in answer to questions asked by yourself.' Then the Doctor apologised with what grace
he could. But when he left the house his heart was
still bitter against Mr. Puddicombe.

He was almost ashamed of himself as he rode
back to Bowick,—first, because he had condescended to ask advice, and then because, after
having asked it, he had been so thoroughly scolded.
There was no one whom Mr. Puddicombe would
admit to have been wrong in the matter except the
Doctor himself. And yet though he had been so
counselled and so scolded, he had found himself
obliged to apologise before he left the house ! And,
too, he had been made to understand that he had
better not rush into print. Though the 'Broughton
Gazette' should come to the attack again and again,
he must hold his peace. That reference to Mr.
Puddicombe's dirty boot had convinced him. He
could see the thoroughly squalid look of the boot

that had been scraped in vain, and appreciate the wholesomeness of the unadulterated mud. There was more in the man than he had ever acknowledged before. There was a consistency in him, and a courage, and an honesty of purpose. But there was no softness of heart. Had there been a grain of tenderness there, he could not have spoken so often as he had done of Mrs. Peacocke without expressing some grief at the unmerited sorrows to which that poor lady had been subjected.

His own heart melted with ruth as he thought, while riding home, of the cruelty to which she had been and was subjected. She was all alone there, waiting, waiting, waiting, till the dreary days should have gone by. And if no good news should come, if Mr. Peacocke should return with tidings that her husband was alive and well, what should she do then? What would the world then have in store for her? 'If it were me,' said the Doctor to himself, 'I'd take her to some other home and treat her as my wife in spite of all the Puddicombes in creation;—in spite of all the bishops.'

The Doctor, though he was a self-asserting and somewhat violent man, was thoroughly soft-hearted. It is to be hoped that the reader has already learned as much as that;—a man with a kind, tender, affectionate nature. It would perhaps be unfair to raise a question whether he would have done as much, been so willing to sacrifice himself, for a plain woman. Had Mr. Stantiloup, or Sir Samuel Griffin* if he had suddenly come again to life, been found to have prior wives also living, would the Doctor have found shelter for them in their ignominy and trouble? Mrs. Wortle, who

knew her husband thoroughly, was sure that he
would not have done so. Mrs. Peacocke was a very
beautiful woman, and the Doctor was a man who
thoroughly admired beauty. To say that Mrs.
Wortle was jealous would be quite untrue. She
liked to see her husband talking to a pretty woman,
because he would be sure to be in a good humour
and sure to make the best of himself. She loved
to see him shine. But she almost wished that Mrs.
Peacocke had been ugly, because there would not
then have been so much danger about the school.

'I'm just going up to see her,' said the Doctor,
as soon as he got home,—'just to ask her what she
wants.'

'I don't think she wants anything,' said Mrs.
Wortle, weakly.

'Does she not? She must be a very odd woman
if she can live there all day alone, and not want to
see a human creature.'

'I was with her yesterday.'

'And therefore I will call to-day,' said the Doctor, leaving the room with his hat on.

When he was shown up into the sitting-room
he found Mrs. Peacocke with a newspaper in her
hand. He could see at a glance that it was a copy
of the 'Broughton Gazette,' and could see also the
length and outward show of the very article which
he had been discussing with Mr. Puddicombe.
'Dr. Wortle,' she said, 'if you don't mind, I will
go away from this.'

'But I do mind. Why should you go away?'

'They have been writing about me in the newspapers.'

'That was to be expected.'

'But they have been writing about you.'

'That was to have been expected also. You don't suppose they can hurt me?' This was a false boast, but in such conversations he was almost bound to boast.

'It is I, then, am hurting you?'

'You;—oh dear, no; not in the least.'

'But I do. They talk of boys going away from the school.'

'Boys will go and boys will come, but we run on for ever,' said the Doctor, playfully.

'I can well understand that it should be so,' said Mrs. Peacocke, passing over the Doctor's parody as though unnoticed; 'and I perceive that I ought not to be here.'

'Where ought you to be, then?' said he, intending simply to carry on his joke.

'Where indeed! There is no where. But wherever I may do least injury to innocent people,—to people who have not been driven by storms out of the common path of life. For this place I am peculiarly unfit.'

'Will you find any place where you will be made more welcome?'

'I think not.'

'Then let me manage the rest. You have been reading that dastardly article in the paper. It will have no effect upon me. Look here, Mrs. Peacocke;'—then he got up and held her hand as though he were going, but he remained some moments while he was still speaking to her,—still holding her hand;—'it was settled between your husband and me, when he went away, that you should remain here under my charge till his return.

I am bound to him to find a home for you. I think
you are as much bound to obey him,—which you
can only do by remaining here.'

' I would wish to obey him, certainly.'

' You ought to do so,—from the peculiar circumstances more especially. Don't trouble your mind
about the school, but do as he desired. There is
no question but that you must do so. Good-bye.
Mrs. Wortle or I will come and see you to-morrow.'
Then, and not till then, he dropped her hand.

On the next day Mrs. Wortle did call, though
these visits were to her an intolerable nuisance.
But it was certainly better that she should alternate
the visits with the Doctor than that he should go
every day. The Doctor had declared that charity
required that one of them should see the poor
woman daily. He was quite willing that they
should perform the task day and day about,—but
should his wife omit the duty he must go in his
wife's place. What would all the world of Bowick
say if the Doctor were to visit a lady, a young and
a beautiful lady, every day, whereas his wife
visited the lady not at all ? Therefore they took
it turn about, except that sometimes the Doctor
accompanied his wife. The Doctor had once suggested that his wife should take the poor lady out
in her carriage. But against this even Mrs. Wortle
had rebelled. ' Under such circumstances as hers
she ought not to be seen driving about,' said Mrs.
Wortle. The Doctor had submitted to this, but still
thought that the world of Bowick was very cruel.

Mrs. Wortle, though she made no complaint,
thought that she was used cruelly in the matter.
There had been an intention of going into Brittany

during these summer holidays. The little tour had
been almost promised. But the affairs of Mrs. Peacocke were of such a nature as not to allow the
Doctor to be absent. ' You and Mary can go, and
Henry will go with you.' Henry was a bachelor
brother of Mrs. Wortle, who was always very much
at the Doctor's disposal, and at hers. But certainly
she was not going to quit England, not going to quit
home at all, while her husband remained there, and
while Mrs. Peacocke was an inmate of the school.
It was not that she was jealous. The idea was
absurd. But she knew very well what Mrs. Stantiloup would say.

CHAPTER II

' EVERYBODY'S BUSINESS '

But there arose a trouble greater than that
occasioned by the ' Broughton Gazette.' There
came out an article in a London weekly newspaper,
called ' Everybody's Business,' which nearly drove
the Doctor mad. This was on the last Saturday of
the holidays. The holidays had been commenced
in the middle of July, and went on till the end of
August. Things had not gone well at Bowick
during these weeks. The parents of all the four
newly-expected boys had—changed their minds.
One father had discovered that he could not afford
it. Another declared that the mother could not
be got to part with her darling quite so soon as he
had expected. A third had found that a private
tutor at home would best suit his purposes. While
the fourth boldly said that he did not like to send
his boy because of the ' fuss ' which had been made

about Mr. and Mrs. Peacocke. Had this last come
alone, the Doctor would probably have resented
such a communication ; but following the others
as it did, he preferred the fourth man to any of the
other three. 'Miserable cowards,' he said to himself, as he docketed the letters and put them away.
But the greatest blow of all,—of all blows of this
sort,—came to him from poor Lady Anne Clifford.
She wrote a piteous letter to him, in which she implored him to allow her to take her two boys away.

'My dear Doctor Wortle,' she said, 'so many
people have been telling so many dreadful things
about this horrible affair, that I do not dare to
send my darling boys back to Bowick again. Uncle
Clifford and Lord Robert both say that I should
be very wrong. The Marchioness has said so much
about it that I dare not go against her. You know
what my own feelings are about you and dear Mrs.
Wortle ; but I am not my own mistress. They all
tell me that it is my first duty to think about the
dear boys' welfare ; and of course that is true. I
hope you won't be very angry with me, and will
write one line to say that you forgive me.—Yours
most sincerely,

'ANNE CLIFFORD.'

In answer to this the Doctor did write as follows ;—

'MY DEAR LADY ANNE,—Of course your duty
is very plain,—to do what you think best for the
boys ; and it is natural enough that you should
follow the advice of your relatives and theirs.—
Faithfully yours,

'JEFFREY WORTLE.'

He could not bring himself to write in a more friendly tone, or to tell her that he forgave her. His sympathies were not with her. His sympathies at the present moment were only with Mrs. Peacocke. But then Lady Anne Clifford was not a beautiful woman, as was Mrs. Peacocke.

This was a great blow. Two other boys had also been summoned away, making five in all, whose premature departure was owing altogether to the virulent tongue of that wretched old Mother Shipton. And there had been four who were to come in the place of four others, who, in the course of nature, were going to carry on their more advanced studies elsewhere. Vacancies such as these had always been pre-occupied long beforehand by ambitious parents. These very four places had been pre-occupied, but now they were all vacant. There would be nine empty beds in the school when it met again after the holidays ; and the Doctor well understood that nine beds remaining empty would soon cause others to be emptied. It is success that creates success, and decay that produces decay. Gradual decay he knew that he could not endure. He must shut up his school,—give up his employment,—and retire altogether from the activity of life. He felt that if it came to this with him he must in very truth turn his face to the wall and die. Would it,—would it really come to that, that Mrs. Stantiloup should have altogether conquered him in the combat that had sprung up between them ?

But yet he would not give up Mrs. Peacocke. Indeed, circumstanced as he was, he could not give her up. He had promised not only her, but her

absent husband, that until his return there should
be a home for her in the school-house.   There
would be a cowardice in going back from his word
which was altogether foreign to his nature.   He
could not bring himself to retire from the fight,
even though by doing so he might save himself
from the actual final slaughter which seemed to
be imminent.   He thought only of making fresh
attacks upon his enemy, instead of meditating
flight from those which were made upon him.   As
a dog, when another dog has got him well by the
ear, thinks not at all of his own wound, but only
how he may catch his enemy by the lip, so was the
Doctor in regard to Mrs. Stantiloup.   When the
two Clifford boys were taken away, he took some
joy to himself in remembering that Mr. Stantiloup
could not pay his butcher's bill.

Then, just at the end of the holidays, some good-
natured friend sent to him a copy of ' Everybody's
Business.'   There is no duty which a man owes to
himself more clearly than that of throwing into
the waste-paper basket, unsearched and even un-
opened, all newspapers sent to him without a
previously-declared purpose.   The sender has either
written something himself which he wishes to force
you to read, or else he has been desirous of wound-
ing you by some ill-natured criticism upon yourself.   ' Everybody's Business ' was a paper which,
in the natural course of things, did not find its way
into the Bowick Rectory ;   and the Doctor, though
he was no doubt acquainted with the title, had
never even looked at its columns.   It was the purpose of the periodical to amuse its readers, as its
name declared, with the private affairs of their

neighbours. It went boldly about its work, excusing itself by the assertion that Jones was just as well inclined to be talked about as Smith was to hear whatever could be said about Jones. As both parties were served, what could be the objection? It was in the main good-natured, and probably did most frequently gratify the Joneses, while it afforded considerable amusement to the listless and numerous Smiths of the world. If you can't read and understand Jones's speech in Parliament, you may at any rate have mind enough to interest yourself with the fact that he never composed a word of it in his own room without a ring on his finger and a flower in his button-hole. It may also be agreeable to know that Walker the poet always takes a mutton-chop and two glasses of sherry at half-past one. 'Everybody's Business' did this for everybody to whom such excitement was agreeable. But in managing everybody's business in that fashion, let a writer be as good-natured as he may and let the principle be ever so well-founded that nobody is to be hurt, still there are dangers. It is not always easy to know what will hurt and what will not. And then sometimes there will come a temptation to be, not spiteful, but specially amusing. There must be danger, and a writer will sometimes be indiscreet. Personalities will lead to libels even when the libeller has been most innocent. It may be that after all the poor poet never drank a glass of sherry before dinner in his life,— it may be that a little toast-and-water, even with his dinner, gives him all the refreshment that he wants, and that two glasses of alcoholic mixture in the middle of the day shall seem, when imputed

to him, to convey a charge of downright inebriety.
But the writer has perhaps learned to regard two
glasses of meridian wine as but a moderate amount
of sustentation. This man is much flattered if it
be given to be understood of him that he falls in
love with every pretty woman that he sees ;—
whereas another will think that he has been made
subject to a foul calumny by such insinuation.

' Everybody's Business ' fell into some such mistake as this, in that very amusing article which
was written for the delectation of its readers in
reference to Dr. Wortle and Mrs. Peacocke. The
' Broughton Gazette ' no doubt confined itself to
the clerical and highly moral views of the case,
and, having dealt with the subject chiefly on behalf of the Close and the admirers of the Close, had
made no allusion to the fact that Mrs. Peacocke
was a very pretty woman. One or two other local
papers had been more scurrilous, and had, with
ambiguous and timid words, alluded to the Doctor's
personal admiration for the lady. These, or the
rumours created by them, had reached one of the
funniest and lightest-handed of the contributors
to ' Everybody's Business,' and he had concocted
an amusing article,—which he had not intended to
be at all libellous, which he had thought to be only
funny. He had not appreciated, probably, the
tragedy of the lady's position, or the sanctity of
that of the gentleman. There was comedy in the
idea of the Doctor having sent one husband away
to America to look after the other while he consoled
the wife in England. ' It must be admitted,' said
the writer, ' that the Doctor has the best of it.
While one gentleman is gouging the other,—as

cannot but be expected,—the Doctor will be at
any rate in security, enjoying the smiles of beauty
under his own fig-tree at Bowick. After a hot
morning with " τυπτω " in the school, there will be
" amo " in the cool of the evening."* And this was
absolutely sent to him by some good-natured friend!

The funny writer obtained a popularity wider
probably than he had expected. His words reached
Mrs. Stantiloup, as well as the Doctor, and were
read even in the Bishop's palace. They were quoted
even in the ' Broughton Gazette,' not with appro-
bation, but in a high tone of moral severity. ' See
the nature of the language to which Dr. Wortle's
conduct has subjected the whole of the diocese ! '
That was the tone of the criticism made by the
' Broughton Gazette ' on the article in ' Everybody's Business.' ' What else has he a right to
expect ? ' said Mrs. Stantiloup to Mrs. Rolland,
having made quite a journey into Broughton for
the sake of discussing it at the palace. There she
explained it all to Mrs. Rolland, having herself
studied the passage so as fully to appreciate the
virus contained in it. ' He passes all the morning
in the school whipping the boys himself because
he has sent Mr. Peacocke away, and then amuses
himself in the evening by making love to Mr. Peacocke's wife, as he calls her.' Dr. Wortle, when he
read and re-read the article, and when the jokes
which were made upon it reached his ears, as they
were sure to do, was nearly maddened by what he
called the heartless iniquity of the world ; but his
state became still worse when he received an affectionate but solemn letter from the Bishop warning
him of his danger. An affectionate letter from a

bishop must surely be the most disagreeable mis-
sive which a parish clergyman can receive. Affection from one man to another is not natural in
letters. A bishop never writes affectionately unless
he means to reprove severely. When he calls a
clergyman his 'dear brother in Christ,' he is sure
to go on to show that the man so called is altogether
unworthy of the name. So it was with a letter now
received at Bowick, in which the Bishop expressed
his opinion that Dr. Wortle ought not to pay any
further visits to Mrs. Peacocke till she should have
settled herself down with one legitimate husband,
let that legitimate husband be who it might. The
Bishop did not indeed, at first, make reference by
name to 'Everybody's Business,' but he stated
that the 'metropolitan press' had taken up the
matter, and that scandal would take place in the
diocese if further cause were given. 'It is not
enough to be innocent,' said the Bishop, 'but men
must know that we are so.'

Then there came a sharp and pressing correspondence between the Bishop and the Doctor, which
lasted four or five days. The Doctor, without
referring to any other portion of the Bishop's letter,
demanded to know to what 'metropolitan newspaper' the Bishop had alluded, as, if any such
paper had spread scandalous imputations as to
him, the Doctor, respecting the lady in question,
it would be his, the Doctor's, duty to proceed
against that newspaper for libel. In answer to
this the Bishop, in a note much shorter and much
less affectionate than his former letter, said that
he did not wish to name any metropolitan newspaper. But the Doctor would not, of course, put

up with such an answer as this. He wrote very
solemnly now, if not affectionately. ' His lordship
had spoken of " scandal in the diocese." The
words,' said the Doctor, ' contained a most grave
charge. He did not mean to say that any such
accusation had been made by the Bishop himself ;
but such accusation must have been made by some
one at least of the London newspapers or the
Bishop would not have been justified in what he
has written. Under such circumstances he, Dr.
Wortle, thought himself entitled to demand from
the Bishop the name of the newspaper in question,
and the date on which the article had appeared.'

In answer to this there came no written reply,
but a copy of the ' Everybody's Business ' which
the Doctor had already seen. He had, no doubt,
known from the first that it was the funny paragraph about ' τυπτω ' and ' amo ' to which the
Bishop had referred. But in the serious steps
which he now intended to take, he was determined
to have positive proof from the hands of the Bishop
himself. The Bishop had not directed the perni-
cious newspaper with his own hands, but if called
upon, could not deny that it had been sent from
the palace by his orders. Having received it, the
Doctor wrote back at once as follows ;—

' RIGHT REVEREND AND DEAR LORD,—Any word
coming from your lordship to me is of grave importance, as should, I think, be all words coming from
a bishop to his clergy ; and they are of special
importance when containing a reproof, whether
deserved or undeserved. The scurrilous and vulgar
attack made upon me in the newspaper which your

lordship has sent to me would not have been worthy of my serious notice had it not been made worthy by your lordship as being the ground on which such a letter was written to me as that of your lordship's of the 12th instant. Now it has been invested with so much solemnity by your lordship's notice of it that I feel myself obliged to defend myself against it by public action.

' If I have given just cause of scandal to the diocese I will retire both from my living and from my school. But before doing so I will endeavour to prove that I have done neither. This I can only do by publishing in a court of law all the circumstances in reference to my connection with Mr. and Mrs. Peacocke. As regards myself, this, though necessary, will be very painful. As regards them, I am inclined to think that the more the truth is known, the more general and the more generous will be the sympathy felt for their position.

' As the newspaper sent to me, no doubt by your lordship's orders, from the palace, has been accompanied by no letter, it may be necessary that your lordship should be troubled by a subpœna, so as to prove that the newspaper alluded to by your lordship is the one against which my proceedings will be taken. It will be necessary, of course, that I should show that the libel in question has been deemed important enough to bring down upon me ecclesiastical rebuke of such a nature as to make my remaining in the diocese unbearable,—unless it is shown that that rebuke was undeserved.'

There was consternation in the palace when this was received. So stiffnecked a man, so obstinate,

so unclerical,—so determined to make much of
little ! The Bishop had felt himself bound to warn
a clergyman that, for the sake of the Church, he
could not do altogether as other men might. No
doubt certain ladies had got around him,—especially Lady Margaret Momson,—filling his ears
with the horrors of the Doctor's proceedings. The
gentleman who had written the article about the
Greek and the Latin words had seen the truth of
the thing at once,—so said Lady Margaret. The
Doctor had condoned the offence committed by
the Peacockes because the woman had been beautiful, and was repaying himself for his mercy by
basking in her loveliness. There was no saying
that there was not some truth in this ? Mrs.
Wortle herself entertained a feeling of the same
kind. It was palpable, on the face of it, to all
except Dr. Wortle himself,—and to Mrs. Peacocke.
Mrs. Stantiloup, who had made her way into the
palace, was quite convincing on this point. Everybody knew, she said, that the Doctor went across,
and saw the lady all alone, every day. Everybody
did not know that. If everybody had been accurate,
everybody would have asserted that he did this
thing every other day. But the matter, as it was
represented to the Bishop by the ladies, with the
assistance of one or two clergymen in the Close,
certainly seemed to justify his lordship's interference.

But this that was threatened was very terrible.
There was a determination about the Doctor which
made it clear to the Bishop that he would be as bad
as he said. When he, the Bishop, had spoken of
scandal, of course he had not intended to say that

the Doctor's conduct was scandalous ; nor had he
said anything of the kind. He had used the word
in its proper sense,—and had declared that offence
would be created in the minds of people unless an
injurious report were stopped. ' It is not enough
to be innocent,' he had said, ' but men must know
that we are so.' He had declared in that his belief
in Dr. Wortle's innocence. But yet there might,
no doubt, be an action for libel against the newspaper. And when damages came to be considered,
much weight would be placed naturally on the
attention which the Bishop had paid to the article.
The result of this was that the Bishop invited the
Doctor to come and spend a night with him in the
palace.

The Doctor went, reaching the palace only just
before dinner. During dinner and in the drawing-
room Dr. Wortle made himself very pleasant. He
was a man who could always be soft and gentle in
a drawing-room. To see him talking with Mrs.
Rolland and the Bishop's daughters, you would
not have thought that there was anything wrong
with him. The discussion with the Bishop came
after that, and lasted till midnight. ' It will be
for the disadvantage of the diocese that this matter
should be dragged into Court,—and for the disadvantage of the Church in general that a clergyman should seem to seek such redress against his
bishop.' So said the Bishop.

But the Doctor was obdurate. ' I seek no
redress,' he said, ' against my bishop. I seek
redress against a newspaper which has calumni-
ated me. It is your good opinion, my lord,—your
good opinion or your ill opinion which is the breath

of my nostrils. I have to refer to you in order that
I may show that this paper, which I should otherwise have despised, has been strong enough to
influence that opinion.'

CHAPTER III

' " AMO " IN THE COOL OF THE EVENING '

THE Doctor went up to London, and was told
by his lawyers that an action for damages probably
would lie. ' " Amo " in the cool of the evening,'
certainly meant making love. There could be no
doubt that allusion was made to Mrs. Peacocke.
To accuse a clergyman of a parish, and a schoolmaster, of making love to a lady so circumstanced
as Mrs. Peacocke, no doubt was libellous. Presum-
ing that the libel could not be justified, he would
probably succeed. ' Justified ! ' said the Doctor,
almost shrieking, to his lawyers ; ' I never said a
word to the lady in my life except in pure kindness
and charity. Every word might have been heard
by all the world.' Nevertheless, had all the world
been present, he would not have held her hand so
tenderly or so long as he had done on a certain
occasion which has been mentioned.

' They will probably apologise,' said the lawyer.

' Shall I be bound to accept their apology ? '

' No ; not bound ; but you would have to show,
if you went on with the action, that the damage
complained of was of so grievous a nature that the
apology would not salve it.'

' The damage has been already done,' said the
Doctor, eagerly. ' I have received the Bishop's

rebuke,—a rebuke in which he has said that I have brought scandal upon the diocese.'

' Rebukes break no bones,' said the lawyer. ' Can you show that it will serve to prevent boys from coming to your school ? '

' It may not improbably force me to give up the living. I certainly will not remain there subject to the censure of the Bishop. I do not in truth want any damages. I would not accept money. I only want to set myself right before the world.' It was then agreed that the necessary communication should be made by the lawyer to the newspaper proprietors, so as to put the matter in a proper train for the action.

After this the Doctor returned home, just in time to open his school with his diminished forces. At the last moment there was another defaulter, so that there were now no more than twenty pupils. The school had not been so low as this for the last fifteen years. There had never been less than eight-and-twenty before, since Mrs. Stantiloup had first begun her campaign. It was heartbreaking to him. He felt as though he were almost ashamed to go into his own school. In directing his housekeeper to send the diminished orders to the tradesmen he was thoroughly ashamed of himself ; in giving his directions to the usher as to the redivided classes he was thoroughly ashamed of himself. He wished that there was no school, and would have been contented now to give it all up, and to confine Mary's fortune to £10,000 instead of £20,000, had it not been that he could not bear to confess that he was beaten. The boys themselves seemed almost to carry their tails between their legs, as though even they were ashamed of their own school. If, as was too probable, another half-dozen should go at Christmas, then the thing must be abandoned. And how could he go on as rector of the parish with the abominable empty building staring him in the face every moment of his life ?

'I hope you are not really going to law,' said his wife to him.

'I must, my dear. I have no other way of defending my honour.'

'Go to law with the Bishop ? '

'No, not with the Bishop.'

'But the Bishop would be brought into it ? '

'Yes ; he will certainly be brought into it.'

'And as an enemy. What I mean is, that he will be brought in very much against his own will.'

'Not a doubt about it,' said the Doctor. 'But he will have brought it altogether upon himself. How he can have condescended to send that scurrilous newspaper is more than I can understand. That one gentleman should have so treated another is to me incomprehensible. But that a bishop should have done so to a clergyman of his own diocese shakes all my old convictions. There is a vulgarity about it, a meanness of thinking, an aptitude to suspect all manner of evil, which I cannot fathom. What ! did he really think that I was making love to the woman ; did he doubt that I was treating her and her husband with kindness, as one human being is bound to treat another in affliction ; did he believe, in his heart, that I sent the man away in order that I might have an opportunity for a wicked purpose of my own ? It is impossible. When I think of myself and of him, I cannot be-

lieve it. That woman who has succeeded at last
in stirring up all this evil against me,—even she
could not believe it. Her malice is sufficient to
make her conduct intelligible ;—but there is no
malice in the Bishop's mind against me. He would
infinitely sooner live with me on pleasant terms if
he could justify his doing so to his conscience. He
has been stirred to do this in the execution of some
presumed duty. I do not accuse him of malice.
But I do accuse him of a meanness of intellect
lower than what I could have presumed to have
been possible in a man so placed. I never thought
him clever ; I never thought him great ; I never
thought him even to be a gentleman, in the fullest
sense of the word ; but I did think he was a man.
This is the performance of a creature not worthy
to be called so.'

' Oh, Jeffrey, he did not believe all that.'

' What did he believe ? When he read that
article, did he see in it a true rebuke against a
hypocrite, or did he see in it a scurrilous attack
upon a brother clergyman, a neighbour, and a
friend ? If the latter, he certainly would not have
been instigated by it to write to me such a letter
as he did. He certainly would not have sent the
paper to me had he felt it to contain a foul-mouthed
calumny.'

' He wanted you to know what people of that
sort were saying.'

' Yes ; he wanted me to know that, and he
wanted me to know also that the knowledge had
come to me from my bishop. I should have thought
evil of any one who had sent me the vile ribaldry.
But coming from him, it fills me with despair.'

'Despair !' she said, repeating his word.

'Yes ; despair as to the condition of the Church when I see a man capable of such meanness holding so high place. "'Amo' in the cool of the evening !" That words such as those should have been sent to me by the Bishop, as showing what the "metropolitan press" of the day was saying about my conduct ! Of course, my action will be against him,—against the Bishop. I shall be bound to expose his conduct. What else can I do ? There are things which a man cannot bear and live. Were I to put up with this I must leave the school, leave the parish ;—nay, leave the country. There is a stain upon me which I must wash out, or I cannot remain here.'

'No, no, no,' said his wife, embracing him.

'" 'Amo' in the cool of the evening !" And that when, as God is my judge above me, I have done my best to relieve what has seemed to me the unmerited sorrows of two poor sufferers ! Had it come from Mrs. Stantiloup, it would, of course, have been nothing. I could have understood that her malice should have condescended to anything, however low. But from the Bishop !'

'How will you be the worse ? Who will know ?'

'I know it,' said he, striking his breast. 'I know it. The wound is here. Do you think that when a coarse libel is welcomed in the Bishop's palace, and treated there as true, that it will not be spread abroad among other houses ? When the Bishop has thought it necessary to send it me, what will other people do,—others who are not bound to be just and righteous in their dealings with me as he is ? " ' Amo ' in the cool of the evening !" '

Then he seized his hat and rushed out into the garden.

The gentleman who had written the paragraph certainly had had no idea that his words would have been thus effectual. The little joke had seemed to him to be good enough to fill a paragraph, and it had gone from him without further thought. Of the Doctor or of the lady he had conceived no idea whatsoever. Somebody else had said somewhere that a clergyman had sent a lady's reputed husband away to look for another husband, while he and the lady remained together. The joke had not been much of a joke, but it had been enough. It had gone forth, and had now brought the whole palace of Broughton into grief, and had nearly driven our excellent Doctor mad! ' " Amo " in the cool of the evening ! ' The words stuck to him like the shirt of Nessus,* lacerating his very spirit. That words such as those should have been sent to him in a solemn sober spirit by the bishop of his diocese ! It never occurred to him that he had, in truth, been imprudent when paying his visits alone to Mrs. Peacocke.

It was late in the evening, and he wandered away up through the green rides of a wood the borders of which came down to the glebe fields. He had been boiling over with indignation while talking to his wife. But as soon as he was alone he endeavoured, —purposely endeavoured to rid himself for a while of his wrath. This matter was so important to him that he knew well that it behoved him to look at it all round in a spirit other than that of anger. He had talked of giving up his school, and giving up his parish, and had really for a time almost persuaded himself that he must do so unless he could induce the Bishop publicly to withdraw the censure which he felt to have been expressed against him.

And then what would his life be afterwards? His parish and his school had not been only sources of income to him. The duty also had been dear, and had been performed on the whole with conscientious energy. Was everything to be thrown up, and his whole life hereafter be made a blank to him, because the Bishop had been unjust and injudicious? He could see that it well might be so, if he were to carry this contest on. He knew his own temper well enough to be sure that, as he fought, he would grow hotter in the fight, and that when he was once in the midst of it nothing would be possible to him but absolute triumph or absolute annihilation. If once he should succeed in getting the Bishop into court as a witness, either the Bishop must be crushed or he himself. The Bishop must be got to say why he had sent that low ribaldry to a clergyman in his parish. He must be asked whether he had himself believed it, or whether he had not believed it. He must be made to say that there existed no slightest reason for believing the insinuation contained; and then, having confessed so much, he must be asked why he had sent that letter to Bowick parsonage. If it were false as well as ribald, slanderous as well as vulgar, malicious as well as mean, was the sending of it a mode of communication between a bishop and a clergyman of which he as a bishop could approve? Questions such as these must be asked him; and the Doctor, as he walked alone, arranging these questions within his own bosom, putting them into the strongest language which he could find, almost assured himself that the Bishop would be crushed in answering them. The Bishop had made a great mistake. So the Doctor assured himself. He had been entrapped by bad advisers, and had fallen into a pit. He had gone wrong, and had lost himself. When cross-questioned, as the Doctor suggested to himself that he should be cross-questioned, the Bishop would have to own all this ;—and then he would be crushed.

But did he really want to crush the Bishop ? Had this man been so bitter an enemy to him that, having him on the hip, he wanted to strike him down altogether ? In describing the man's character to his wife, as he had done in the fury of his indignation, he had acquitted the man of malice. He was sure now, in his calmer moments, that the man had not intended to do him harm. If it were left in the Bishop's bosom, his parish, his school, and his character would all be made safe to him. He was sure of that. There was none of the spirit of Mrs. Stantiloup in the feeling that had prevailed at the palace. The Bishop, who had never yet been able to be masterful over him, had desired in a mild way to become masterful. He had liked the opportunity of writing that affectionate letter. That reference to the ' metropolitan press ' had slipt from him unawares ; and then, when badgered for his authority, when driven to give an instance from the London newspapers, he had sent the objectionable periodical. He had, in point of fact, made a mistake ;—a stupid, foolish mistake, into which a really well-bred man would hardly have fallen. ' Ought I to take advantage of it ? ' said the Doctor to himself when he had wandered for an hour or more alone through the wood. He certainly did not wish to be crushed himself. Ought he to be anxious to crush the Bishop because of this error ?

'As for the paper,' he said to himself, walking quicker as his mind turned to this side of the subject,—'as for the paper itself, it is beneath my notice. What is it to me what such a publication, or even the readers of it, may think of me ? As for damages, I would rather starve than soil my hands with their money. Though it should succeed in ruining me, I could not accept redress in that shape.' And thus having thought the matter fully over, he returned home, still wrathful, but with mitigated wrath.

A Saturday was fixed on which he should again go up to London to see the lawyer. He was obliged now to be particular about his days, as, in the absence of Mr. Peacocke, the school required his time. Saturday was a half-holiday, and on that day he could be absent on condition of remitting the classical lessons in the morning. As he thought of it all he began to be almost tired of Mr. Peacocke. Nevertheless, on the Saturday morning, before he started, he called on Mrs. Peacocke,—in company with his wife,—and treated her with all his usual cordial kindness. 'Mrs. Wortle,' he said, 'is going up to town with me ; but we shall be home to-night, and we will see you on Monday if not to-morrow.' Mrs. Wortle was going with him, not with the view of being present at his interview with the lawyer, which she knew would not be allowed, but on the pretext of shopping. Her real reason for making the request to be taken up to town was,

that she might use the last moment possible in
mitigating her husband's wrath against the Bishop.

' I have seen one of the proprietors and the
editor,' said the lawyer, ' and they are quite willing
to apologise. I really do believe they are very
sorry. The words had been allowed to pass without
being weighed. Nothing beyond an innocent joke
was intended.'

' I dare say. It seems innocent enough to them.
If soot be thrown at a chimney-sweeper the joke is
innocent, but very offensive when it is thrown at
you.'

' They are quite aware that you have ground to
complain. Of course you can go on if you like.
The fact that they have offered to apologise will no
doubt be a point in their favour. Nevertheless you
would probably get a verdict.'

' We could bring the Bishop into court ? '

' I think so. You have got his letter speaking of
the " metropolitan press " ? '

' Oh yes.'

' It is for you to think, Dr. Wortle, whether there
would not be a feeling against you among clergymen.'

' Of course there will. Men in authority always
have public sympathy with them in this country.
No man more rejoices that it should be so than
I do. But not the less is it necessary that now and
again a man shall make a stand in his own defence.
He should never have sent me that paper.'

' Here,' said the lawyer, ' is the apology they
propose to insert if you approve of it. They will
also pay my bill,—which, however, will not, I am
sorry to say, be very heavy.' Then the lawyer

handed to the Doctor a slip of paper, on which the following words were written ;—

'Our attention has been called to a notice which was made in our impression of the — ultimo on the conduct of a clergyman in the diocese of Broughton. A joke was perpetrated which, we are sorry to find, has given offence where certainly no offence was intended. We have since heard all the details of the case to which reference was made, and are able to say that the conduct of the clergyman in question has deserved neither censure nor ridicule. Actuated by the purest charity he has proved himself a sincere friend to persons in great trouble.'

'They'll put in your name if you wish it,' said the lawyer, ' or alter it in any way you like, so that they be not made to eat too much dirt.'

' I do not want them to alter it,' said the Doctor, sitting thoughtfully. ' Their eating dirt will do no good to me. They are nothing to me. It is the Bishop.' Then, as though he were not thinking of what he did, he tore the paper and threw the fragments down on the floor. ' They are nothing to me.'

' You will not accept their apology ? ' said the lawyer.

' Oh yes ;—or rather, it is unnecessary. You may tell them that I have changed my mind, and that I will ask for no apology. As far as the paper is concerned, it will be better to let the thing die a natural death. I should never have troubled myself about the newspaper if the Bishop had not sent it to me. Indeed I had seen it before the Bishop sent it, and thought little or nothing of it. Animals will after their kind. The wasp stings, and the polecat stinks, and the lion tears its prey asunder.

Such a paper as that of course follows its own bent. One would have thought that a bishop would have done the same.'

' I may tell them that the action is withdrawn ? '

' Certainly ; certainly. Tell them also that they will oblige me by putting in no apology. And as for your bill, I would prefer to pay it myself. I will exercise no anger against them. It is not they who in truth have injured me.' As he returned home he was not altogether happy, feeling that the Bishop would escape him ; but he made his wife happy by telling her the decision to which he had come.

CHAPTER IV

' IT IS IMPOSSIBLE '

THE absence of Dr. and Mrs. Wortle was pecu-liarly unfortunate on that afternoon, as a visitor rode over from a distance to make a call,—a visitor whom they both would have been very glad to welcome, but of whose coming Mrs. Wortle was not so delighted to hear when she was told by Mary that he had spent two or three hours at the Rectory. Mrs. Wortle began to think whether the visitor could have known of her intended absence and the Doctor's. That Mary had not known that the visitor was coming she was quite certain. Indeed she did not really suspect the visitor, who was one too ingenuous in his nature to preconcert so subtle and so wicked a scheme. The visitor, of course, had been Lord Carstairs.

' Was he here long ? ' asked Mrs. Wortle anxiously.

' Two or three hours, mamma. He rode over

from Buttercup where he is staying, for a cricket match, and of course I got him some lunch.'

'I should hope so,' said the Doctor. 'But I didn't think that Carstairs was so fond of the Momson lot as all that.'

Mrs. Wortle at once doubted the declared purpose of this visit to Buttercup. Buttercup was more than half-way between Carstairs and Bowick.

'And then we had a game of lawn-tennis. Talbot and Monk came through to make up sides.' So much Mary told at once, but she did not tell more till she was alone with her mother.

Young Carstairs had certainly not come over on the sly, as we may call it, but nevertheless there had been a project in his mind, and fortune had favoured him. He was now about nineteen, and had been treated for the last twelve months almost as though he had been a man. It had seemed to him that there was no possible reason why he should not fall in love as well as another. Nothing more sweet, nothing more lovely, nothing more lovable than Mary Wortle had he ever seen. He had almost made up his mind to speak on two or three occasions before he left Bowick; but either his courage or the occasion had failed him. Once, as he was walking home with her from church, he had said one word;—but it had amounted to nothing. She had escaped from him before she was bound to understand what he meant. He did not for a moment suppose that she had understood anything. He was only too much afraid that she regarded him as a mere boy. But when he had been away from Bowick two months he resolved that he would not be regarded as a mere boy any longer. Therefore he took an opportunity of going to Buttercup, which he certainly would not have done for the sake of the Momsons or for the sake of the cricket.

He ate his lunch before he said a word, and then, with but poor grace, submitted to the lawn-tennis with Talbot and Monk. Even to his youthful mind it seemed that Talbot and Monk were brought in on purpose. They were both of them boys he had liked, but he hated them now. However, he played his game, and when that was over, managed to get rid of them, sending them back through the gate to the school-ground.

'I think I must say good-bye now,' said Mary, 'because there are ever so many things in the house which I have got to do.'

'I am going almost immediately,' said the young lord.

'Papa will be so sorry not to have seen you.' This had been said once or twice before.

'I came over,' he said, 'on purpose to see you.'

They were now standing on the middle of the lawn, and Mary had assumed a look which intended to signify that she expected him to go. He knew the place well enough to get his own horse, or to order the groom to get it for him. But instead of that, he stood his ground, and now declared his purpose.

'To see me, Lord Carstairs!'

'Yes, Miss Wortle. And if the Doctor had been here, or your mother, I should have told them.'

'Have told them what?' she asked. She knew; she felt sure that she knew; and yet she could not refrain from the question.

'I have come here to ask if you can love me.'

It was a most decided way of declaring his purpose, and one which made Mary feel that a great difficulty was at once thrown upon her. She really did not know whether she could love him or not. Why shouldn't she have been able to love him? Was it not natural enough that she should be able? But she knew that she ought not to love him, whether able or not. There were various reasons which were apparent enough to her though it might be very difficult to make him see them. He was little more than a boy, and had not yet finished his education. His father and mother would not expect him to fall in love, at any rate till he had taken his degree. And they certainly would not expect him to fall in love with the daughter of his tutor. She had an idea that, circumstanced as she was, she was bound by loyalty both to her own father and to the lad's father not to be able to love him. She thought that she would find it easy enough to say that she did not love him; but that was not the question. As for being able to love him,—she could not answer that at all.

' Lord Carstairs,' she said, severely, ' you ought not to have come here when papa and mamma are away.'

' I didn't know they were away. I expected to find them here.'

' But they ain't. And you ought to go away.'

' Is that all you can say to me? '

' I think it is. You know you oughtn't to talk to me like that. Your own papa and mamma would be angry if they knew it.'

' Why should they be angry? Do you think that I shall not tell them? '

'I am sure they would disapprove it altogether,' said Mary. 'In fact it is all nonsense, and you really must go away.'

Then she made a decided attempt to enter the house by the drawing-room window, which opened out on a gravel terrace.

But he stopped her, standing boldly by the window. 'I think you ought to give me an answer, Mary,' he said.

'I have; and I cannot say anything more. You must let me go in.'

'If they say that it's all right at Carstairs, then will you love me?'

'They won't say that it's all right; and papa won't think that it's right. It's very wrong. You haven't been to Oxford yet, and you'll have to remain there for three years. I think it's very ill-natured of you to come and talk to me like this. Of course it means nothing. You are only a boy, but yet you ought to know better.'

'It does mean something. It means a great deal. As for being a boy, I am older than you are, and have quite as much right to know my own mind.'

Hereupon she took advantage of some little movement in his position, and, tripping by him hastily, made good her escape into the house. Young Carstairs, perceiving that his occasion for the present was over, went into the yard and got upon his horse. He was by no means contented with what he had done, but still he thought that he must have made her understand his purpose.

Mary, when she found herself safe within her own room, could not refrain from asking herself the

question which her lover had asked her. ' Could
she love him ? ' She didn't see any reason why she
couldn't love him. It would be very nice, she
thought, to love him. He was sweet-tempered,
handsome, bright, and thoroughly good-humoured;
and then his position in the world was very high.
Not for a moment did she tell herself that she would
love him. She did not understand all the differ-
ences in the world's ranks quite as well as did her
father, but still she felt that because of his rank,—
because of his rank and his youth combined,—she
ought not to allow herself to love him. There was
no reason why the son of a peer should not marry
the daughter of a clergyman. The peer and the
clergyman might be equally gentlemen. But young
Carstairs had been there in trust. Lord Bracy
had sent him there to be taught Latin and Greek,
and had a right to expect that he should not be
encouraged to fall in love with his tutor's daughter.
It was not that she did not think herself good
enough to be loved by any young lord, but that she
was too good to bring trouble on the people who
had trusted her father. Her father would despise
her were he to hear that she had encouraged the
lad, or as some might say, had entangled him. She
did not know whether she should not have spoken
to Lord Carstairs more decidedly. But she could,
at any rate, comfort herself with the assurance that
she had given him no encouragement. Of course
she must tell it all to her mother, but in doing so
could declare positively that she had given the
young man no encouragement.

' It was very unfortunate that Lord Carstairs
should have come just when I was away,' said Mrs.

Wortle to her daughter as soon as they were alone together.

' Yes, mamma ; it was.'

' And so odd. I haven't been away from home any day all the summer before.'

' He expected to find you.'

' Of course he did. Had he anything particular to say ? '

' Yes, mamma.'

' He had ? What was it, my dear ? '

' I was very much surprised, mamma, but I couldn't help it. He asked me——'

' Asked you what, Mary ? '

' Oh, mamma ! ' Here she knelt down and hid her face in her mother's lap.

' Oh, my dear, this is very bad ;—very bad indeed.'

' It needn't be bad for you, mamma ; or for papa.'

' Is it bad for you, my child ? '

' No, mamma ; except of course that I am sorry that it should be so.'

' What did you say to him ? '

' Of course I told him that it was impossible. He is only a boy, and I told him so.'

' You made him no promise ? '

' No, mamma ; no ! A promise ! Oh dear no ! Of course it is impossible. I knew that. I never dreamed of anything of the kind ; but he said it all there out on the lawn.'

' Had he come on purpose ? '

' Yes ;—so he said. I think he had. But he will go to Oxford, and will of course forget it.'

' He is such a nice boy,' said Mrs. Wortle, who, in all her anxiety, could not but like the lad the better for having fallen in love with her daughter.

' Yes, mamma ; he is. I always liked him. But
this is quite out of the question. What would his
papa and mamma say ? '

' It would be very dreadful to have a quarrel,
wouldn't it,—and just at present, when there are
so many things to trouble your papa.' Though
Mrs. Wortle was quite honest and true in the feeling
she had expressed as to the young lord's visit, yet
she was alive to the glory of having a young lord
for her son-in-law.

' Of course it is out of the question, mamma. It
has never occurred to me for a moment as otherwise. He has got to go to Oxford and take his
degree before he thinks of such a thing. I shall be
quite an old woman by that time, and he will have
forgotten me. You may be sure, mamma, that
whatever I did say to him was quite plain. I wish
you could have been here and heard it all, and seen
it all.'

' My darling,' said the mother, embracing her,
' I could not believe you more thoroughly even
though I saw it all, and héard it all.'

That night Mrs. Wortle felt herself constrained
to tell the whole story to her husband. It was
indeed impossible for her to keep any secret from
her husband. When Mary, in her younger years,
had torn her frock or cut her finger, that was always
told to the Doctor. If a gardener was seen idling
his time, or a housemaid flirting with the groom,
that certainly would be told to the Doctor. What
comfort does a woman get out of her husband
unless she may be allowed to talk to him about
everything ? When it had been first proposed that
Lord Carstairs should come into the house as a

private pupil she had expressed her fear to the Doctor,—because of Mary. The Doctor had ridiculed her fears, and this had been the result. Of course she must tell the Doctor. 'Oh, dear,' she said, ' what do you think has happened while we were up in London ? '

' Carstairs was here.'

' Oh, yes ; he was here. He came on purpose to make a regular declaration of love to Mary.'

' Nonsense.'

' But he did, Jeffrey.'

' How do you know he came on purpose ? '

' He told her so.'

' I did not think the boy had so much spirit in him,' said the Doctor. This was a way of looking at it which Mrs. Wortle had not expected. Her husband seemed rather to approve than otherwise of what had been done. At any rate, he had expressed none of that loud horror which she had expected. ' Nevertheless,' continued the Doctor, ' he's a stupid fool for his pains.'

' I don't know that he is a fool,' said Mrs. Wortle.

' Yes ; he is. He is not yet twenty, and he has all Oxford before him. How did Mary behave ? '

' Like an angel,' said Mary's mother.

' That's of course. You and I are bound to believe so. But what did she do, and what did she say ? '

' She told him that it was simply impossible.'

' So it is,—I'm afraid. She at any rate was bound to give him no encouragement.'

' She gave him none. She feels quite strongly that it is altogether impossible. What would Lord Bracy say ? '

'If Carstairs were but three or four years older,' said the Doctor, proudly, 'Lord Bracy would have much to be thankful for in the attachment on the part of his son, if it were met by a return of affection on the part of my daughter. What better could he want ?'

'But he is only a boy,' said Mrs. Wortle.

'No ; that's where it is. And Mary was quite right to tell him that it is impossible. It is impossible. And I trust, for her sake, that his words have not touched her young heart.'

'Oh, no,' said Mrs. Wortle.

'Had it been otherwise how could we have been angry with the child ?'

Now this did seem to the mother to be very much in contradiction to that which the Doctor had himself said when she had whispered to him that Lord Carstairs's coming might be dangerous. 'I was afraid of it, as you know,' said she.

'His character has altered during the last twelve months.'

'I suppose when boys grow into men it is so with them.'

'Not so quickly,' said the Doctor. 'A boy when he leaves Eton is not generally thinking of these things.'

'A boy at Eton is not thrown into such society,' said Mrs. Wortle.

'I suppose his being here and seeing Mary every day has done it. Poor Mary !'

'I don't think she is poor at all,' said Mary's mother.

'I am afraid she must not dream of her young lover.'

'Of course she will not dream of him. She has never entertained any idea of the kind. There never was a girl with less nonsense of that kind than Mary. When Lord Carstairs spoke to her to-day I do not suppose she had thought about him more than any other boy that has been here.'

'But she will think now.'

'No;—not in the least. She knows it is impossible.'

'Nevertheless she will think about it. And so will you.'

'I!'

'Yes,—why not? Why should you be different from other mothers? Why should I not think about it as other fathers might do? It is impossible. I wish it were not. For Mary's sake, I wish he were three or four years older. But he is as he is, and we know that it is impossible. Nevertheless, it is natural that she should think about him. I only hope that she will not think about him too much.' So saying he closed the conversation for that night.

Mary did not think very much about 'it' in such a way as to create disappointment. She at once realised the impossibilities, so far as to perceive that the young lord was the top brick of the chimney as far as she was concerned. The top brick of the chimney may be very desirable, but one doesn't cry for it, because it is unattainable. Therefore Mary did not in truth think of loving her young lover. He had been to her a very nice boy ; and so he was still ; that ;—that, and nothing more. Then had come this little episode in her life which seemed to lend it a gentle tinge of romance. But

had she inquired of her bosom she would have
declared that she had not been in love. With her
mother there was perhaps something of regret. But
it was exactly the regret which may be felt in reference to the top brick. It would have been so sweet
had it been possible ; but then it was so evidently
impossible.

With the Doctor the feeling was somewhat different. It was not quite so manifest to him that
this special brick was altogether unattainable, nor
even that it was quite at the top of the chimney.
There was no reason why his daughter should not
marry an earl's son and heir. No doubt the lad
had been confided to him in trust. No doubt it
would have been his duty to have prevented anything of the kind, had anything of the kind seemed
to him to be probable. Had there been any moment
in which the duty had seemed to him to be a duty,
he would have done it, even though it had been
necessary to caution the Earl to take his son away
from Bowick. But there had been nothing of the
kind. He had acted in the simplicity of his heart,
and this had been the result. Of course it was
impossible. He acknowledged to himself that it
was so, because of the necessity of those Oxford
studies and those long years which would be required for the taking of the degree. But to his
thinking there was no other ground for saying that
it was impossible. The thing must stand as it was.
If this youth should show himself to be more constant than other youths,—which was not probable,
—and if, at the end of three or four years, Mary
should not have given her heart to any other lover,
—which was also improbable,—why, then, it might

come to pass that he should some day find himself
father-in-law to the future Earl Bracy. Though
Mary did not think of it, nor Mrs. Wortle, he
thought of it,—so as to give an additional interest
to these disturbed days.

CHAPTER V

CORRESPONDENCE WITH THE PALACE

THE possible glory of Mary's future career did
not deter the Doctor from thinking of his troubles,
—and especially that trouble with the Bishop
which was at present heavy on his hand. He had
determined not to go on with his action, and had so
resolved because he had felt, in his more sober
moments, that in bringing the Bishop to disgrace,
he would be as a bird soiling its own nest. It was
that conviction, and not any idea as to the sufficiency or insufficiency, as to the truth or falsehood,
of the editor's apology, which had actuated him.
As he had said to his lawyer, he did not in the least
care for the newspaper people. He could not condescend to be angry with them. The abominable
joke as to the two verbs was altogether in their line.
As coming from them, they were no more to him
than the ribald words of boys which he might hear
in the street. The offence to him had come from
the Bishop,—and he resolved to spare the Bishop
because of the Church. But yet something must be
done. He could not leave the man to triumph over
him. If nothing further were done in the matter,
the Bishop would have triumphed over him. As
he could not bring himself to expose the Bishop, he

must see whether he could not reach the man by means of his own power of words ;—so he wrote as follows ;—

'My dear Lord,—I have to own that this letter is written with feelings which have been very much lacerated by what your lordship has done. I must tell you, in the first place, that I have abandoned my intention of bringing an action against the proprietors of the scurrilous newspaper which your lordship sent me, because I am unwilling to bring to public notice the fact of a quarrel between a clergyman of the Church of England and his Bishop. I think that, whatever may be the difficulty between us, it should be arranged without bringing down upon either of us adverse criticism from the public press. I trust your lordship will appreciate my feeling in this matter. Nothing less strong could have induced me to abandon what seems to be the most certain means by which I could obtain redress.

'I had seen the paper which your lordship sent to me before it came to me from the palace. The scurrilous, unsavoury, and vulgar words which it contained did not matter to me much. I have lived long enough to know that, let a man's own garments be as clean as they may be, he cannot hope to walk through the world without rubbing against those who are dirty. It was only when those words came to me from your lordship,—when I found that the expressions which I found in that paper were those to which your lordship had before alluded as being criticisms on my conduct in the metropolitan press,—criticisms so grave as to

make your lordship think it necessary to admonish
me respecting them,—it was only then, I say, that
I considered them to be worthy of my notice.
When your lordship, in admonishing me, found it
necessary to refer me to the metropolitan press, and
to caution me to look to my conduct because the
metropolitan press had expressed its dissatisfaction, it was, I submit to you, natural for me to ask
you where I should find that criticism which had so
strongly affected your lordship's judgment.   There
are perhaps half a score of newspapers published in
London whose animadversions I, as a clergyman,
might have reason to respect,—even if I did not
fear them.   Was I not justified in thinking that at
least some two or three of these had dealt with my
conduct, when your lordship held the metropolitan
press *in terrorem**over my head ?   I applied to your
lordship for the names of these newspapers, and
your lordship, when pressed for a reply, sent to me
—that copy of " Everybody's Business."

' I ask your lordship to ask yourself whether, so
far, I have overstated anything.   Did not that
paper come to me as the only sample you were able
to send me of criticism made on my conduct in the
metropolitan press ?   No doubt my conduct was
handled there in very severe terms.   No doubt the
insinuations, if true,—or if of such kind as to be
worthy of credit with your lordship, whether true
or false,—were severe, plain-spoken, and damning.
The language was so abominable, so vulgar, so
nauseous, that I will not trust myself to repeat it.
Your lordship, probably, when sending me one
copy, kept another.   Now, I must ask your lordship,—and I must beg of your lordship for a reply,

—whether the periodical itself has such a character as to justify your lordship in founding a complaint against a clergyman on its unproved statements, and also whether the facts of the case, as they were known to you, were not such as to make your lordship well aware that the insinuations were false. Before these ribald words were printed, your lordship had heard all the facts of the case from my own lips. Your lordship had known me and my character for, I think, a dozen years. You know the character that I bear among others as a clergyman, a schoolmaster, and a gentleman. You have been aware how great is the friendship I have felt for the unfortunate gentleman whose career is in question, and for the lady who bears his name. When you read those abominable words did they induce your lordship to believe that I had been guilty of the inexpressible treachery of making love to the poor lady whose misfortunes I was endeavouring to relieve, and of doing so almost in my wife's presence ?

' I defy you to have believed them. Men are various, and their minds work in different ways,— but the same causes will produce the same effects. You have known too much of me to have thought it possible that I should have done as I was accused. I should hold a man to be no less than mad who could so have believed, knowing as much as your lordship knew. Then how am I to reconcile to my idea of your lordship's character the fact that you should have sent me that paper ? What am I to think of the process going on in your lordship's mind when your lordship could have brought yourself to use a narrative which you must have known to be

false, made in a newspaper which you knew to be
scurrilous, as the ground for a solemn admonition
to a clergyman of my age and standing ? You
wrote to me, as is evident from the tone and context of your lordship's letter, because you found
that the metropolitan press had denounced my conduct. And this was the proof you sent to me that
such had been the case !

' It occurred to me at once that, as the paper in
question had vilely slandered me, I could redress
myself by an action of law, and that I could prove
the magnitude of the evil done me by showing the
grave importance which your lordship had attached
to the words. In this way I could have forced an
answer from your lordship to the questions which
I now put to you. Your lordship would have been
required to state on oath whether you believed
those insinuations or not ; and, if so, why you
believed them. On grounds which I have already
explained I have thought it improper to do so.
Having abandoned that course, I am unable to
force any answer from your lordship. But I appeal
to your sense of honour and justice whether you
should not answer my questions ;—and I also ask
from your lordship an ample apology, if, on consideration, you shall feel that you have done me an
undeserved injury.—I have the honour to be, my
lord, your lordship's most obedient, very humble
servant,

' JEFFREY WORTLE.'

He was rather proud of this letter as he read it
to himself, and yet a little afraid of it, feeling that he
had addressed his Bishop in very strong language.

It might be that the Bishop should send him
no answer at all, or some curt note from his
chaplain in which it would be explained that the
tone of the letter precluded the Bishop from answering it. What should he do then ? It was not,
he thought, improbable, that the curt note from the
chaplain would be all that he might receive. He
let the letter lie by him for four-and-twenty hours
after he had composed it, and then determined that
not to send it would be cowardly. He sent it,
and then occupied himself for an hour or two in
meditating the sort of letter he would write to the
Bishop when that curt reply had come from the
chaplain.

That further letter must be one which must
make all amicable intercourse between him and the
Bishop impossible. And it must be so written as
to be fit to meet the public eye if he should be ever
driven by the Bishop's conduct to put it in print.
A great wrong had been done him ;—a great wrong !
The Bishop had been induced by influences which
should have had no power over him to use his
episcopal rod and to smite him,—him, Dr. Wortle !
He would certainly show the Bishop that he should
have considered beforehand whom he was about to
smite. ' " Amo " in the cool of the evening ! ' And
that given as an expression of opinion from the
metropolitan press in general ! He had spared the
Bishop as far as that action was concerned, but he
would not spare him should he be driven to further
measures by further injustice. In this way he
lashed himself again into a rage. Whenever those
odious words occurred to him he was almost mad
with anger against the Bishop.

When the letter had been two days sent, so that he might have had a reply had a reply come to him by return of post, he put a copy of it into his pocket and rode off to call on Mr. Puddicombe. He had thought of showing it to Mr. Puddicombe before he sent it, but his mind had revolted from such submission to the judgment of another. Mr. Puddicombe would no doubt have advised him not to send it, and then he would have been almost compelled to submit to such advice. But the letter was gone now. The Bishop had read it, and no doubt re-read it two or three times. But he was anxious that some other clergyman should see it,—that some other clergyman should tell him that, even if inexpedient, it had still been justified. Mr. Puddicombe had been made acquainted with the former circumstances of the affair ; and now, with his mind full of his own injuries, he went again to Mr. Puddicombe.

' It is just the sort of letter that you would write, as a matter of course,' said Mr. Puddicombe.

' Then I hope that you think it is a good letter ? '

' Good as being expressive, and good also as being true, I do think it.'

' But not good as being wise ? '

' Had I been in your case I should have thought it unnecessary. But you are self-demonstrative, and cannot control your feelings.'

' I do not quite understand you.'

' What did it all matter ? The Bishop did a foolish thing in talking of the metropolitan press. But he had only meant to put you on your guard.'

' I do not choose to be put on my guard in that way,' said the Doctor.

' No ; exactly. And he should have known you better than to suppose you would bear it. Then you pressed him, and he found himself compelled to send you that stupid newspaper. Of course he had made a mistake. But don't you think that the world goes easier when mistakes are forgiven ? '

' I did forgive it, as far as foregoing the action.'

' That, I think, was a matter of course. If you had succeeded in putting the poor Bishop into a witness-box you would have had every sensible clergyman in England against you. You felt that yourself.'

' Not quite that,' said the Doctor.

' Something very near it ; and therefore you withdrew. But you cannot get the sense of the injury out of your mind, and, therefore, you have persecuted the Bishop with that letter.'

' Persecuted ? '

' He will think so. And so should I, had it been addressed to me. As I said before, all your arguments are true,—only I think you have made so much more of the matter than was necessary ! He ought not to have sent you that newspaper, nor ought he to have talked about the metropolitan press. But he did you no harm ; nor had he wished to do you harm ;—and perhaps it might have been as well to pass it over.'

' Could you have done so ? '

' I cannot imagine myself in such a position. I could not, at any rate, have written such a letter as that, even if I would ; and should have been afraid to write it if I could. I value peace and quiet too greatly to quarrel with my bishop,—unless, indeed, he should attempt to impose upon my conscience. There was nothing of that kind here. I think I should have seen that he had made a mistake, and have passed it over.'

The Doctor, as he rode home, was, on the whole, better pleased with his visit than he had expected to be. He had been told that his letter was argumentative and true, and that in itself had been much.

At the end of the week he received a reply from the Bishop, and found that it was not, at any rate, written by the chaplain.

'MY DEAR DR. WORTLE,' said the reply; 'your letter has pained me exceedingly, because I find that I have caused you a degree of annoyance which I am certainly very sorry I have inflicted. When I wrote to you in my letter,—which I certainly did not intend as an admonition,—about the metropolitan press, I only meant to tell you, for your own information, that the newspapers were making reference to your affair with Mr. Peacocke. I doubt whether I knew anything of the nature of "Everybody's Business." I am not sure even whether I had ever actually read the words to which you object so strongly. At any rate, they had had no weight with me. If I had read them,—which I probably did very cursorily,—they did not rest on my mind at all when I wrote to you. My object was to caution you, not at all as to your own conduct, but as to others who were speaking evil of you.

' As to the action of which you spoke so strongly when I had the pleasure of seeing you here, I am very glad that you abandoned it, for your own sake and for mine, and the sake of all us generally to whom the peace of the Church is dear.

' As to the nature of the language in which you have found yourself compelled to write to me, I must remind you that it is unusual as coming from a clergyman to a bishop. I am, however, ready to admit that the circumstances of the case were unusual, and I can understand that you should have felt the matter severely. Under these circumstances, I trust that the affair may now be allowed to rest without any breach of those kind feelings which have hitherto existed between us.—Yours very faithfully,

'C. BROUGHTON.'

' It is a beastly letter,' the Doctor said to himself, when he had read it, ' a beastly letter ; ' and then he put it away without saying any more about it to himself or to any one else. It had appeared to him to be a ' beastly letter,' because it had exactly the effect which the Bishop had intended. It did not eat ' humble pie ; ' it did not give him the full satisfaction of a complete apology ; and yet it left no room for a further rejoinder. It had declared that no censure had been intended, and expressed sorrow that annoyance had been caused. But yet to the Doctor's thinking it was an unmanly letter. ' Not intended as an admonition ! ' Then why had the Bishop written in that severely affectionate and episcopal style ? He had intended it as an admonition, and the excuse was false. So thought the Doctor, and comprised all his criticism in the one epithet given above. After that he put the letter away, and determined to think no more about it.

' Will you come in and see Mrs. Peacocke after lunch ? ' the Doctor said to his wife the next morning. They paid their visit together ; and after that, when the Doctor called on the lady, he was generally accompanied by Mrs. Wortle. So much had been effected by ' Everybody's Business,' and its abominations.

CHAPTER VI

THE JOURNEY

WE will now follow Mr. Peacocke for a while upon his journey. He began his close connection with Robert Lefroy by paying the man's bill at the inn before he left Broughton, and after that found himself called upon to defray every trifle of expense incurred as they went along. Lefroy was very anxious to stay for a week in town. It would, no doubt, have been two weeks or a month had his companion given way ;—but on this matter a line of conduct had been fixed by Mr. Peacocke in conjunction with the Doctor from which he never departed. ' If you will not be guided by me, I will go without you,' Mr. Peacocke had said, ' and leave you to follow your own devices on your own resources.'

' And what can you do by yourself ? '

' Most probably I shall be able to learn all that I want to learn. It may be that I shall fail to learn anything either with you or without you. I am willing to make the attempt with you if you will come along at once ;—but I will not be delayed for a single day. I shall go whether you go or stay.' Then Lefroy had yielded, and had agreed to be put

on board a German steamer starting from Southampton to New York.

But an hour or two before the steamer started he
made a revelation. 'This is all gammon, Peacocke,'
he said, when on board.

'What is all gammon?'

'My taking you across to the States.'

'Why is it gammon?'

'Because Ferdinand died more than a year since;
—almost immediately after you took her off.'

'Why did you not tell me that at Bowick?'

'Because you were so uncommon uncivil. Was
it likely I should have told you that when you cut
up so uncommon rough?'

'An honest man would have told me the very
moment that he saw me.'

'When one's poor brother has died, one does not
blurt it like that all at once.'

'Your poor brother!'

'Why not my poor brother as well as anybody
else's? And her husband too! How was I to let
it out in that sort of way? At any rate he is dead
as Julius Cæsar. I saw him buried,—right away
at 'Frisco.'

'Did he go to San Francisco?'

'Yes,—we both went there right away from St.
Louis. When we got up to St. Louis we were on our
way with them other fellows. Nobody meant to
disturb you; but Ferdy got drunk, and would go
and have a spree, as he called it.'

'A spree, indeed!'

'But we were off by train to Kansas at five
o'clock the next morning. The devil wouldn't keep
him sober, and he died of D.T.*the day after we got

him to 'Frisco. So there's the truth of it, and you needn't go to New York at all. Hand me the dollars. I'll be off to the States ; and you can go back and marry the widow,—or leave her alone, just as you please.'

They were down below when this story was told, sitting on their portmanteaus in the little cabin in which they were to sleep. The prospect of the journey certainly had no attraction for Mr. Peacocke. His companion was most distasteful to him ; the ship was abominable ; the expense was most severe. How glad would he avoid it all if it were possible ! ' You know it all as well as if you were there,' said Robert, ' and were standing on his grave.' He did believe it. The man in all probability had at the last moment told the true story. Why not go back and be married again ? The Doctor could be got to believe it.

But then if it were not true ? It was only for a moment that he doubted. ' I must go to 'Frisco all the same,' he said.

' Why so ? '

' Because I must in truth stand upon his grave. I must have proof that he has been buried there.'

' Then you may go by yourself,' said Robert Lefroy. He had said this more than once or twice already, and had been made to change his tone. He could go or stay as he pleased, but no money would be paid to him until Peacocke had in his possession positive proof of Ferdinand Lefroy's death. So the two made their unpleasant journey to New York together. There was complaining on the way, even as to the amount of liquor that should be allowed. Peacocke would pay for nothing that he did not himself order. Lefroy had some small funds of his own, and was frequently drunk while on board. There were many troubles ; but still they did at last reach New York.

Then there was a great question whether they would go on direct from thence to San Francisco, or delay themselves three or four days by going round by St. Louis. Lefroy was anxious to go to St. Louis,—and on that account Peacocke was almost resolved to take tickets direct through for San Francisco. Why should Lefroy wish to go to St. Louis ? But then, if the story were altogether false, some truth might be learned at St. Louis ; and it was at last decided that thither they would go. As they went on from town to town, changing carriages first at one place and then at another, Lefroy's manner became worse and worse, and his language more and more threatening. Peacocke was asked whether he thought a man was to be brought all that distance without being paid for his time. ' You will be paid when you have performed your part of the bargain,' said Peacocke.

' I'll see some part of the money at St. Louis,' said Lefroy, ' or I'll know the reason why. A thousand dollars ! What are a thousand dollars ? Hand out the money.' This was said as they were sitting together in a corner or separated portion of the smoking-room of a little hotel at which they were waiting for a steamer which was to take them down the Mississippi to St. Louis. Peacocke looked round and saw that they were alone.

' I shall hand out nothing till I see your brother's grave,' said Peacocke.

' You won't ? '

'Not a dollar! What is the good of your going on like that? You ought to know me well enough by this time.'

'But you do not know me well enough. You must have taken me for a very tame sort o' critter.'

'Perhaps I have.'

'Maybe you'll change your mind.'

'Perhaps I shall. It is quite possible that you should murder me. But you will not get any money by that.'

'Murder you. You ain't worth murdering.' Then they sat in silence, waiting another hour and a half till the steamboat came. The reader will understand that it must have been a bad time for Mr. Peacocke.

They were on the steamer together for about twenty-four hours, during which Lefroy hardly spoke a word. As far as his companion could understand he was out of funds, because he remained sober during the greater part of the day, taking only what amount of liquor was provided for him. Before, however, they reached St. Louis, which they did late at night, he had made acquaintance with certain fellow-travellers, and was drunk and noisy when they got out upon the quay. Mr. Peacocke bore his position as well as he could, and accompanied him up to the hotel. It was arranged that they should remain two days at St. Louis, and then start for San Francisco by the railway which runs across the State of Kansas. Before he went to bed Lefroy insisted on going into the large hall in which, as is usual in American hotels, men sit and loafe and smoke and read the newspapers. Here, though it was twelve o'clock, there was still a crowd ; and Lefroy, after he had seated himself and lit his cigar, got up from his seat and addressed all the men around him.

' Here's a fellow,' said he, ' has come out from England to find out what's become of Ferdinand Lefroy.'

' I knew Ferdinand Lefroy,' said one man, ' and I know you too, Master Robert.'

' What has become of Ferdinand Lefroy ? ' asked Mr. Peacocke.

' He's gone where all the good fellows go,' said another.

' You mean that he is dead ? ' asked Peacocke.

' Of course he's dead,' said Robert. ' I've been telling him so ever since we left England ; but he is such a d—— unbelieving infidel that he wouldn't credit the man's own brother. He won't learn much here about him.'

' Ferdinand Lefroy,' said the first man, ' died on the way as he was going out West. I was over the road the day after.'

' You know nothing about it,' said Robert. ' He died at 'Frisco two days after we'd got him there.'

' He died at Ogden Junction,* where you turn down to Utah City.'

' You didn't see him dead,' said the other.

' If I remember right,' continued the first man, ' they'd taken him away to bury him somewhere just there in the neighbourhood. I didn't care much about him, and I didn't ask any particular questions. He was a drunken beast,—better dead than alive.'

' You've been drunk as often as him, I guess,' said Robert.

' I never gave nobody the trouble to bury me at any rate,' said the other.

' Do you mean to say positively of your own knowledge,' asked Peacocke, ' that Ferdinand Lefroy died at that station ? '

' Ask him ; he's his brother, and he ought to know best.'

' I tell you,' said Robert, earnestly, ' that we carried him on to 'Frisco, and there he died. If you think you know best, you can go to Utah City and wait there till you hear all about it. I guess they'll make you one of their elders if you wait long enough.' Then they all went to bed.

It was now clear to Mr. Peacocke that the man as to whose life or death he was so anxious had really died. The combined evidence of these men, which had come out without any preconcerted arrangement, was proof to his mind. But there was no evidence which he could take back with him to England and use there as proof in a court of law, or even before the Bishop and Dr. Wortle. On the next morning, before Robert Lefroy was up, he got hold of the man who had been so positive that death had overtaken the poor wretch at the railway station which is distant from San Francisco two days' journey. Had the man died there, and been buried there, nothing would be known of him in San Francisco. The journey to San Francisco would be entirely thrown away, and he would be as badly off as ever.

' I wouldn't like to say for certain,' said the man when he was interrogated. ' I only tell you what they told me. As I was passing along somebody said as Ferdy Lefroy had been taken dead out of the cars on to the platform. Now you know as much about it as I do.'

He was thus assured that at any rate the journey to San Francisco had not been altogether a fiction. The man had gone ' West,' as had been said, and nothing more would be known of him at St. Louis. He must still go on upon his journey and make such inquiry as might be possible at the Ogden Junction.

On the day but one following they started again, taking their tickets as far as Leavenworth.* They were told by the officials that they would find a train at Leavenworth waiting to take them on across country into the regular San Francisco line. But, as is not unusual with railway officials in that part of the world, they were deceived. At Leavenworth they were forced to remain for four-and-twenty hours, and there they put themselves up at a miserable hotel in which they were obliged to occupy the same room. It was a rough, uncouth place, in which, as it seemed to Mr. Peacocke, the men were more uncourteous to him, and the things around more unlike to what he had met elsewhere, than in any other town of the Union. Robert Lefroy, since the first night at St. Louis, had become sullen rather than disobedient. He had not refused to go on when the moment came for starting, but had left it in doubt till the last moment whether he did or did not intend to prosecute his journey. When the ticket was taken for him he pretended to be altogether indifferent about it, and would himself give no help whatever in any of the usual troubles of travelling. But as far as this little town of Leavenworth he had been carried, and Peacocke now began to think it probable that he might succeed in taking him to San Francisco.

On that night he endeavoured to induce him to go first to bed, but in this he failed. Lefroy insisted on remaining down at the bar, where he had ordered for himself some liquor for which Mr. Peacocke, in spite of all his efforts to the contrary, would have to pay. If the man would get drunk and lie there, he could not help himself. On this he was determined, that whether with or without the man, he would go on by the first train;—and so he took himself to his bed.

He had been there perhaps half-an-hour when his companion came into the room,—certainly not drunk. He seated himself on his bed, and then, pulling to him a large travelling-bag which he used, he unpacked it altogether, laying all the things which it contained out upon the bed. 'What are you doing that for?' said Mr. Peacocke; 'we have to start from here to-morrow morning at five.'

'I'm not going to start to-morrow at five, nor yet to-morrow at all, nor yet next day.'

'You are not?'

'Not if I know it. I have had enough of this game. I am not going further West for any one. Hand out the money. You have been told everything about my brother, true and honest, as far as I know it. Hand out the money.'

'Not a dollar,' said Peacocke. 'All that I have heard as yet will be of no service to me. As far as I can see, you will earn it; but you will have to come on a little further yet.'

'Not a foot; I ain't a-going out of this room to-morrow.'

' Then I must go without you ;—that's all.'

' You may go and be ——. But you'll have to shell out the money first, old fellow.'

' Not a dollar.'

' You won't ?'

' Certainly I will not. How often have I told you so.'

' Then I shall take it.'

' That you will find very difficult. In the first place, if you were to cut my throat——'

' Which is just what I intend to do.'

' If you were to cut my throat,—which in itself will be difficult,—you would only find the trifle of gold which I have got for our journey as far as 'Frisco. That won't do you much good. The rest is in circular notes,* which to you would be of no service whatever.'

' My God,' said the man suddenly, ' I am not going to be done in this way.' And with that he drew out a bowie-knife* which he had concealed among the things which he had extracted from the bag. ' You don't know the sort of country you're in now. They don't think much here of the life of such a skunk as you. If you mean to live till to-morrow morning you must come to terms.'

The room was a narrow chamber in which two beds ran along the wall, each with its foot to the other, having a narrow space between them and the other wall. Peacocke occupied the one nearest to the door. Lefroy now got up from the bed in the further corner, and with the bowie-knife in his hand rushed against the door as though to prevent his companion's escape. Peacocke, who was in bed undressed, sat up at once ; but as he did so he brought a revolver out from under his pillow. 'So you have been and armed yourself, have you?' said Robert Lefroy.

'Yes,' said Peacocke;—'if you come nearer me with that knife I shall shoot you. Put it down.'

'Likely I shall put it down at your bidding.'

With the pistol still held at the other man's head, Peacocke slowly extracted himself from his bed. 'Now,' said he, 'if you don't come away from the door I shall fire one barrel just to let them know in the house what sort of affair is going on. Put the knife down. You know that I shall not hurt you then.'

After hesitating for a moment or two, Lefroy did put the knife down. 'I didn't mean anything, old fellow,' said he. 'I only wanted to frighten you.'

'Well; you have frightened me. Now, what's to come next?'

'No, I ain't;—not frightened you a bit. A pistol's always better than a knife any day. Well now, I'll tell ye how it all is.' Saying this, he seated himself on his own bed, and began a long narration. He would not go further West than Leavenworth. Whether he got his money or whether he lost it, he would not travel a foot further. There were reasons which would make it disagreeable for him to go into California. But he made a proposition. If Peacocke would only give him money enough to support himself for the necessary time, he would remain at Leavenworth till his companion should return there, or would make his way to Chicago, and stay there till Peacocke should come to him. Then he proceeded to explain how absolute evidence might be obtained at San Francisco as to

his brother's death. 'That fellow was lying altogether,' he said, 'about my brother dying at the
Ogden station. He was very bad there, no doubt,
and we thought it was going to be all up with him.
He had the horrors*there, worse than I ever saw
before, and I hope never to see the like again. But
we did get him on to San Francisco; and when he
was able to walk into the city on his own legs, I
thought that, might be, he would rally and come
round. However, in two days he died ;—and we
buried him in the big cemetery just out of the
town.'

'Did you put a stone over him ?'

'Yes; there is a stone as large as life. You'll find
the name on it,—Ferdinand Lefroy of Kilbrack,
Louisiana. Kilbrack was the name of our planta-
tion, where we should be living now as gentlemen
ought, with three hundred niggers of our own, but
for these accursed Northern hypocrites.'*

'How can I find the stone ?'

'There's a chap there who knows, I guess, where
all them graves are to be found. But it's on the
right hand, a long way down, near the far wall at
the bottom, just where the ground takes a little dip
to the north. It ain't so long ago but what the
letters on the stone will be as fresh as if they were
cut yesterday.'

'Does no one in San Francisco know of his
death ?'

'There's a chap named Burke at Johnson's, the
cigar-shop in Montgomery Street. He was brother
to one of our party, and he went out to the funeral.
Maybe you'll find him, or, any way, some traces of
him.'

The two men sat up discussing the matter nearly the whole of the night, and Peacocke, before he started, had brought himself to accede to Lefroy's last proposition. He did give the man money enough to support him for two or three weeks and also to take him to Chicago, promising at the same time that he would hand to him the thousand dollars at Chicago should he find him there at the appointed time, and should he also have found Ferdinand Lefroy's grave at San Francisco in the manner described.

CHAPTER VII

'NOBODY HAS CONDEMNED YOU HERE'

Mrs. Wortle, when she perceived that her husband no longer called on Mrs. Peacocke alone, became herself more assiduous in her visits, till at last she too entertained a great liking for the woman. When Mr. Peacocke had been gone for nearly a month she had fallen into a habit of going across every day after the performance of her own domestic morning duties, and remaining in the school-house for an hour. On one morning she found that Mrs. Peacocke had just received a letter from New York, in which her husband had narrated his adventures so far. He had written from Southampton, but not after the revelation which had been made to him there as to the death of Ferdinand. He might have so done, but the information given to him had, at the spur of the moment, seemed to be so doubtful that he had refrained. Then he had been able to think of it all during the voyage, and from New York he had

written at great length, detailing everything. Mrs.
Peacocke did not actually read out loud the letter,
which was full of such terms of affection as are
common between man and wife, knowing that her
title to be called a wife was not admitted by Mrs.
Wortle ; but she read much of it, and told all the
circumstances as they were related.

'Then,' said Mrs. Wortle, ' he certainly is—no
more.' There came a certain accession of sadness
to her voice, as she reflected that, after all, she
was talking to this woman of the death of her
undoubted husband.

'Yes ; he is dead—at last.' Mrs. Wortle uttered
a deep sigh. It was dreadful to her to think that a
woman should speak in that way of the death of her
husband. ' I know all that is going on in your
mind,' said Mrs. Peacocke, looking up into her face.

'Do you ? '

'Every thought. You are telling yourself how
terrible it is that a woman should speak of the
death of her husband without a tear in her eye,
without a sob,—without one word of sorrow.'

'It is very sad.'

'Of course it is sad. Has it not all been sad ?
But what would you have me do ? It is not because
he was always bad to me,—because he marred all
my early life, making it so foul a blotch that I
hardly dare to look back upon it from the quiet-
ness and comparative purity of these latter days.
It is not because he has so treated me as to make
me feel that it has been a misfortune to me to be
born, that I now receive these tidings with joy. It
is because of him who has always been good to me
as the other was bad, who has made me wonder

at the noble instincts of a man, as the other has made me shudder at his possible meanness.'

'It has been very hard upon you,' said Mrs. Wortle.

'And hard upon him, who is dearer to me than my own soul. Think of his conduct to me! How he went away to ascertain the truth when he first heard tidings which made him believe that I was free to become his! How he must have loved me then, when, after all my troubles, he took me to himself at the first moment that was possible! Think, too, what he has done for me since,——and I for him! How I have marred his life, while he has striven to repair mine! Do I not owe him everything?'

'Everything,' said Mrs. Wortle,—'except to do what is wrong.'

'I did do what was wrong. Would not you have done so under such circumstances? Would not you have obeyed the man who had been to you so true a husband while he believed himself entitled to the name? Wrong! I doubt whether it was wrong. It is hard to know sometimes what is right and what is wrong. What he told me to do, that to me was right. Had he told me to go away and leave him, I should have gone,—and have died. I suppose that would have been right.' She paused as though she expected an answer. But the subject was so difficult that Mrs. Wortle was unable to make one. 'I have sometimes wished that he had done so. But as I think of it when I am alone, I feel how impossible that would have been to him. He could not have sent me away. That which you call right would have been impossible to him whom

I regard as the most perfect of human beings. As far as I know him, he is faultless ;—and yet, according to your judgment, he has committed a sin so deep that he must stand disgraced before the eyes of all men.'

' I have not said so.'

' It comes to that. I know how good you are ; how much I owe to you. I know that Dr. Wortle and yourself have been so kind to us, that were I not grateful beyond expression I should be the meanest human creature. Do not suppose that I am angry or vexed with you because you condemn me. It is necessary that you should do so. But how can I condemn myself ;—or how can I condemn him ? '

' If you are both free now, it may be made right.'

' But how about repentance ? Will it be all right though I shall not have repented ? I will never repent. There are laws in accordance with which I will admit that I have done wrong ; but had I not broken those laws when he bade me, I should have hated myself through all my life afterwards.'

' It was very different.'

' If you could know, Mrs. Wortle, how difficult it would have been to go away and leave him ! It was not till he came to me and told me that he was going down to Texas, to see how it had been with my husband, that I ever knew what it was to love a man. He had never said a word. He tried not to look it. But I knew that I had his heart and that he had mine. From that moment I have thought of him day and night. When I gave him my hand then as he parted from me, I gave it him as his own.

It has been his to do what he liked with it ever since, let who might live or who might die. Ought I not to rejoice that he is dead ? ' Mrs. Wortle could not answer the question. She could only shudder. ' It was not by any will of my own,' continued the eager woman, ' that I married Ferdinand Lefroy. Everything in our country was then destroyed. All that we loved and all that we valued had been taken away from us. War had destroyed everything.* When I was just springing out of childhood, we were ruined. We had to go, all of us ; women as well as men, girls as well as boys ;—and be something else than we had been. I was told to marry him.'

' That was wrong.'

' When everything is in ruin about you, what room is there for ordinary well-doing ? It seemed then that he would have some remnant of property. Our fathers had known each other long. The wretched man whom drink afterwards made so vile might have been as good a gentleman as another, if things had gone well with him. He could not have been a hero like him whom I will always call my husband ; but it is not given to every man to be a hero.'

' Was he bad always from the first ? '

' He always drank,—from his wedding-day ; and then Robert was with him, who was worse than he. Between them they were very bad. My life was a burden to me. It was terrible. It was a comfort to me even to be deserted and to be left. Then came this Englishman in my way ; and it seemed to me, on a sudden, that the very nature of mankind was altered. He did not lie when he spoke. He was never debased by drink. He had other care than for himself. For himself, I think, he never cared. Since he has been here, in the school, have you found any cause of fault in him ? '

' No, indeed.'

' No, indeed ! nor ever will ;—unless it be a fault to love a woman as he loves me. See what he is doing now,—where he has gone,—what he has to suffer, coupled as he is with that wretch ! And all for my sake ! '

' For both your sakes.'

' He would have been none the worse had he chosen to part with me. He was in no trouble. I was not his wife ; and he need only—bid me go. There would have been no sin with him then,—no wrong. Had he followed out your right and your wrong, and told me that, as we could not be man and wife, we must just part, he would have been in no trouble ;—would he ? '

' I don't know how it would have been then,' said Mrs. Wortle, who was by this time sobbing aloud in tears.

' No ; nor I, nor I. I should have been dead ; —but he ? He is a sinner now, so that he may not preach in your churches, or teach in your schools ; so that your dear husband has to be ruined almost because he has been kind to him. He then might have preached in any church,—have taught in any school. What am I to think that God will think of it ? Will God condemn him ? '

' We must leave that to Him,' sobbed Mrs. Wortle.

' Yes ; but in thinking of our souls we must reflect a little as to what we believe to be probable.

He, you say, has sinned,—is sinning still in calling me his wife. Am I not to believe that if he were called to his long account he would stand there pure and bright, in glorious garments,—one fit for heaven, because he has loved others better than he has loved himself, because he has done to others as he might have wished that they should do to him ? I do believe it ! Believe ! I know it. And if so, what am I to think of his sin, or of my own ? Not to obey him, not to love him, not to do in everything as he counsels me,—that, to me, would be sin. To the best of my conscience he is my husband and my master. I will not go into the rooms of such as you, Mrs. Wortle, good and kind as you are ; but it is not because I do not think myself fit. It is because I will not injure you in the estimation of those who do not know what is fit and what is unfit. I am not ashamed of myself. I owe it to him to blush for nothing that he has caused me to do. I have but two judges,—the Lord in heaven, and he, my husband, upon earth.'

' Nobody has condemned you here.'

' Yes ;—they have condemned me. But I am not angry at that. You do not think, Mrs. Wortle, that I can be angry with you,—so kind as you have been, so generous, so forgiving ;—the more kind because you think that we are determined, headstrong sinners ? Oh no ! It is natural that you should think so,—but I think differently. Circumstances have so placed me that they have made me unfit for your society. If I had no decent gown to wear, or shoes to my feet, I should be unfit also ;— but not on that account disgraced in my own estimation. I comfort myself by thinking that I can-

not be altogether bad when a man such as he has
loved me and does love me.'

The two women, when they parted on that morning, kissed each other, which they had not done
before ; and Mrs. Wortle had been made to doubt
whether, after all, the sin had been so very sinful.
She did endeavour to ask herself whether she would
not have done the same in the same circumstances.
The woman, she thought, must have been right to
have married the man whom she loved, when she
heard that that first horrid husband was dead.
There could, at any rate, have been no sin in that.
And then, what ought she to have done when the
dead man,—dead as he was supposed to have been,
—burst into her room ? Mrs. Wortle,—who found
it indeed extremely difficult to imagine herself to
be in such a position,—did at last acknowledge
that, in such circumstances, she certainly would
have done whatever Dr. Wortle had told her. She
could not bring it nearer to herself than that. She
could not suggest to herself two men as her own
husbands. She could not imagine that the Doctor
had been either the bad husband, who had unex-
pectedly come to life,—or the good husband, who
would not, in truth, be her husband at all ; but she
did determine, in her own mind, that, however all
that might have been, she would clearly have done
whatever the Doctor told her. She would have
sworn to obey him, even though, when swearing, she
should not have really married him. It was terrible
to think of,—so terrible that she could not quite
think of it ; but in struggling to think of it her heart
was softened towards this other woman. After that
day she never spoke further of the woman's sin.

Of course she told it all to the Doctor,—not indeed explaining the working of her own mind as to that suggestion that he should have been, in his first condition, a very bad man, and have been reported dead, and have come again, in a second shape, as a good man. She kept that to herself. But she did endeavour to describe the effect upon herself of the description the woman had given her of her own conduct.

'I don't quite know how she could have done otherwise,' said Mrs. Wortle.

'Nor I either; I have always said so.'

'It would have been so very hard to go away, when he told her not.'

'It would have been very hard to go away,' said the Doctor, 'if he had told her to do so. Where was she to go? What was she to do? They had been brought together by circumstances, in such a manner that it was, so to say, impossible that they should part. It is not often that one comes across events like these, so altogether out of the ordinary course that the common rules of life seem to be insufficient for guidance. To most of us it never happens; and it is better for us that it should not happen. But when it does, one is forced to go beyond the common rules. It is that feeling which has made me give them my protection. It has been a great misfortune; but, placed as I was, I could not help myself. I could not turn them out. It was clearly his duty to go, and almost as clearly mine to give her shelter till he should come back.'

'A great misfortune, Jeffrey?'

'I am afraid so. Look at this.' Then he handed to her a letter from a nobleman living at a great

distance,—at a distance so great that Mrs. Stantiloup would hardly have reached him there,—
expressing his intention to withdraw his two boys
from the school at Christmas.

' He doesn't give this as a reason.'

' No ; we are not acquainted with each other
personally, and he could hardly have alluded to my
conduct in this matter. It was easier for him to
give a mere notice such as this. But not the less
do I understand it. The intention was that the
elder Mowbray should remain for another year, and
the younger for two years. Of course he is at
liberty to change his mind ; nor do I feel myself
entitled to complain. A school such as mine must
depend on the credit of the establishment. He has
heard, no doubt, something of the story which has
injured our credit, and it is natural that he should
take the boys away.'

' Do you think that the school will be put an
end to ? '

' It looks very like it.'

' Altogether ? '

' I shall not care to drag it on as a failure. I am
too old now to begin again with a new attempt if
this collapses. I have no offers to fill up the
vacancies. The parents of those who remain, of
course, will know how it is going with the school.
I shall not be disposed to let it die of itself. My
idea at present is to carry it on without saying anything till the Christmas holidays, and then to give
notice to the parents that the establishment will be
closed at Midsummer.'

' Will it make you very unhappy ? '

' No doubt it will. A man does not like to fail.

I am not sure but what I am less able to bear such failure than most men.'

'But you have sometimes thought of giving it up.'

'Have I? I have not known it. Why should I give it up? Why should any man give up a profession while he has health and strength to carry it on?'

'You have another.'

'Yes; but it is not the one to which my energies have been chiefly applied. The work of a parish such as this can be done by one person. I have always had a curate. It is, moreover, nonsense to say that a man does not care most for that by which he makes his money. I am to give up over £2,000 a-year, which I have had not a trouble but a delight in making! It is like coming to the end of one's life.'

'Oh, Jeffrey!'

'It has to be looked in the face, you know.'

'I wish,—I wish they had never come.'

'What is the good of wishing? They came, and according to my way of thinking I did my duty by them. Much as I am grieved by this, I protest that I would do the same again were it again to be done. Do you think that I would be deterred from what I thought to be right by the machinations of a she-dragon such as that?'

'Has she done it?'

'Well, I think so,' said the Doctor, after some little hesitation. 'I think it has been, in truth, her doing. There has been a grand opportunity for slander, and she has used it with uncommon skill. It was a wonderful chance in her favour. She has

been enabled without actual lies,—lies which could
be proved to be lies,—to spread abroad reports
which have been absolutely damning. And she has
succeeded in getting hold of the very people through
whom she could injure me. Of course all this
correspondence with the Bishop has helped. The
Bishop hasn't kept it as a secret. Why should he ? '

' The Bishop has had nothing to do with the
school,' said Mrs. Wortle.

' No ; but the things have been mixed up together. Do you think it would have no effect with
such a woman as Lady Anne Clifford, to be told
that the Bishop had censured my conduct severely?
If it had not been for Mrs. Stantiloup, the Bishop
would have heard nothing about it. It is her doing.
And it pains me to feel that I have to give her
credit for her skill and her energy.'

' Her wickedness, you mean.'

' What does it signify whether she has been
wicked or not in this matter ? '

' Oh, Jeffrey ! '

' Her wickedness is a matter of course. We all
knew that beforehand. If a person has to be wicked,
it is a great thing for him to be successful in his
wickedness. He would have to pay the final penalty
even if he failed. To be wicked and to do nothing
is to be mean all round. I am afraid that Mrs.
Stantiloup will have succeeded in her wickedness.'

CHAPTER VIII

THE school and the parish went on through
August and September, and up to the middle of
October, very quietly. The quarrel between the
Bishop and the Doctor had altogether subsided.
People in the diocese had ceased to talk continually
of Mr. and Mrs. Peacocke. There was still alive
a certain interest as to what might be the ultimate
fate of the poor lady; but other matters had come
up, and she no longer formed the one topic of conversation at all meetings. The twenty boys at
the school felt that, as their numbers had been
diminished, so also had their reputation. They were
less loud, and, as other boys would have said of
them, less ' cocky ' than of yore. But they ate and
drank and played, and, let us hope, learnt their
lessons as usual. Mrs. Peacocke had from time to
time received letters from her husband, the last up
to the time of which we speak having been written
at the Ogden junction, at which Mr. Peacocke had
stopped for four-and-twenty hours with the object
of making inquiry as to the statement made to him
at St. Louis. Here he learned enough to convince
him that Robert Lefroy had told him the truth in
regard to what had there occurred. The people
about the station still remembered the condition of
the man who had been taken out of the car when
suffering from delirium tremens; and remembered
also that the man had not died there, but had been
carried on by the next train to San Francisco. One
of the porters also declared that he had heard a few

days afterwards that the sufferer had died almost immediately on his arrival at San Francisco. Information as far as this Mr. Peacocke had sent home to his wife, and had added his firm belief that he should find the man's grave in the cemetery, and be able to bring home with him testimony to which no authority in England, whether social, episcopal, or judicial, would refuse to give credit.

' Of course he will be married again,' said Mrs. Wortle to her husband.

' They shall be married here, and I will perform the ceremony. I don't think the Bishop himself would object to that; and I shouldn't care a straw if he did.'

' Will he go on with the school ? ' whispered Mrs. Wortle.

' Will the school go on ? If the school goes on, he will go on, I suppose. About that you had better ask Mrs. Stantiloup.'

'I will ask nobody but you,' said the wife, putting up her face to kiss him. As this was going on, everything was said to comfort Mrs. Peacocke, and to give her hopes of new life. Mrs. Wortle told her how the Doctor had promised that he himself would marry them as soon as the forms of the Church and the legal requisitions would allow. Mrs. Peacocke accepted all that was said to her quietly and thankfully, but did not again allow herself to be roused to such excitement as she had shown on the one occasion recorded.

It was at this time that the Doctor received a letter which greatly affected his mode of thought at the time. He had certainly become hipped*and low-spirited, if not despondent, and clearly showed to his wife, even though he was silent, that his mind was still intent on the injury which that wretched woman had done him by her virulence. But the letter of which we speak for a time removed this feeling, and gave him, as it were, a new life. The letter, which was from Lord Bracy, was as follows ;—

'MY DEAR DOCTOR WORTLE.—Carstairs left us for Oxford yesterday, and before he went, startled his mother and me considerably by a piece of information. He tells us that he is over head and ears in love with your daughter. The communication was indeed made three days ago, but I told him that I should take a day or two to think of it before I wrote to you. He was very anxious, when he told me, to go off at once to Bowick, and to see you and your wife, and of course the young lady ; —but this I stopped by the exercise of somewhat peremptory parental authority. Then he informed me that he had been to Bowick, and had found his lady-love at home, you and Mrs. Wortle having by chance been absent at the time. It seems that he declared himself to the young lady, who, in the exercise of a wise discretion, ran away from him and left him planted on the terrace. That is his account of what passed, and I do not in the least doubt its absolute truth. It is at any rate quite clear, from his own showing, that the young lady gave him no encouragement.

' Such having been the case, I do not think that I should have found it necessary to write to you at all had not Carstairs persevered with me till I promised to do so. He was willing, he said, not to go to Bowick on condition that I would write to

you on the subject. The meaning of this is, that
had he not been very much in earnest, I should
have considered it best to let the matter pass on as
such matters do, and be forgotten. But he is very
much in earnest. However foolish it is,—or perhaps I had better say unusual,—that a lad should
be in love before he is twenty, it is, I suppose, possible. At any rate it seems to be the case with him,
and he has convinced his mother that it would be
cruel to ignore the fact.

'I may at once say that, as far as you and your
girl are concerned, I should be quite satisfied that
he should choose for himself such a marriage. I
value rank, at any rate, as much as it is worth;
but that he will have of his own, and does not need
to strengthen it by intermarriage with another
house of peculiarly old lineage. As far as that is
concerned, I should be contented. As for money,
I should not wish him to think of it in marrying.
If it comes, *tant mieux*.* If not, he will have enough
of his own. I write to you, therefore, exactly as
I should do if you had happened to be a brother
peer instead of a clergyman.

'But I think that long engagements are very
dangerous; and you probably will agree with me
that they are likely to be more prejudicial to the
girl than to the man. It may be that, as difficulties
arise in the course of years, he can forget the affair,
and that she cannot. He has many things of which
to think; whereas she, perhaps, has only that one.
She may have made that thing so vital to her that
it cannot be got under and conquered; whereas,
without any fault or heartlessness on his part, occu-
pation has conquered it for him. In this case I fear

that the engagement, if made, could not but be long. I should be sorry that he should not take his degree. And I do not think it wise to send a lad up to the University hampered with the serious feeling that he has already betrothed himself.

' I tell you all just as it is, and I leave it to your wisdom to suggest what had better be done. He wished me to promise that I would undertake to induce you to tell Miss Wortle of his conversation with me. He said that he had a right to demand so much as that, and that, though he would not for the present go to Bowick, he should write to you. The young gentleman seems to have a will of his own,—which I cannot say that I regret. What you will do as to the young lady,—whether you will or will not tell her what I have written,—I must leave to yourself. If you do, I am to send word to her from Lady Bracy to say that she shall be delighted to see her here. She had better, however, come when that inflammatory young gentleman shall be at Oxford. Yours very faithfully,

' BRACY.'

This letter certainly did a great deal to invigorate the Doctor, and to console him in his troubles. Even though the debated marriage might prove to be impossible, as it had been declared by the voices of all the Wortles one after another, still there was something in the tone in which it was discussed by the young man's father which was in itself a relief. There was, at any rate, no contempt in the letter. ' I may at once say that, as far as you and your girl are concerned, I shall be very well pleased.' That, at any rate, was satisfactory. And the more he looked at it the less he thought that it need be altogether impossible. If Lord Bracy liked it, and Lady Bracy liked it,—and young Carstairs, as to whose liking there seemed to be no reason for any doubt,—he did not see why it should be impossible. As to Mary,—he could not conceive that she should make objection if all the others were agreed. How could she possibly fail to love the young man if encouraged to do so? Suitors who are good-looking, rich, of high rank, sweet-tempered, and at the same time thoroughly devoted, are not wont to be discarded. All the difficulty lay in the lad's youth. After all, how many noblemen have done well in the world without taking a degree? Degrees, too, have been taken by married men. And, again, young men have been persistent before now, even to the extent of waiting three years. Long engagements are bad,—no doubt. Everybody has always said so. But a long engagement may be better than none at all.

He at last made up his mind that he would speak to Mary; but he determined that he would consult his wife first. Consulting Mrs. Wortle, on his part, generally amounted to no more than instructing her. He found it sometimes necessary to talk her over, as he had done in that matter of visiting Mrs. Peacocke; but when he set himself to work he rarely failed. She had nowhere else to go for a certain foundation and support. Therefore he hardly doubted much when he began his operation about this suggested engagement.

'I have got that letter this morning from Lord Bracy,' he said, handing her the document.

'Oh dear! Has he heard about Carstairs?'

'You had better read it.'

'He has told it all,' she exclaimed, when she had finished the first sentence.

'He has told it all, certainly. But you had better read the letter through.'

Then she seated herself and read it, almost trembling, however, as she went on with it. 'Oh dear; —that is very nice what he says about you and Mary.'

'It is all very nice as far as that goes. There is no reason why it should not be nice.'

'It might have made him so angry!'

'Then he would have been very unreasonable.'

'He acknowledges that Mary did not encourage him.'

'Of course she did not encourage him. He would have been very unlike a gentleman had he thought so. But in truth, my dear, it is a very good letter. Of course there are difficulties.'

'Oh;—it is impossible!'

'I do not see that at all. It must rest very much with him, no doubt;—with Carstairs; and I do not like to think that our girl's happiness should depend on any young man's constancy. But such dangers have to be encountered. You and I were engaged for three years before we were married, and we did not find it so very bad.'

'It was very good. Oh, I was so happy at the time.'

'Happier than you've been since?'

'Well; I don't know. It was very nice to know that you were my lover.'

'Why shouldn't Mary think it very nice to have a lover?'

'But I knew that you would be true.'

'Why shouldn't Carstairs be true?'

'Remember he is so young. You were in orders.'

'I don't know that I was at all more likely to be true on that account. A clergyman can jilt a girl just as well as another. It depends on the nature of the man.'

'And you were so good.'

'I never came across a better youth than Carstairs. You see what his father says about his having a will of his own. When a young man shows a purpose of that kind he generally sticks to it.'

The upshot of it all was, that Mary was to be told, and that her father was to tell her.

'Yes, papa, he did come,' she said. 'I told mamma all about me.'

'And she told me, of course. You did what was quite right, and I should not have thought it necessary to speak to you had not Lord Bracy written to me.'

'Lord Bracy has written!' said Mary. It seemed to her, as it had done to her mother, that Lord Bracy must have written angrily; but though she thought so, she plucked up her spirit gallantly, telling herself that though Lord Bracy might be angry with his own son, he could have no cause to be displeased with her.

'Yes; I have a letter, which you shall read. The young man seems to have been very much in earnest.'

'I don't know,' said Mary, with some little exultation at her heart.

'It seems but the other day that he was a boy, and now he has become suddenly a man.' To this

Mary said nothing ; but she also had come to the
conclusion that, in this respect, Lord Carstairs had
lately changed,—very much for the better. ' Do
you like him, Mary ? '

' Like him, papa ? '

' Well, my darling ; how am I to put it ? He is
so much in earnest that he has got his father to
write to me. He was coming over himself again
before he went to Oxford ; but he told his father
what he was going to do, and the Earl stopped him.
There's the letter, and you may read it.'

Mary read the letter, taking herself apart to a
corner of the room, and seemed to her father to take
a long time in reading it. But there was very much
on which she was called upon to make up her mind
during those few minutes. Up to the present time,
—up to the moment in which her father had now
summoned her into his study, she had resolved that
it was ' impossible.' She had become so clear on
the subject that she would not ask herself the question whether she could love the young man. Would
it not be wrong to love the young man ? Would it
not be a longing for the top brick of the chimney,
which she ought to know was out of her reach ?
So she had decided it, and had therefore already
taught herself to regard the declaration made to
her as the ebullition of a young man's folly. But
not the less had she known how great had been the
thing suggested to her,—how excellent was this top
brick of the chimney ; and as to the young man
himself, she could not but feel that, had matters
been different, she might have loved him. Now
there had come a sudden change ; but she did not
at all know how far she might go to meet the change,

nor what the change altogether meant. She had
been made sure by her father's question that he
had taught himself to hope. He would not have
asked her whether she liked him,—would not, at
any rate, have asked that question in that voice,
—had he not been prepared to be good to her had
she answered in the affirmative. But then this
matter did not depend upon her father's wishes,
—or even on her father's judgment. It was necessary that, before she said another word, she should
find out what Lord Bracy said about it. There she
had Lord Bracy's letter in her hand, but her mind
was so disturbed that she hardly knew how to read
it aright at the spur of the moment.

'You understand what he says, Mary?'

'I think so, papa.'

'It is a very kind letter.'

'Very kind indeed. I should have thought that
he would not have liked it at all.'

'He makes no objection of that kind. To tell
the truth, Mary, I should have thought it unreasonable had he done so. A gentleman can do no better
than marry a lady. And though it is much to be
a nobleman, it is more to be a gentleman.'

'Some people think so much of it. And then
his having been here as a pupil! I was very sorry
when he spoke to me.'

'All that is past and gone. The danger is that
such an engagement would be long.'

'Very long.'

'You would be afraid of that, Mary?' Mary
felt that this was hard upon her, and unfair. Were
she to say that the danger of a long engagement
did not seem to her to be very terrible, she would

at once be giving up everything. She would have
declared then that she did love the young man;
or, at any rate, that she intended to do so. She
would have succumbed at the first hint that such
succumbing was possible to her. And yet she had
not known that she was very much afraid of a long
engagement. She would, she thought, have been
much more afraid had a speedy marriage been
proposed to her. Upon the whole, she did not
know whether it would not be nice to go on knowing that the young man loved her, and to rest secure
on her faith in him. She was sure of this,—that the
reading of Lord Bracy's letter had in some way
made her happy, though she was unwilling at once
to express her happiness to her father. She was
quite sure that she could make no immediate reply
to that question, whether she was afraid of a long
engagement. 'I must answer Lord Bracy's letter,
you know,' said the Doctor.

'Yes, papa.'

'And what shall I say to him?'

'I don't know, papa.'

'And yet you must tell me what to say, my
darling.'

'Must I, papa?'

'Certainly! Who else can tell me? But I will
not answer it to-day. I will put it off till Monday.'
It was Saturday morning on which the letter was
being discussed,—a day of which a considerable
portion was generally appropriated to the preparation of a sermon. 'In the mean time you had
better talk to mamma; and on Monday we will
settle what is to be said to Lord Bracy.'

CHAPTER IX

AT CHICAGO

Mr. Peacocke went on alone to San Francisco from the Ogden Junction, and there obtained full information on the matter which had brought him upon this long and disagreeable journey. He had no difficulty in obtaining the evidence which he required. He had not been twenty-four hours in the place before he was, in truth, standing on the stone which had been placed over the body of Ferdinand Lefroy, as he had declared to Robert Lefroy that he would stand before he would be satisfied. On the stone was cut simply the names, Ferdinand Lefroy of Kilbrack, Louisiana ; and to these were added the dates of the days on which the man had been born and on which he died. Of this stone he had a photograph made, of which he took copies with him ; and he obtained also from the minister who had buried the body and from the custodian who had charge of the cemetery certificates of the interment. Armed with these he could no longer doubt himself, or suppose that others would doubt, that Ferdinand Lefroy was dead.

Having thus perfected his object, and feeling but little interest in a town to which he had been brought by such painful circumstances, he turned round, and on the second day after his arrival, again started for Chicago. Had it been possible, he would fain have avoided any further meeting with Robert Lefroy. Short as had been his stay at San Francisco he had learnt that Robert, after

his brother's death, had been concerned in buying
mining shares and paying for them with forged
notes. It was not supposed that he himself had
been engaged in the forgery, but that he had come
into the city with men who had been employed for
years on this operation, and had bought shares and
endeavoured to sell them on the following day. He
had, however, managed to leave the place before
the police had got hold of him, and had escaped,
so that no one had been able to say at what station
he had got upon the railway. Nor did any one in
San Francisco know where Robert Lefroy was now
to be found. His companions had been taken,
tried, and convicted, and were now in the State
prison,—where also would Robert Lefroy soon be
if any of the officers of the State could get hold of
him. Luckily Mr. Peacocke had said little or
nothing of the man in making his own inquiries.
Much as he had hated and dreaded the man;
much as he had suffered from his companionship,
—good reason as he had to dislike the whole family,
—he felt himself bound by their late companionship not to betray him. The man had assisted
Mr. Peacocke simply for money; but still he had
assisted him. Mr. Peacocke therefore held his
peace and said nothing. But he would have been
thankful to have been able to send the money that
was now due to him without having again to see
him. That, however, was impossible.

On reaching Chicago he went to an hotel far
removed from that which Lefroy had designated.
Lefroy had explained to him something of the
geography of the town, and had explained that
for himself he preferred a ' modest, quiet hotel.'

The modest, quiet hotel was called Mrs. Jones's
boarding-house, and was in one of the suburbs far
from the main street. ' You needn't say as you're
coming to me,' Lefroy had said to him ; ' nor need
you let on as you know anything of Mrs. Jones at
all. People are so curious ; and it may be that a
gentleman sometimes likes to lie *perdu*.'* Mr. Peacocke, although he had but small sympathy for the
taste of a gentleman who likes to lie *perdu*, nevertheless did as he was bid, and found his way to
Mrs. Jones's boarding-house without telling any
one whither he was going.

Before he started he prepared himself with a
thousand dollars in bank-notes, feeling that this
wretched man had earned them in accordance with
their compact. His only desire now was to hand
over the money as quickly as possible, and to hurry
away out of Chicago. He felt as though he himself were almost guilty of some crime in having to
deal with this man, in having to give him money
secretly, and in carrying out to the end an arrangement of which no one else was to know the details.
How would it be with him if the police of Chicago
should come upon him as a friend, and probably
an accomplice, of one who was ' wanted ' on account of forgery at San Francisco ? But he had
no help for himself, and at Mrs. Jones's he found
his wife's brother-in-law seated in the bar of the
public-house,—that everlasting resort for American
loungers,—with a cigar as usual stuck in his mouth,
loafing away his time as only American frequenters
of such establishments know how to do. In England such a man would probably be found in such
a place with a glass of some alcoholic mixture

beside him, but such is never the case with an
American. If he wants a drink he goes to the bar
and takes it standing,—will perhaps take two or
three, one after another ; but when he has settled
himself down to loafe, he satisfies himself with
chewing a cigar, and covering a circle around him
with the results. With this amusement he will
remain contented hour after hour ;—nay, throughout the entire day if no harder work be demanded
of him. So was Robert Lefroy found now. When
Peacocke entered the hall or room the man did
not rise from his chair, but accosted him as though
they had parted only an hour since. 'So, old
fellow, you've got back all alive.'

'I have reached this place at any rate.'

'Well ; that's getting back, ain't it ? '

'I have come back from San Francisco.'

'H'sh ! ' exclaimed Lefroy, looking round the
room, in which, however, there was no one but
themselves. 'You needn't tell everybody where
you've been.'

'I have nothing to conceal.'

'That is more than anybody knows of himself.
It's a good maxim to keep your own affairs quiet
till they're wanted. In this country everybody
is spry enough to learn all about everything. I
never see any good in letting them know without
a reason. Well ;—what did you do when you got
there ? '

'It was all as you told me.'

'Didn't I say so ? What was the good of bringing me all this way, when, if you'd only believed
me, you might have saved me the trouble. Ain't
I to be paid for that ? '

' You are to be paid. I have come here to pay you.'

' That's what you owe for the knowledge. But for coming ? Ain't I to be paid extra for the journey ?'

' You are to have a thousand dollars.'

' H'sh !—you speak of money as though every one has a business to know that you have got your pockets full. What's a thousand dollars, seeing all that I have done for you ! '

' It's all that you're going to get. It's all, indeed, that I have got to give you.'

' Gammon.'

' It's all, at any rate, that you're going to get. Will you have it now ? '

' You found the tomb, did you ? '

' Yes ; I found the tomb. Here is a photograph of it. You can keep a copy if you like it.'

'What do I want of a copy ?' said the man, taking the photograph in his hand. ' He was always more trouble than he was worth,—was Ferdy. It's a pity she didn't marry me. I'd 've made a woman of her.' Peacocke shuddered as he heard this, but he said nothing. ' You may as well give us the picter ;—it'll do to hang up somewhere if ever I have a room of my own. How plain it is. Ferdinand Lefroy,—of Kilbrack ! Kilbrack indeed ! It's little either of us was the better for Kilbrack. Some of them psalm-singing rogues from New England* has it now ;—or perhaps a right-down nigger. I shouldn't wonder. One of our own lot, maybe ! Oh ; that's the money, is it ?—A thousand dollars ; all that I'm to have for coming to England and telling you, and bringing you back, and showing

you where you could get this pretty picter made.'
Then he took the money, a thick roll of notes, and
crammed them into his pocket.

'You'd better count them.'

'It ain't worth the while with such a trifle as
that.'

'Let me count them then.'

'You'll never have that plunder in your fists
again, my fine fellow.'

'I do not want it.'

'And now about my expenses out to England,
on purpose to tell you all this. You can go and
make her your wife now,—or can leave her, just
as you please. You couldn't have done neither if
I hadn't gone out to you.'

'You have got what was promised.'

'But my expenses,—going out ?'

'I have promised you nothing for your expenses
going out,—and will pay you nothing.'

'You won't ?'

'Not a dollar more.'

'You won't ?'

'Certainly not. I do not suppose that you
expect it for a moment, although you are so persistent in asking for it.'

'And you think you've got the better of me,
do you ? You think you've carried me along with
you, just to do your bidding and take whatever
you please to give me ? That's your idea of
me ?'

'There was a clear bargain between us. I have
not got the better of you at all.'

'I rather think not, Peacocke. I rather think
not. You'll have to get up earlier before you get

the better of Robert Lefroy. You don't expect to
get this money back again,—do you ? '

' Certainly not,—any more than I should expect
a pound of meat out of a dog's jaw.' Mr. Peacocke,
as he said this, was waxing angry.

' I don't suppose you do ;—but you expected
that I was to earn it by doing your bidding ;—
didn't you ? '

' And you have.'

' Yes, I have ; but how ? You never heard of my
cousin, did you ;—Ferdinand Lefroy of Kilbrack,
Louisiana ? '

' Heard of whom ? '

' My cousin ; Ferdinand Lefroy. He was very
well known in his own State, and in California too,
till he died. He was a good fellow, but given to
drink. We used to tell him that if he would marry
it would be better for him ;—but he never would ;—
he never did.' Robert Lefroy as he said this put
his left hand into his trousers-pocket over the notes
which he had placed there, and drew a small
revolver out of his pocket with the other hand.
' I am better prepared now,' he said, ' than when
you had your six-shooter under your pillow at
Leavenworth.'

' I do not believe a word of it. It's a lie,' said
Peacocke.

' Very well. You're a chap that's fond of
travelling, and have got plenty of money. You'd
better go down to Louisiana and make your way
straight from New Orleans to Kilbrack. It ain't
above forty miles to the south-west, and there's a
rail goes within fifteen miles of it. You'll learn
there all about Ferdinand Lefroy as was our

cousin,—him as never got married up to the day
he died of drink and was buried at San Francisco.
They'll be very glad, I shouldn't wonder, to see
that pretty little picter of yours, because they was
always uncommon fond of cousin Ferdy at Kilbrack. And I'll tell you what; you'll be sure to
come across my brother Ferdy in them parts, and
can tell him how you've seen me. You can give
him all the latest news, too, about his own wife.
He'll be glad to hear about her, poor woman.' Mr.
Peacocke listened to this without saying a word
since that last exclamation of his. It might be true.
Why should it not be true ? If in truth there had
been these two cousins of the same name, what
could be more likely than that his money should be
lured out of him by such a fraud as this ? But
yet,—yet, as he came to think of it all, it could not
be true. The chance of carrying such a scheme
to a successful issue would have been too small to
induce the man to act upon it from the day of his
first appearance at Bowick. Nor was it probable
that there should have been another Ferdinand
Lefroy unknown to his wife ; and the existence of
such a one, if known to his wife, would certainly
have been made known to him.

'It's a lie,' said he, ' from beginning to end.'

'Very well ; very well. I'll take care to make
the truth known by letter to Dr. Wortle and the
Bishop and all them pious swells over there. To
think that such a chap as you, a minister of the
gospel, living with another man's wife and looking
as though butter wouldn't melt in your mouth ! I
tell you what ; I've got a little money in my pocket
now, and I don't mind going over to England again

and explaining the whole truth to the Bishop myself. I could make him understand how that photograph ain't worth nothing, and how I explained to you myself as the lady's righteous husband is all alive, keeping house on his own property down in Louisiana. Do you think we Lefroys hadn't any place beside Kilbrack among us ? '

' Certainly you are a liar,' said Peacocke.

' Very well. Prove it.'

' Did you not tell me that your brother was buried at San Francisco ? '

' Oh, as for that, that don't matter. It don't count for much whether I told a crammer*or not. That picter counts for nothing. It ain't my word you were going on as evidence. You is able to prove that Ferdy Lefroy was buried at 'Frisco. True enough. I buried him. I can prove that. And I would never have treated you this way, and not have said a word as to how the dead man was only a cousin, if you'd treated me civil over there in England. But you didn't.'

' I am going to treat you worse now,' said Peacocke, looking him in the face.

' What are you going to do now ? It's I that have the revolver this time.' As he said this he turned the weapon round in his hand.

' I don't want to shoot you,—nor yet to frighten you, as I did in the bed-room at Leavenworth. Not but what I have a pistol too.' And he slowly drew his out of his pocket. At this moment two men sauntered in and took their places in the further corner of the room. ' I don't think there is to be any shooting between us.'

' There may,' said Lefroy.

'The police would have you.'

'So they would—for a time. What does that matter to me? Isn't a fellow to protect himself when a fellow like you comes to him armed?'

'But they would soon know that you are the swindler who escaped from San Francisco eighteen months ago. Do you think it wouldn't be found out that it was you who paid for the shares in forged notes?'

'I never did. That's one of your lies.'

'Very well. Now you know what I know; and you had better tell me over again who it is that lies buried under the stone that's been photographed there.'

'What are you men doing with them pistols?' said one of the strangers, walking across the room, and standing over the backs of their chairs.

'We are alooking at 'em,' said Lefroy.

'If you're agoing to do anything of that kind you'd better go and do it elsewhere,' said the stranger.

'Just so,' said Lefroy. 'That's what I was thinking myself.'

'But we are not going to do anything,' said Mr. Peacocke. 'I have not the slightest idea of shooting the gentleman; and he has just as little of shooting me.'

'Then what do you sit with 'em out in your hands in that fashion for?' said the stranger. 'It's a decent widow woman as keeps this house, and I won't see her set upon. Put 'em up.' Whereupon Lefroy did return his pistol to his pocket,—upon which Mr. Peacocke did the same. Then the stranger slowly walked back to his seat at the other side of the room.

'So they told you that lie; did they,—at 'Frisco?' asked Lefroy.

'That was what I heard over there when I was inquiring about your brother's death.'

'You'd believe anything if you'd believe that.'

'I'd believe anything if I'd believe in your cousin.' Upon this Lefroy laughed, but made no further allusion to the romance which he had craftily invented on the spur of the moment. After that the two men sat without a word between them for a quarter of an hour, when the Englishman got up to take his leave. 'Our business is over now,' he said, 'and I will bid you good-bye.'

'I'll tell you what I'm athinking,' said Lefroy. Mr. Peacocke stood with his hand ready for a final adieu, but he said nothing. 'I've half a mind to go back with you to England. There ain't nothing to keep me here.'

'What could you do there?'

'I'd be evidence for you, as to Ferdy's death, you know.'

'I have evidence. I do not want you.'

'I'll go, nevertheless.'

'And spend all your money on the journey.'

'You'd help;—wouldn't you now?'

'Not a dollar,' said Peacocke, turning away and leaving the room. As he did so he heard the wretch laughing loud at the excellence of his own joke.

Before he made his journey back again to England he only once more saw Robert Lefroy. As he was seating himself in the railway car that was to take him to Buffalo the man came up to him with an affected look of solicitude. 'Peacocke,' he said, 'there was only nine hundred dollars in that roll.'

' There were a thousand. I counted them half-an-hour before I handed them to you.'

' There was only nine hundred when I got 'em.'

' There were all that you will get. What kind of notes were they you had when you paid for the shares at 'Frisco ? ' This question he asked out loud, before all the passengers. Then Robert Lefroy left the car, and Mr. Peacocke never saw him or heard from him again.

CONCLUSION

CHAPTER X

THE DOCTOR'S ANSWER

WHEN the Monday came there was much to be done and to be thought of at Bowick. Mrs. Peacocke on that day received a letter from San Francisco, giving her all the details of the evidence that her husband had obtained, and enclosing a copy of the photograph. There was now no reason why she should not become the true and honest wife of the man whom she had all along regarded as her husband in the sight of God. The writer declared that he would so quickly follow his letter that he might be expected home within a week, or, at the longest, ten days, from the date at which she would receive it. Immediately on his arrival at Liverpool, he would, of course, give her notice by telegraph.

When this letter reached her, she at once sent a message across to Mrs. Wortle. Would Mrs. Wortle kindly come and see her ? Mrs. Wortle was, of course, bound to do as she was asked, and started at once. But she was, in truth, but little able to give counsel on any subject outside the one which was at the moment nearest to her heart. At one o'clock, when the boys went to their dinner, Mary was to instruct her father as to the purport of the letter which was to be sent to Lord Bracy, —and Mary had not as yet come to any decision. She could not go to her father for aid ;—she could

not, at any rate, go to him until the appointed hour
should come ; and she was, therefore, entirely
thrown upon her mother. Had she been old enough
to understand the effect and the power of character,
she would have known that, at the last moment,
her father would certainly decide for her,—and had
her experience of the world been greater, she might
have been quite sure that her father would decide
in her favour. But as it was, she was quivering
and shaking in the dark, leaning on her mother's
very inefficient aid, nearly overcome with the feeling that by one o'clock she must be ready to say
something quite decided.

And in the midst of this her mother was taken
away from her, just at ten o'clock. There was not,
in truth, much that the two ladies could say to each
other. Mrs. Peacocke felt it to be necessary to
let the Doctor know that Mr. Peacocke would be
back almost at once, and took this means of doing
so. ' In a week ! ' said Mrs. Wortle, as though
painfully surprised by the suddenness of the coming
arrival.

' In a week or ten days. He was to follow his
letter as quickly as possible from San Francisco.'

' And he has found it all out ? '

' Yes ; he has learned everything, I think.
Look at this ! ' And Mrs. Peacocke handed to her
friend the photograph of the tombstone.

' Dear me ! ' said Mrs. Wortle. ' Ferdinand
Lefroy ! And this was his grave ? '

' That is his grave,' said Mrs. Peacocke, turning
her face away.

' It is very sad ; very sad indeed ;—but you had
to learn it, you know.'

'It will not be sad for him, I hope,' said Mrs. Peacocke. 'In all this, I endeavour to think of him rather than of myself. When I am forced to think of myself, it seems to me that my life has been so blighted and destroyed that it must be indifferent what happens to me now. What has happened to me has been so bad that I can hardly be injured further. But if there can be a good time coming for him,—something at least of relief, something perhaps of comfort,—then I shall be satisfied.'

'Why should there not be comfort for you both?'

'I am almost as dead to hope as I am to shame. Some year or two ago I should have thought it impossible to bear the eyes of people looking at me, as though my life had been sinful and impure. I seem now to care nothing for all that. I can look them back again with bold eyes and a brazen face, and tell them that their hardness is at any rate as bad as my impurity.'

'We have not looked at you like that,' said Mrs. Wortle.

'No; and therefore I send to you in my trouble, and tell you all this. The strangest thing of all to me is that I should have come across one man so generous as your husband, and one woman so soft-hearted as yourself.' There was nothing further to be said then. Mrs. Wortle was instructed to tell her husband that Mr. Peacocke was to be expected in a week or ten days, and then hurried back to give what assistance she could in the much more important difficulties of her own daughter.

Of course they were much more important to her. Was her girl to become the wife of a young

lord,—to be a future countess ? Was she destined
to be the mother-in-law of an earl ? Of course
this was much more important to her. And then
through it all,—being as she was a dear, good,
Christian, motherly woman,—she was well aware
that there was something, in truth, much more
important even than that. Though she thought
much of the earl-ship, and the countess-ship, and
the great revenue, and the big house at Carstairs,
and the fine park with its magnificent avenues,
and the carriage in which her daughter would be
rolled about to London parties, and the diamonds
which she would wear when she should be presented
to the Queen as the bride of the young Lord Carstairs, yet she knew very well that she ought not
in such an emergency as the present to think of
these things as being of primary importance. What
would tend most to her girl's happiness,—and welfare in this world and the next ? It was of that she
ought to think,—of that only. If some answer
were now returned to Lord Bracy, giving his lordship to understand that they, the Wortles, were
anxious to encourage the idea, then in fact her girl
would be tied to an engagement whether the young
lord should hold himself to be so tied or no ! And
how would it be with her girl if the engagement
should be allowed to run on in a doubtful way for
years, and then be dropped by reason of the young
man's indifference ? How would it be with her if,
after perhaps three or four years, a letter should
come saying that the young lord had changed his
mind, and had engaged himself to some nobler
bride ? Was it not her duty, as a mother, to save
her child from the too probable occurrence of some

crushing grief such as this ?   All of it was clear to
her mind ;—but then it was clear also that, if this
opportunity of greatness were thrown away, no
such chance in all probability would ever come
again.   Thus she was so tossed to and fro between
a prospect of glorious prosperity for her child on
one side, and the fear of terrible misfortune for
her child on the other, that she was altogether
unable to give any salutary advice.   She, at any
rate, ought to have known that her advice would
at last be of no importance.   Her experience ought
to have told her that the Doctor would certainly
settle the matter himself.   Had it been her own
happiness that was in question, her own conduct,
her own greatness, she would not have dreamed
of having an opinion of her own.   She would have
consulted the Doctor, and simply have done as he
directed.   But all this was for her child, and in a
vague, vacillating way she felt that for her child
she ought to be ready with counsel of her own.

' Mamma,' said Mary, when her mother came
back from Mrs. Peacocke, ' what am I to say when
he sends for me ? '

' If you think that you can love him, my dear——'

' Oh, mamma, you shouldn't ask me ! '

' My dear ! '

' I do like him,—very much.'

' If so—— '

' But I never thought of it before ;—and then,
if he,—if he—— '

' If he what, my dear ? '

' If he were to change his mind ? '

' Ah, yes ;—there it is.   It isn't as though you
could be married in three months' time.'

' Oh, mamma !   I shouldn't like that at all.'

' Or even in six.'

' Oh, no.'

' Of course he is very young.'

' Yes, mamma.'

' And when a young man is so very young, I suppose he doesn't quite know his own mind.'

' No, mamma.   But——'

' Well, my dear.'

' His father says that he has got—such a strong will of his own,' said poor Mary, who was anxious, unconsciously anxious, to put in a good word on her own side of the question, without making her own desire too visible.

' He always had that.   When there was any game to be played, he always liked to have his own way. But then men like that are just as likely to change as others.'

' Are they, mamma ? '

' But I do think that he is a lad of very high principle.'

' Papa has always said that of him.'

' And of fine generous feeling.   He would not change like a weather-cock.'

' If you think he would change at all, I would rather,—rather,—rather——.   Oh, mamma, why did you tell me ? '

' My darling, my child, my angel !   What am I to tell you ?   I do think of all the young men I ever knew he is the nicest, and the sweetest, and the most thoroughly good and affectionate.'

' Oh, mamma, do you ? ' said Mary, rushing at her mother and kissing her and embracing her.

' But if there were to be no regular engagement,

and you were to let him have your heart,—and then things were to go wrong ! '

Mary left the embracings, gave up the kissings, and seated herself on the sofa alone. In this way the morning was passed ;—and when Mary was summoned to her father's study, the mother and daughter had not arrived between them at any decision.

' Well, my dear,' said the Doctor, smiling, ' what am I to say to the Earl ? '

' Must you write to-day, papa ? '

' I think so. His letter is one that should not be left longer unanswered. Were we to do so, he would only think that we didn't know what to say for ourselves.'

' Would he, papa ? '

' He would fancy that we are half-ashamed to accept what has been offered to us, and yet anxious to take it.'

' I am not ashamed of anything.'

' No, my dear ; you have no reason.'

' Nor have you, papa.'

' Nor have I. That is quite true. I have never been wont to be ashamed of myself ;—nor do I think that you ever will have cause to be ashamed of yourself. Therefore, why should we hesitate ? Shall I help you, my darling, in coming to a decision on the matter ? '

' Yes, papa.'

' If I can understand your heart on this matter, it has never as yet been given to this young man.'

' No, papa.' This Mary said not altogether with that complete power of asseveration which the negative is sometimes made to bear.

' But there must be a beginning to such things.
A man throws himself into it headlong,—as my
Lord Carstairs seems to have done. At least all the
best young men do.' Mary at this point felt a great
longing to get up and kiss her father; but she
restrained herself. ' A young woman, on the other
hand, if she is such as I think you are, waits till she
is asked. Then it has to begin.' The Doctor, as he
said this, smiled his sweetest smile.

' Yes, papa.'

' And when it has begun, she does not like to
blurt it out at once, even to her loving old father.'

' Papa ! '

'That's about it, isn't it ? Haven't I hit it off ? '
He paused, as though for a reply, but she was not
as yet able to make him any. ' Come here, my dear.'
She came and stood by him, so that he could put his
arm round her waist. ' If it be as I suppose, you
are better disposed to this young man than you are
likely to be to any other, just at present.'

' Oh yes, papa.'

' To all others you are quite indifferent ? '

' Yes,—indeed, papa.'

' I am sure you are. But not quite indifferent to
this one ? Give me a kiss, my darling, and I will
take that for your speech.' Then she kissed him,—
giving him her very best kiss. ' And now, my
child, what shall I say to the Earl ? '

' I don't know, papa.'

' Nor do I, quite. I never do know what to say
till I've got the pen in my hand. But you'll commission me to write as I may think best ? '

' Oh yes, papa.'

' And I may presume that I know your mind ? '

' Yes, papa.'

' Very well. Then you had better leave me, so that I can go to work with the paper straight before me, and my pen fixed in my fingers. I can never begin to think till I find myself in that position.' Then she left him, and went back to her mother.

' Well, my dear,' said Mrs. Wortle.

' He is going to write to Lord Bracy.'

' But what does he mean to say ? '

' I don't know at all, mamma.'

' Not know ! '

' I think he means to tell Lord Bracy that he has got no objection.'

Then Mrs. Wortle was sure that the Doctor meant to face all the dangers, and that therefore it would behove her to face them also.

The Doctor, when he was left alone, sat a while thinking of the matter before he put himself into the position fitted for composition which he had described to his daughter. He acknowledged to himself that there was a difficulty in making a fit reply to the letter which he had to answer. When his mind was set on sending an indignant epistle to the Bishop, the words flew from him like lightning out of the thunder-clouds. But now he had to think much of it before he could make any light to come which should not bear a different colour from that which he intended. 'Of course such a marriage would suit my child, and would suit me,' he wished to say ;—' not only, or not chiefly, because your son is a nobleman, and will be an earl and a man of great property. That goes a long way with· us. We are too true to deny it. We hate humbug, and want you to know simply the truth about us. The

title and the money go far,—but not half so far as
the opinion which we entertain of the young man's
own good gifts. I would not give my girl to the
greatest and richest nobleman under the British
Crown, if I did not think that he would love her
and be good to her, and treat her as a husband
should treat his wife. But believing this young
man to have good gifts such as these, and a fine
disposition, I am willing, on my girl's behalf,—and
she also is willing,—to encounter the acknowledged
danger of a long engagement in the hope of realising
all the good things which would, if things went for-
tunately, thus come within her reach.' This was what
he wanted to say to the Earl, but he found it very
difficult to say it in language that should be natural.

'My DEAR LORD BRACY,—When I learned,
through Mary's mother, that Carstairs had been
here in our absence and made a declaration of love
to our girl, I was, I must confess, annoyed. I felt,
in the first place, that he was too young to have
taken in hand such a business as that ; and, in the
next, that you might not unnaturally have been
angry that your son, who had come here simply for
tuition, should have fallen into a matter of love.
I imagine that you will understand exactly what
were my feelings. There was, however, nothing to
be said about it. The evil, so far as it was an evil, had
been done, and Carstairs was going away to Oxford,
where, possibly, he might forget the whole affair.
I did not, at any rate, think it necessary to make
a complaint to you of his coming.

' To all this your letter has given altogether a
different aspect. I think that I am as little likely

as another to spend my time or thoughts in looking for external advantages, but I am as much alive as another to the great honour to myself and advantage to my child of the marriage which is suggested to her. I do not know how any more secure prospect of happiness could be opened to her than that which such a marriage offers. I have thought myself bound to give her your letter to read because her heart and her imagination have naturally been affected by what your son said to her. I think I may say of my girl that none sweeter, none more innocent, none less likely to be over-anxious for such a prospect could exist. But her heart has been touched; and though she had not dreamt of him but as an acquaintance till he came here and told his own tale, and though she then altogether declined to entertain his proposal when it was made, now that she has learnt so much more through you, she is no longer indifferent. This, I think, you will find to be natural.

' I and her mother also are of course alive to the dangers of a long engagement, and the more so because your son has still before him a considerable portion of his education. Had he asked advice either of you or of me he would of course have been counselled not to think of marriage as yet. But the very passion which has prompted him to take this action upon himself shows,—as you yourself say of him,—that he has a stronger will than is usual to be found at his years. As it is so, it is probable that he may remain constant to this as to a fixed idea.

' I think you will now understand my mind and Mary's and her mother's.' Lord Bracy as he read this declared to himself that though the Doctor's mind was very clear, Mrs. Wortle, as far as he knew, had no mind in the matter at all. 'I would suggest that the affair should remain as it is, and that each of the young people should be made to understand that any future engagement must depend, not simply on the persistency of one of them, but on the joint persistency of the two.

'If, after this, Lady Bracy should be pleased to receive Mary at Carstairs, I need not say that Mary will be delighted to make the visit.—Believe me, my dear Lord Bracy, yours most faithfully.

'JEFFREY WORTLE.'

The Earl, when he read this, though there was not a word in it to which he could take exception, was not altogether pleased. 'Of course it will be an engagement,' he said to his wife.

'Of course it will,' said the Countess. 'But then Carstairs is so very much in earnest. He would have done it for himself if you hadn't done it for him.'

'At any rate the Doctor is a gentleman,' the Earl said, comforting himself.

CHAPTER XI

MR. PEACOCKE'S RETURN

THE Earl's rejoinder to the Doctor was very short : 'So let it be.' There was not another word in the body of the letter ; but there was appended to it a postscript almost equally short ; 'Lady Bracy will write to Mary and settle with her some period for her visit.' And so it came to be understood by the Doctor, by Mrs. Wortle, and by Mary herself, that Mary was engaged to Lord Carstairs.

The Doctor, having so far arranged the matter, said little or nothing more on the subject, but turned his mind at once to that other affair of Mr. and Mrs. Peacocke. It was evident to his wife, who probably alone understood the buoyancy of his spirit and its corresponding susceptibility to depression, that he at once went about Mr. Peacocke's affairs with renewed courage. Mr. Peacocke should resume his duties as soon as he was remarried, and let them see what Mrs. Stantiloup or the Bishop would dare to say then ! It was impossible, he thought, that parents would be such asses as to suppose that their boys' morals could be affected to evil by connection with a man so true, so gallant, and so manly as this. He did not at this time say anything further as to abandoning the school, but seemed to imagine that the vacancies would get themselves filled up as in the course of nature. He ate his dinner again as though he liked it, and abused the Liberals, and was anxious about the grapes and peaches, as was always the case with him when things were going well. All this, as Mrs. Wortle understood, had come to him from the brilliancy of Mary's prospects.

But though he held his tongue on the subject, Mrs. Wortle did not. She found it absolutely impossible not to talk of it when she was alone with Mary, or alone with the Doctor. As he counselled her not to make Mary think too much about it, she was obliged to hold her peace when both were with her ; but with either of them alone she was always full of it. To the Doctor she communicated all her fears and all her doubts, showing only too plainly that she would be altogether broken-hearted if any-

thing should interfere with the grandeur and prosperity which seemed to be partly within reach, but
not altogether within reach of her darling child. If
he, Carstairs, should prove to be a recreant young
lord ! If Aristotle and Socrates should put love out
of his heart ! * If those other wicked young lords at
Christ-Church* were to teach him that it was a
foolish thing for a young lord to become engaged to
his tutor's daughter before he had taken his degree !
If some better born young lady were to come in his
way and drive Mary out of his heart ! No more
lovely or better girl could be found to do so ;—of
that she was sure. To the latter assertion the
Doctor agreed, telling her that, as it was so, she
ought to have a stronger trust in her daughter's
charms,—telling her also, with somewhat sterner
voice, that she should not allow herself to be so
disturbed by the glories of the Bracy coronet. In
this there was, I think, some hypocrisy. Had the
Doctor been as simple as his wife in showing her
own heart, it would probably have been found that
he was as much set upon the coronet as she.

Then Mrs. Wortle would carry the Doctor's
wisdom to her daughter. 'Papa says, my dear,
that you shouldn't think of it too much.'

'I do think of him, mamma. I do love him now,
and of course I think of him.'

'Of course you do, my dear ;—of course you do.
How should you not think of him when he is all in
all to you ? But papa means that it can hardly be
called an engagement yet.'

'I don't know what it should be called ; but
of course I love him. He can change it if he
likes.'

'But you shouldn't think of it, knowing his rank and wealth.'

'I never did, mamma ; but he is what he is, and I must think of him.'

Poor Mrs. Wortle did not know what special advice to give when this declaration was made. To have held her tongue would have been the wisest, but that was impossible to her. Out of the full heart the mouth speaks,* and her heart was very full of Lord Carstairs and of Carstairs House, and of the diamonds which her daughter would certainly be called upon to wear before the Queen,—if only that young man would do his duty.

Poor Mary herself probably had the worst of it. No provision was made either for her to see her lover or to write to him. The only interview which had ever taken place between them as lovers was that on which she had run by him into the house, leaving him, as the Earl had said, planted on the terrace. She had never been able to whisper one single soft word into his ear, to give him even one touch of her fingers in token of her affection. She did not in the least know when she might be allowed to see him,— whether it had not been settled among the elders that they were not to see each other as real lovers till he should have taken his degree,—which would be almost in a future world, so distant seemed the time. It had been already settled that she was to go to Carstairs in the middle of November and stay till the middle of December ; but it was altogether settled that her lover was not to be at Carstairs during the time. He was to be at Oxford then, and would be thinking only of his Greek and Latin,— or perhaps amusing himself, in utter forgetfulness

that he had a heart belonging to him at Bowick
Parsonage. In this way Mary, though no doubt
she thought the most of it all, had less opportunity
of talking of it than either her father or her
mother.

In the mean time Mr. Peacocke was coming
home. The Doctor, as soon as he heard that the
day was fixed, or nearly fixed, being then, as has
been explained, in full good humour with all the
world except Mrs. Stantiloup and the Bishop, be-
thought himself as to what steps might best be
taken in the very delicate matter in which he was
called upon to give advice. He had declared at
first that they should be married at his own parish
church ; but he felt that there would be difficulties
in this. ' She must go up to London and meet him
there,' he said to Mrs. Wortle. ' And he must not
show himself here till he brings her down as his
actual wife.' Then there was very much to be
done in arranging all this. And something to be
done also in making those who had been his friends,
and perhaps more in making those who had been
his enemies, understand exactly how the matter
stood. Had no injury been inflicted upon him, as
though he had done evil to the world in general
in befriending Mr. Peacocke, he would have been
quite willing to pass the matter over in silence
among his friends ; but as it was he could not afford
to hide his own light under a bushel. He was being
punished almost to the extent of ruin by the cruel
injustice which had been done him by the evil
tongue of Mrs. Stantiloup, and, as he thought, by
the folly of the Bishop. He must now let those
who had concerned themselves know as accurately

as he could what he had done in the matter, and
what had been the effect of his doing. He wrote a
letter, therefore, which was not, however, to be
posted till after the Peacocke marriage had been
celebrated, copies of which he prepared with his
own hand in order that he might send them to the
Bishop and to Lady Ann Clifford, and to Mr. Talbot and,—not, indeed, to Mrs. Stantiloup, but to
Mrs. Stantiloup's husband. There was a copy also
made for Mr. Momson, though in his heart he despised Mr. Momson thoroughly. In this letter he
declared the great respect which he had entertained, since he had first known them, both for Mr.
and Mrs. Peacocke, and the distress which he had
felt when Mr. Peacocke had found himself obliged
to explain to him the facts,—the facts which need
not be repeated, because the reader is so well acquainted with them. ' Mr. Peacocke,' he went on
to say, ' has since been to America, and has found
that the man whom he believed to be dead when he
married his wife, has died since his calamitous reappearance. Mr. Peacocke has seen the man's
grave, with the stone on it bearing his name, and
has brought back with him certificates and evidence
as to his burial.

' Under these circumstances, I have no hesitation in re-employing both him and his wife ; and
I think that you will agree that I could not do less.
I think you will agree, also, that in the whole
transaction I have done nothing of which the parent
of any boy intrusted to me has a right to complain.'

Having done this, he went up to London, and
made arrangements for having the marriage celebrated there as soon as possible after the arrival of

Mr. Peacocke. And on his return to Bowick, he
went off to Mr. Puddicombe with a copy of his
letter in his pocket. He had not addressed a copy
to his friend, nor had he intended that one should
be sent to him. Mr. Puddicombe had not interfered
in regard to the boys, and had, on the whole, shown
himself to be a true friend. There was no need for
him to advocate his cause to Mr. Puddicombe. But
it was right, he thought, that that gentleman
should know what he did ; and it might be that he
hoped that he would at length obtain some praise
from Mr. Puddicombe. But Mr. Puddicombe did
not like the letter. ' It does not tell the truth,' he
said.

' Not the truth ! '

' Not the whole truth.'

' As how ! Where have I concealed anything ? '

' If I understand the question rightly, they who
have thought proper to take their children away
from your school because of Mr. Peacocke, have
done so because that gentleman continued to live
with that lady when they both knew that they were
not man and wife.'

' That wasn't my doing.'

' You condoned it. I am not condemning you.
You condoned it, and now you defend yourself in
this letter. But in your defence you do not really
touch the offence as to which you are, according to
your own showing, accused. In telling the whole
story, you should say : " They did live together
though they were not married ;—and, under all
the circumstances, I did not think that they were
on that account unfit to be left in charge of my
boys." '

'But I sent him away immediately,—to America.'

'You allowed the lady to remain.'

'Then what would you have me say?' demanded the Doctor.

'Nothing,' said Mr. Puddicombe ;—' not a word. Live it down in silence. There will be those, like myself, who, though they could not dare to say that in morals you were strictly correct, will love you the better for what you did.' The Doctor turned his face towards the dry, hard-looking man and showed that there was a tear in each of his eyes. 'There are few of us not so infirm as sometimes to love best that which is not best. But when a man is asked a downright question, he is bound to answer the truth.'

'You would say nothing in your own defence.'

'Not a word. You know the French proverb : "Who excuses himself is his own accuser."* The truth generally makes its way. As far as I can see, a slander never lives long.'

'Ten of my boys are gone!' said the Doctor, who had not hitherto spoken a word of this to any one out of his own family ;—' ten out of twenty.'

'That will only be a temporary loss.'

'That is nothing,—nothing. It is the idea that the school should be failing.'

'They will come again. I do not believe that that letter would bring a boy. I am almost inclined to say, Dr. Wortle, that a man should never defend himself.'

'He should never have to defend himself.'

'It is much the same thing. But I'll tell you what I'll do, Dr. Wortle,—if it will suit your plans. I will go up with you and will assist at the marriage.

I do not for a moment think that you will require
any countenance, or that if you did, that I could
give it you.'

' No man that I know so efficiently.'

' But it may be that Mr. Peacocke will like to
find that the clergymen from his neighbourhood are
standing with him.' And so it was settled, that
when the day should come on which the Doctor
would take Mrs. Peacocke up with him to London,
Mr. Puddicombe was to accompany them.

The Doctor when he left Mr. Puddicombe's parsonage had by no means pledged himself not to
send the letters. When a man has written a letter,
and has taken some trouble with it, and more
especially when he has copied it several times himself so as to have made many letters of it,—when
he has argued his point successfully to himself, and
has triumphed in his own mind, as was likely to be
the case with Dr. Wortle in all that he did, he does
not like to make waste paper of his letters. As
he rode home he tried to persuade himself that he
might yet use them. He could not quite admit his
friend's point. Mr. Peacocke, no doubt, had known
his own condition, and him a strict moralist might
condemn. But he,—he,—Dr. Wortle,—had known
nothing. All that he had done was not to condemn
the other man when he did know ! '

Nevertheless as he rode into his own yard, he
made up his mind that he would burn the letters.
He had shown them to no one else. He had not
even mentioned them to his wife. He could burn
them without condemning himself in the opinion
of any one. And he burned them. When Mr.
Puddicombe found him at the station at Broughton

as they were about to proceed to London with Mrs.
Peacocke, he simply whispered the fate of the
letters. 'After what you said I destroyed what
I had written.'

'Perhaps it was as well,' said Mr. Puddicombe.

When the telegram came to say that Mr. Peacocke was at Liverpool, Mrs. Peacocke was anxious
immediately to rush up to London. But she was
restrained by the Doctor,—or rather by Mrs.
Wortle under the Doctor's orders. 'No, my dear ;
no. You must not go till all will be ready for you
to meet him in the church. The Doctor says so.'

'Am I not to see him till he comes up to the
altar ? '

On this there was another consultation between
Mrs. Wortle and the Doctor, at which she explained how impossible it would be for the woman
to go through the ceremony with due serenity and
propriety of manner unless she should be first
allowed to throw herself into his arms, and to welcome him back to her. 'Yes,' she said, 'he can
come and see you at the hotel on the evening before,
and again in the morning,—so that if there be a
word to say you can say it. Then when it is over he
will bring you down here. The Doctor and Mr.
Puddicombe will come down by a later train. Of
course it is painful,' said Mrs. Wortle, 'but you
must bear up.' To her it seemed to be so painful
that she was quite sure that she could not have
borne it. To be married for the third time, and for
the second time to the same husband ! To Mrs.
Peacocke, as she thought of it, the pain did not so
much rest in that, as in the condition of life which
these things had forced upon her.

'I must go up to town to-morrow, and must be away for two days,' said the Doctor out loud in the school, speaking immediately to one of the ushers, but so that all the boys present might hear him. 'I trust that we shall have Mr. Peacocke with us the day after to-morrow.'

'We shall be very glad of that,' said the usher.

'And Mrs. Peacocke will come and eat her dinner again like before?' asked a little boy.

'I hope so, Charley.'

'We shall like that, because she has to eat it all by herself now.'

All the school, down even to Charley, the smallest boy in it, knew all about it. Mr. Peacocke had gone to America, and Mrs. Peacocke was going up to London to be married once more to her own husband,—and the Doctor and Mr. Puddicombe were both going to marry them. The usher of course knew the details more clearly than that,—as did probably the bigger boys. There had even been a rumour of the photograph which had been seen by one of the maid-servants,—who had, it is to be feared, given the information to the French teacher. So much, however, the Doctor had felt it wise to explain, not thinking it well that Mr. Peacocke should make his reappearance among them without notice.

On the afternoon of the next day but one, Mr. and Mrs. Peacocke were driven up to the school in one of the Broughton flys. She went quickly up into her own house, when Mr. Peacocke walked into the school. The boys clustered round him, and the three assistants, and every word said to him was kind and friendly;—but in the whole course of his troubles there had never been a moment to him more difficult than this,—in which he found it so nearly impossible to say anything or to say nothing. ' Yes, I have been over very many miles since I saw you last.' This was an answer to young Talbot, who asked him whether he had not been a great traveller whilst he was away.

' In America,' suggested the French usher, who had heard of the photograph, and knew very well where it had been taken.

' Yes, in America.'

' All the way to San Francisco,' suggested Charley.

' All the way to San Francisco, Charley,—and back again.'

' Yes; I know you're come back again,' said Charley, ' because I see you here.'

' There are only twenty boys this half,' said one of the twenty.

' Then I shall have more time to attend to you now.'

' I suppose so,' said the lad, not seeming to find any special consolation in that view of the matter.

Painful as this first re-introduction had been, there was not much more in it than that. No questions were asked, and no explanations expected. It may be that Mrs. Stantiloup was affected with fresh moral horrors when she heard of the return, and that the Bishop said that the Doctor was foolish and headstrong as ever. It may be that there was a good deal of talk about it in the Close at Broughton. But at the school there was very little more said about it than what has been stated above.

CHAPTER XII

MARY'S SUCCESS

IN this last chapter of our short story I will venture to run rapidly over a few months so as to explain how the affairs of Bowick arranged themselves up to the end of the current year. I cannot pretend that the reader shall know, as he ought to be made to know, the future fate and fortunes of our personages. They must be left still struggling. But then is not such always in truth the case, even when the happy marriage has been celebrated ?— even when, in the course of two rapid years, two normal children make their appearance to gladden the hearts of their parents ?

Mr. and Mrs. Peacocke fell into their accustomed duties in the diminished school, apparently without difficulty. As the Doctor had not sent those ill-judged letters he of course received no replies, and was neither troubled by further criticism nor consoled by praise as to his conduct. Indeed, it almost seemed to him as though the thing, now that it was done, excited less observation than it deserved. He heard no more of the metropolitan press, and was surprised to find that the ' Broughton Gazette ' inserted only a very short paragraph, in which it stated that ' they had been given to understand that Mr. and Mrs. Peacocke had resumed their usual duties at the Bowick School, after the performance of an interesting ceremony in London, at which Dr. Wortle and Mr. Puddicombe had assisted.' The press, as far as the Doctor was aware, said nothing more on the subject. And if remarks injurious to his conduct were made by the Stantiloups and the Momsons, they did not reach his ears. Very soon after the return of the Peacockes there was a grand dinner-party at the palace, to which the Doctor and his wife were invited. It was not a clerical dinner-party, and so the honour was the greater. The aristocracy of the neighbourhood were there, including Lady Anne Clifford, who was devoted, with almost repentant affection, to her old friend. And Lady Margaret Momson was there, the only clergyman's wife besides his own, who declared to him with unblushing audacity that she had never regretted anything so much in her life as that Augustus should have been taken away from the school. It was evident that there had been an intention at the palace to make what amends the palace could for the injuries it had done.

' Did Lady Anne say anything about the boys ? ' asked Mrs. Wortle, as they were going home.

' She was going to, but I would not let her. I managed to show her that I did not wish it, and she was clever enough to stop.'

' I shouldn't wonder if she sent them back,' said Mrs. Wortle.

' She won't do that. Indeed, I doubt whether I should take them. But if it should come to pass that she should wish to send them back, you may be sure that others will come. In such a matter she is very good as a weathercock, showing how the wind blows.' In this way the dinner-party at the palace was in a degree comforting and consolatory.

But an incident which of all was most comforting

and most consolatory to one of the inhabitants of
the parsonage took place two or three days after
the dinner-party. On going out of his own hall-
door one Saturday afternoon, immediately after
lunch, whom should the Doctor see driving himself
into the yard in a hired gig from Broughton—but
young Lord Carstairs. There had been no promise,
or absolute compact made, but it certainly had
seemed to be understood by all of them that
Carstairs was not to show himself at Bowick till
at some long distant period, when he should have
finished all the trouble of his education. It was
understood even that he was not to be at Carstairs
during Mary's visit,—so imperative was it that the
young people should not meet. And now here he
was getting out of a gig in the Rectory yard!
'Halloa! Carstairs, is that you?'

'Yes, Dr. Wortle,—here I am.'

'We hardly expected to see you, my boy.'

'No,—I suppose not. But when I heard that
Mr. Peacocke had come back, and all about his
marriage, you know, I could not but come over to
see him. He and I have always been such great
friends.'

'Oh,—to see Mr. Peacocke?'

'I thought he'd think it unkind if I didn't look
him up. He has made it all right; hasn't he?'

'Yes;—he has made it all right, I think. A
finer fellow never lived. But he'll tell you all about
it. He travelled with a pistol in his pocket, and
seemed to want it too. I suppose you must come
in and see the ladies after we have been to Peacocke?'

'I suppose I can just see them,' said the young

lord, as though moved by equal anxiety as to the mother and as to the daughter.

'I'll leave word that you are here, and then we'll go into the school.' So the Doctor found a servant, and sent what message he thought fit into the house.

'Lord Carstairs here?'

'Yes, indeed, Miss! He's with your papa, going across to the school. He told me to take word in to Missus that he supposes his lordship will stay to dinner.' The maid who carried the tidings, and who had received no commission to convey them to Miss Mary, was, no doubt, too much interested in an affair of love, not to take them first to the one that would be most concerned with them.

That very morning Mary had been bemoaning herself as to her hard condition. Of what use was it to her to have a lover, if she was never to see him, never to hear from him,—only to be told about him,—that she was not to think of him more than she could help? She was already beginning to think that a long engagement carried on after this fashion would have more of suffering in it than she had anticipated. It seemed to her that while she was, and always would be, thinking of him, he never, never would continue to think of her. If it could be only a word once a month it would be something,—just one or two written words under an envelope,—even that would have sufficed to keep her hope alive! But never to see him;—never to hear from him! Her mother had told her that very morning that there was to be no meeting,—probably for three years, till he should have done with Oxford. And here he was

in the house,—and her papa had sent in word to
say that he was to eat his dinner there! It so
astonished her that she felt that she would be
afraid to meet him. Before she had had a minute
to think of it all, her mother was with her. ' Carstairs, love, is here ! '

' Oh mamma, what has brought him ? '

' He has gone into the school with your papa to
see Mr. Peacocke. He always was very fond of
Mr. Peacocke.' For a moment something of a
feeling of jealousy crossed her heart,—but only
for a moment. He would not surely have come
to Bowick if he had begun to be indifferent to her
already ! ' Papa says that he will probably stay
to dinner.'

' Then I am to see him ? '

' Yes ;—of course you must see him.'

' I didn't know, mamma.'

' Don't you wish to see him ? '

' Oh yes, mamma. If he were to come and go,
and we were not to meet at all, I should think it
was all over then. Only,—I don't know what to
say to him.'

' You must take that as it comes, my dear.'

Two hours afterwards they were walking, the
two of them alone together, out in the Bowick
woods. When once the law,—which had been
rather understood than spoken,—had been in-
fringed and set at naught, there was no longer
any use in endeavouring to maintain a semblance
of its restriction. The two young people had met
in the presence both of the father and mother, and
the lover had had her in his arms before either of
them could interfere. There had been a little

scream from Mary, but it may probably be said of her that she was at the moment the happiest young lady in the diocese.

' Does your father know you are here ? ' said the Doctor, as he led the young lord back from the school into the house.

' He knows I'm coming, for I wrote and told my mother. I always tell everything ; but it 's sometimes best to make up your mind before you get an answer.' Then the Doctor made up his mind that Lord Carstairs would have his own way in anything that he wished to accomplish.

' Won't the Earl be angry ? ' Mrs. Wortle asked.

' No ;—not angry. He knows the world too well not to be quite sure that something of the kind would happen. And he is too fond of his son not to think well of anything that he does. It wasn't to be supposed that they should never meet. After all that has passed I am bound to make him welcome if he chooses to come here, and as Mary's lover to give him the best welcome that I can. He won't stay, I suppose, because he has got no clothes.'

' But he has ;—John brought in a portmanteau and a dressing-bag out of the gig.' So that was settled.

In the meantime Lord Carstairs had taken Mary out for a walk into the wood, and she, as she walked beside him, hardly knew whether she was going on her head or her heels. This, indeed, it was to have a lover. In the morning she was thinking that when three years were past he would hardly care to see her ever again. And now they were together among the falling leaves, and sitting about under the branches as though there was nothing in the

world to separate them. Up to that day there had
never been a word between them but such as is
common to mere acquaintances, and now he was
calling her every instant by her Christian name,
and telling her all his secrets.

'We have such jolly woods at Carstairs,' he
said; 'but we shan't be able to sit down when
we're there, because it will be winter. We shall
be hunting, and you must come out and see us.'

'But you won't be there when I am,' she said,
timidly.

'Won't I? That's all you know about it. I can
manage better than that.'

'You'll be at Oxford.'

'You must stay over Christmas, Mary; that's
what you must do. You musn't think of going till
January.'

'But Lady Bracy won't want me.'

'Yes, she will. We must make her want you.
At any rate they'll understand this; if you don't
stay for me, I shall come home even if it's in the
middle of term. I'll arrange that. You don't
suppose I'm not going to be there when you make
your first visit to the old place.'

All this was being in Paradise. She felt when she
walked home with him, and when she was alone
afterwards in her own room, that, in truth, she had
only liked him before. Now she loved him. Now
she was beginning to know him, and to feel that she
would really,—really die of a broken heart if anything were to rob her of him. But she could let
him go now, without a feeling of discomfort, if she
thought that she was to see him again when she
was at Carstairs.

But this was not the last walk in the woods, even
on this occasion. He remained two days at Bowick,
so necessary was it for him to renew his intimacy
with Mr. Peacocke. He explained that he had got
two days' leave from the tutor of his College, and
that two days, in college parlance, always meant
three. He would be back on the third day, in time
for ' gates '; and that was all which the strictest
college discipline would require of him. It need
hardly be said of him that the most of his time he
spent with Mary; but he did manage to devote an
hour or two to his old friend, the school-assistant.

Mr. Peacocke told his whole story, and Carstairs,
whose morals were perhaps not quite so strict as
those of Mr. Puddicombe, gave him all his sympathy. ' To think that a man can be such a brute
as that,' he said, when he heard that Ferdinand
Lefroy had shown himself to his wife at St. Louis,
—' only on a spree.'

' There is no knowing to what depth utter ruin
may reduce a man who has been born to better
things. He falls into idleness, and then comforts
himself with drink. So it seems to have been with
him.'

' And that other fellow ;—do you think he meant
to shoot you ? '

' Never. But he meant to frighten me. And
when he brought out his knife in the bedroom at
Leavenworth he did. My pistol was not loaded.'

' Why not ? '

' Because little as I wish to be murdered, I should
prefer that to murdering any one else. But he
didn't mean it. His only object was to get as much
out of me as he could. As for me, I couldn't give

him more because I hadn't got it.' After that they
made a league of friendship, and Mr. Peacocke
promised that he would, on some distant occasion,
take his wife with him on a visit to Carstairs.

It was about a month after this that Mary was
packed up and sent on her journey to Carstairs.
When that took place, the Doctor was in supreme
good-humour. There had come a letter from the
father of the two Mowbrays, saying that he had
again changed his mind. He had, he said, heard
a story told two ways. He trusted Dr. Wortle
would understand him and forgive him, when he
declared that he had believed both the stories. If
after this the Doctor chose to refuse to take his
boys back again, he would have, he acknowledged,
no ground for offence. But if the Doctor would
take them, he would intrust them to the Doctor's
care with the greatest satisfaction in the world,—
as he had done before.

For a while the Doctor had hesitated ; but here,
perhaps for the first time in her life, his wife was
allowed to persuade him. 'They are such leading
people,' she said.

'Who cares for that ? I have never gone in for
that.' This, however, was hardly true. 'When I
have been sure that a man is a gentleman, I have
taken his son without inquiring much farther. It
was mean of him to withdraw after I had acceded
to his request.'

'But he withdraws his withdrawal in such a
flattering way ! ' Then the Doctor assented, and
the two boys were allowed to come. Lady Anne
Clifford hearing this, learning that the Doctor was
so far willing to relent, became very piteous and

implored forgiveness. The noble relatives were all willing now. It had not been her fault. As far as she was concerned herself she had always been anxious that her boys should remain at Bowick. And so the two Cliffords came back to their old beds in the old room.

Mary, when she first arrived at Carstairs, hardly knew how to carry herself. Lady Bracy was very cordial and the Earl friendly, but for the first two days nothing was said about Carstairs. There was no open acknowledgment of her position. But then she had expected none ; and though her tongue was burning to talk, of course she did not say a word. But before a week was over Lady Bracy had begun, and by the end of the fortnight Lord Bracy had given her a beautiful brooch. ' That means,' said Lady Bracy in the confidence of her own little sitting-room up-stairs, ' that he looks upon you as his daughter.'

' Does it ? '

' Yes, my dear, yes.' Then they fell to kissing each other, and did nothing but talk about Carstairs and all his perfections, and his unalterable love, and how these three years could be made to wear themselves away, till the conversation,— simmering over as such conversation is wont to do,—gave the whole household to understand that Miss Wortle was staying there as Lord Carstairs's future bride.

Of course she stayed over the Christmas, or went back to Bowick for a week, and then returned to Carstairs, so that she might tell her mother everything, and hear of the six new boys who were to come after the holidays. ' Papa couldn't take both

the Buncombes,' said Mrs. Wortle in her triumph,
' and one must remain till midsummer. Sir George
did say that it must be two or none, but he had to
give way. I wanted papa to have another bed in
the east room, but he wouldn't hear of it.'

Mary went back for the Christmas and Carstairs
came ; and the house was full, and everybody
knew of the engagement. She walked with him,
and rode with him, and danced with him, and
talked secrets with him,—as though there were no
Oxford, no degree before him. No doubt it was
very imprudent, but the Earl and the Countess
knew all about it. What might be, or would be,
or was the end of such folly, it is not my purpose
here to tell. I fear that there was trouble before
them. It may, however, be possible that the
degree should be given up on the score of love,
and Lord Carstairs should marry his bride,—at
any rate when he came of age.

As to the school, it certainly suffered nothing by
the Doctor's generosity, and when last I heard of
Mr. Peacocke, the Bishop had offered to grant him
a licence for the curacy. Whether he accepted it
I have not yet heard, but I am inclined to think
that in this matter he will adhere to his old determination.

THE END

NOTES

Passages quoted from Trollope's letter to Blackwood and Blackwood's to Trollope are taken from *The Letters of Anthony Trollope*, ed. N. John Hall, 2 vols. (Stanford, Ca., 1983), II, 856 (Trollope to Blackwood), 859 and 861n (Blackwood to Trollope), respectively.

PART I

1   *D.D.*: Doctor of Divinity. Dr. Wortle is an ordained clergyman. See note to p. 3, below.

     Fellow of Exeter: Exeter College, Oxford.

2   *glebe*: land belonging or yielding revenue to a parish church or ecclesiastical benefice.

     Jupiter: the chief god in Roman mythology; here, lord and master.

3   *Dr. Wortle,—or Mr. Wortle, as he should be called in reference to that period*: in the eighteenth and nineteenth centuries (and even today), after a clergyman had attained a reputation—as, for example, a scholar or headmaster—he was almost always awarded a Doctor of Divinity degree, usually from his old university. Thomas Arnold, for instance, was given a DD from Oxford when he became headmaster of Rugby in 1828. The point is that about this time (see note to p. 4, below) Wortle had gained a professional position respected enough to make him eligible for, and the recipient of, the almost obligatory DD.

4   *Low Church*: that section of the Church of England holding opinions which give a 'low' place to the authority and claims of the Episcopate and the priesthood, to the inherent grace of the sacraments, and to matters of ecclesiastical organization, thus differing little from Protestant Nonconformists and their opinions. By this time the term 'Low Church' was used more specifically to designate the Evangelicals, with whom Trollope was not in sympathy. They were, as he says here, 'more given to interference'—that is, stricter on the subject of moral conduct. Trollope preferred his clergymen to be less strict, and Dr. Wortle is accordingly more easy-going than his Low Church brethren.

     or Dr. Wortle, as he came to be called about this time: see note to p. 3, above.

5 *Dissenters*: those who dissent in matters of religious belief or worship, or separate themselves from any specified church, or disagree with the principle of national or state churches. In Trollope's time the term often designated those who would not take communion in the Established Church of England.

6 *Honourable*: a courtesy title only, suggesting that Mrs. Stantiloup is descended from a titled family.

8 *ushers*: assistant teachers.

cormorant: that is, greedy and rapacious.

she alone knew the length of the Doctor's foot: she alone knew how to get round him, or get from him what she wanted.

12 *Utopian*: suggests the Doctor was being impractically idealistic.

a Classic: that is, a scholar of the classics.

13 *giving up his Fellowship as a matter of course*: in those days, Fellows of colleges could not retain their fellowships if they married.

a thorough-going Tory of the old school . . . bound to hate the name of a republic: Trollope means that Dr. Wortle thinks of himself as being a conservative in politics. In fact, his subsequent behaviour is anything but conservative.

18 *there was something 'rotten in the state of Denmark'*: a reference to Shakespeare's *Hamlet* (1600–1), I. iv; that is, things are not what they should be.

20 *a t'other school*: an English preparatory school—which in England always means preparatory to a public school (as, here, Eton) and not, as in the US, to university. Though some of Dr. Wortle's pupils are old enough to be preparing directly for university, his is primarily a 't'other school' in this sense.

23 *sherry-negus*: a mixture of sherry and, usually, hot water, sugar, lemon juice, and nutmeg.

26 *virago*: shrew.

28 *the 'Black Dwarf' . . . 'The Pirate'*: references to novels by Sir Walter Scott (1771–1832), *The Black Dwarf* (1816) and *The Pirate* (1821), and to the plots of these novels. Trollope means that he is less interested here in melodrama and spectacular revelations of plot than in the nature of his characters. See his letter to the publisher John Blackwood (19 September 1867) regarding his story *Linda Tressel*, serialized in *Blackwood's Magazine* in 1867–8: 'It is hardly possible for a novelist who depends more on character than on incident for his interest always to make the chief personages of his stories pleasant

acquaintances. His object is to shew what is the effect of such and such qualities on the happiness of those on whom they act; and in doing this he can hardly contrive that a nice young man should always be there to be married to the nice young woman. It may be so now & again; but not always—Scott & his followers, who deal with incidents chiefly,—from the taking of a castle . . . down to the elopement of a lady with her groom, have of course always been able at their pleasure to have a Rowena ready for their Ivanhoe,—or a Polly Jones for their Jack Smith as the case may be. Do not suppose that I am turning up my nose at stories of action, which I regard as of far away the highest class if written with the requisite power,—but am simply describing the difference between the work of such workers and my own.' Quoted from *The Letters of Anthony Trollope*, ed. N. John Hall, 2 vols. (Stanford, Ca., 1983), I, 390.

the war of the Secession: the British gave this name to the American Civil War (1861–5).

Abolition: the Abolitionists of the North wished to abolish institutionalized black slavery in the South. Trollope elsewhere makes it clear that in his opinion the Abolitionists were often opportunists and hypocrites seeking a pretext for war—though he was staunchly anti-slavery, and one of the few prominent Englishmen of his time openly to support the Northern cause in the Civil War. There are other references of this sort to the Abolitionists: see notes to pp. 204 and 232, below.

29 *the borders of Texas*: Texas declared its independence from Mexico, of which it was originally a part, in 1863; various kinds of warfare flourished along the hotly disputed Texas–Mexico border for some years afterwards.

PART II

35 *facile princeps*: Latin, meaning the leading man, easily the first; a common school phrase of the day.

46 *'Whither thou goest,' etc.*: Peacocke quotes Ruth, 1:16.

59 *'Dabit Deus his quoque finem'*: Latin, meaning God will assign a limit even to these troubles; that is, God won't give us burdens beyond our capacity to bear. Quoted from Virgil's *Aeneid*, I. 199; Aeneas is comforting his sailors during the great storm.

65 *frogged buttons*: ornamental braiding for fastening the front

of a garment, usually buttons with loops through which they
can pass.

PART III

67 *cut*: drunk.

80 *'Nil conscire sibi,—nulla pallescere culpa'*: quoted from the
Epistles of Horace, Roman poet (65–8 BC): not to be conscious
of any wrongdoing, to have no guilt to make you turn pale.

92 more *'sinned against than sinning'*: Lear's characterization of
himself in Shakespeare's *King Lear* (1605–6), III. ii.

PART IV

120 *quasi*: that is, apparent.

faggot: used here in the sense of cipher, or dummy.

Quixotic: a dreamer or visionary—like the protagonist of
Cervantes' *Don Quixote* (1605–12).

129 *a dowdy*: a woman (or girl) unattractively or shabbily
dressed, without smartness, brightness, or freshness.

132 *Old Mother Shipton*: according to tradition, a witch and
prophetess who lived in the late fifteenth and early sixteenth
centuries, and produced prophecies of notable events. Her
authenticity is not supported by serious historical authority.

133 *Priam*: King of Troy during the Trojan War, in the course of
which the invading and ultimately victorious Greeks slew in
battle his many sons.

PART V

138 *'penny-a-liner'*: someone who is paid a penny a line for his
writing; a hack writer.

144 *Sir Samuel Griffin*: Trollope has misremembered the given
name of Lieutenant-General Sir George Griffin, KCB, who
appears in *The Yellowplush Papers* (1837) of William Makepeace Thackeray (1811–63). Sir George's death, at the age of
seventy-seven, forms the opening incident in a story here
called 'Mr. Deuceace at Paris'. There is an immensely
complicated business over Sir George's will, with his widow,
aged twenty-seven, and his daughter by his deceased first
wife fighting over his fortune. The resurrection of Sir George
and the first Lady Griffin would have made matters, if
possible, even more confusing.

154 *'τυπτω' in the school . . . 'amo' in the cool of the evening*: the
Greek word, pronounced *tupto* (long o), means 'I beat', or 'I
strike'—or perhaps, in a school context, 'I cane'. *Amo* means

'I love'. Both words are conjugated regularly, and *amo* is often the conjugation taught beginners in Latin. τυπτω was frequently assigned by facetious schoolmasters to remind pupils of what might happen if they did not learn their lessons. *Everybody's Business* obviously has a clever, malicious, and classically trained writer working for it. What he says in sum here is that after a hot morning teaching pupils how to conjugate the Greek verb suggesting the beating or caning of his pupils, Dr. Wortle spends the cool of his evenings conjugating with the attractive Mrs. Peacocke the Latin verb to love. There is also a submerged pun here: conjugation/conjugal.

165 *shirt of Nessus*: a poisoned shirt used, according to tradition, by the centaur Nessus to wreak revenge upon Hercules, who shot him with a poisoned arrow. Nessus gave Hercules' wife Deianira his blood-spattered tunic as he was dying, telling her that it had the power to reclaim a husband from unlawful loves. When Hercules was unfaithful to her, Deianira sent him the shirt of Nessus, which caused his death.

185 *in terrorem*: Latin for in fear, in terror.

194 *D.T.*: delirium tremens, brought on by drink; see p. 217 of the text.

198 *Ogden Junction*: a town in northern Utah.

200 *Leavenworth*: north-eastern Kansas town on the Missouri River north-west of Kansas City.

202 *circular notes*: letters of credit, still used by wealthy travellers in preference to travellers' cheques, addressed to various banks along the route of the tour (hence 'circular'), authorizing them to pay the holder up to a certain amount of cash. Only the person to whom they are issued can use them.

bowie-knife: a stout, straight, single-edged hunting knife; after James Bowie (died 1836), an American soldier and hunter.

204 *the horrors*: delirium tremens, brought on by drink.

these accursed Northern hypocrites: see note to p. 28 (3), above.

209 *War had destroyed everything*: that is, the American Civil War.

218 *hipped*: morbidly depressed.

220 *tant mieux*: French, meaning so much the better.

230 *to lie perdu*: that is, to lie low, lost from the sight of others; to hide out.

232 *them psalm-singing rogues from New England*: another
reference to the Northern Abolitionists in the late Civil War;
see note to p. 28 (3), above.

236 *crammer*: someone who tutors students in order to help them
pass examinations; used here contemptuously in reference to
Peacocke's profession of teacher.

CONCLUSION

253 *If Aristotle and Socrates should put love out of his heart!*:
that is, if during his years at university he should forget her,
or cease to love her.

Christ-Church: the Oxford college at which Lord Carstairs is
to be enrolled.

254 *Out of the full heart the mouth speaks*: a paraphrase of
Matthew, 12:34: 'Out of the abundance of the heart the mouth
speaketh.'

258 *'Who excuses himself is his own accuser'*: French proverb:
Qui s'excuse, s'accuse.

THE WORLD'S CLASSICS

A Select List

Oliver Twist
Edited by Kathleen Tillotson

Sikes and Nancy and Other Public Readings
Edited by Philip Collins

ARTHUR CONAN DOYLE
Sherlock Holmes: Selected Stories
With an introduction by S. C. Roberts

GEORGE ELIOT: The Mill on the Floss
Edited by Gordon S. Haight

HENRY FIELDING: Joseph Andrews *and* Shamela
Edited by Douglas Brooks-Davies

GUSTAVE FLAUBERT: Madame Bovary
Translated by Gerard Hopkins
With an introduction by Terence Cave

ELIZABETH GASKELL: Cousin Phillis and Other Tales
Edited by Angus Easson

Cranford
Edited by Elizabeth Porges Watson

North and South
Edited by Angus Easson

Sylvia's Lovers
Edited by Andrew Sanders

OLIVER GOLDSMITH: The Vicar of Wakefield
Edited by Arthur Friedman

KENNETH GRAHAME: The Wind in the Willows
Edited by Peter Green

CHARLES KINGSLEY: Alton Locke
Edited by Elizabeth Cripps

J. SHERIDAN LE FANU: Uncle Silas
Edited by W. J. McCormack

KATHERINE MANSFIELD: Selected Stories
Edited by D. M. Davin

GEORGE MOORE: Esther Waters
Edited by David Skilton

SIDNEY SMITH: Selected Letters
Edited by Nowell C. Smith
With an introduction by Auberon Waugh

R. S. SURTEES: Mr. Facey Romford's Hounds
Edited and with an introduction by Jeremy Lewis

Mr. Sponge's Sporting Tour
With an introduction by Joyce Cary

WILLIAM MAKEPEACE THACKERAY: Barry Lyndon
Edited and with an introduction by Andrew Sanders

Vanity Fair
Edited by John Sutherland

LEO TOLSTOY: Anna Karenina
Translated by Louise and Aylmer Maude
With an introduction by John Bayley

The Raid and Other Stories
Translated by Louise and Aylmer Maude
With an introduction by P. N. Furbank

War and Peace (in two volumes)
Translated by Louise and Aylmer Maude
Edited by Henry Gifford

ANTHONY TROLLOPE: An Autobiography
Edited by P. D. Edwards

Can You Forgive Her?
Edited by Andrew Swarbrick
With an introduction by Kate Flint

Dr. Thorne
Edited by David Skilton

The Duke's Children
Edited by Hermione Lee

The Eustace Diamonds
Edited by W. J. McCormack

Framley Parsonage
Edited by P. D. Edwards

The Kelly's and the O'Kelly's
Edited by W. J. McCormack
With an introduction by William Trevor

The Last Chronicle of Barset
Edited by Stephen Gill

Phineas Finn
Edited by Jacques Berthoud

Phineas Redux
Edited by John C. Whale
Introduction by F. S. L. Lyons

The Prime Minister
Edited by Jennifer Uglow
With an introduction by John McCormick

The Small House at Allington
Edited by James R. Kincaid

The Warden
Edited by David Skilton

The Way We Live Now
Edited by John Sutherland

OSCAR WILDE: Complete Shorter Fiction
Edited by Isobel Murray

The Picture of Dorian Gray
Edited by Isobel Murray

A complete list of Oxford Paperbacks, including books in
The World's Classics, Past Masters, and OPUS Series,
can be obtained from the General Publicity Department,
Oxford University Press, Walton Street, Oxford OX2 6DP.